SEEDS OF TERRA
BOOK ONE OF THE TERRAN SPACE PROJECT

Alex Rath

Theogony Books
Virginia Beach, VA

Copyright © 2020 by Alex Rath.

All rights reserved. No part of this publication may be reproduced, distributed or transmitted in any form or by any means, including photocopying, recording, or other electronic or mechanical methods, without the prior written permission of the publisher, except in the case of brief quotations embodied in critical reviews and certain other noncommercial uses permitted by copyright law. For permission requests, write to the publisher, addressed "Attention: Permissions Coordinator," at the address below.

Chris Kennedy/Theogony Books
2052 Bierce Dr.
Virginia Beach, VA 23454
http://chriskennedypublishing.com/

Publisher's Note: This is a work of fiction. Names, characters, places, and incidents are a product of the author's imagination. Locales and public names are sometimes used for atmospheric purposes. Any resemblance to actual people, living or dead, or to businesses, companies, events, institutions, or locales is completely coincidental.

Cover Design by J Caleb Design.

Ordering Information:
Quantity sales. Special discounts are available on quantity purchases by corporations, associations, and others. For details, contact the "Special Sales Department" at the address above.

Seeds of Terra/Alex Rath -- 1st ed.
ISBN: 978-1648550966

For my daughter, Allison, who helps me explore new worlds every day.

Prologue

As they had every day for the past month, the core team of the Wormhole Traversal Project gathered in the control center in Geneva, Switzerland. Among them, Captain Maxwell Reeves had the most on the line.

Twenty years ago, a theoretical possibility had been proven to be a reality. A wormhole was discovered closer to Earth than expected. Travel in space was as common as driving a hovercar. The development of ion drives and the anti-matter reactors to fuel them had made establishing bases, then habitats on both the Moon and Mars a reality. Now, they hoped to go further.

Four years earlier, a probe was launched through the wormhole and now every telescope they had influence over was watching as much of the sky as possible. There were many theories, but the most prevalent was that the wormhole led to Alpha Centauri, just four light-years away, which meant anything they saw in Alpha Centauri actually happened four years ago.

Since science had not yet found a way to break the speed of light they'd waited four years with a focus on Alpha Centauri to see if the probe emerged.

"There it is!" Kellie Warren shouted, pointing at the large screen with a laser pointer. "Zoom in on that! There!"

A technician manipulated the display and Max's jaw dropped. The probe was visible on the screen. The room erupted in celebration as the culmination of years of hard work by thousands of people finally paid off. He'd hoped, he'd dreamed, and now it was actually happening. He jumped in surprise when Kellie patted him on the back.

"Looks like you'd better get home and finish packing," she yelled with a grin over the cheering. "We have a mission."

He nodded, still in a daze that it was actually happening. "Right," was all he could say.

Max turned and left the command center. Once outside in the hallway, he leaned against the wall and closed his eyes. He was going to Alpha Centauri. There had been thoughts and plans for crewed missions out of the Solar System by the Terran Space Project before, but none of them had gotten the needed funding. This one, on the other hand, had gotten the attention of some very wealthy backers and was a reality.

He stopped by his office to retrieve his backpack, went to his hovercar, and drove to his home a few miles away. Many of the scientists involved in the project lived on a massive campus, but Max and his wife, Annica, had chosen to have their own home so they could have some semblance of a life outside work.

* * *

Max walked through the door and called out, "Annica! Time to pack! The probe arrived; the mission is a go!"

His only response was silence. He went through the house looking and calling for her. When he got to their bedroom, he found half the closet was empty and an old-style paper envelope on his pillow with his name written in her smooth, flowing writing.

He licked his lips, sat on the bed, and opened the envelope to read its contents. It didn't make sense. He'd been on campus for the past few days, and she'd stayed home, but there'd been nothing he could think of that would indicate she would just leave. After re-reading it several times, he tossed it on the ground, grabbed his mission bag, and left the house for what he expected would be the last time.

* * * * *

Chapter One

Transition – 8 Days, 1300 Hours

After going through TSP campus security, Max went to his office, and closed the door behind him. He sighed as he fell into his chair. Today was supposed to be the most exciting day of his life, but all the excitement was gone.

He lost himself in paperwork and reviewed, for the hundredth time, the manifest for the TSP *Traveler*, which would take him and 400 other people out of the Solar System.

After several hours, there was a light knock on the door. "Come," he called.

Kellie walked in and closed the door behind her. She was still excited. "The call has gone out, and we have a 99% response already. Crew and colonists will be loaded in seven days, after their final physicals of course."

Max nodded absently. "Good."

She tilted her head and sat in one of the guest chairs. "Okay, what's going on, Max? Having second thoughts?"

He had known Kellie longer than he'd known Annica and he wasn't trying to hide that he wasn't in the best of moods.

"She's gone, Kellie."

"Who's gone?" Kellie asked, confused.

"Annica. She left me a frigging letter, of all things. She's packed her stuff and left."

Kellie's expression was pained. "What? I'm so sorry, Max."

He shrugged. "It doesn't make sense. I—I just need to focus on the mission."

She nodded. "Okay, but you know if you need to talk…"

Max gave a small smile. "I know. Thanks, Kellie. See if you can track down that one-percent that haven't responded. Everyone was selected for a reason; their skills are vital for survival once we arrive. And, of course, line up our replacement for Annica's spot."

She rose. "I'm on it. Will you stay on campus until launch, then?"

"I might as well."

"Okay, I'll make sure your apartment is freshened up and maybe sanitized a bit?"

He realized what she meant. He and Annica had an apartment on campus for long nights working and there were pictures of the couple everywhere. "Sounds good. Thanks."

She gave him a brief smile and left his office.

He looked at a 3-D projected image of he and Annica in the last inter-planetary shuttle he'd piloted when he'd still been in the military. They were dating when that was taken, but he'd thought they would be together forever. Everyone thought they would. They were the perfect couple, everything in common, shared interests and passions; nothing could stop them. They'd left the United States together after he retired from the military to join the Terran Space Project. The galaxy was going to be theirs to explore. Now he'd do it alone.

Max reached over, turned the projector off, and returned to the many screens of paperwork he had to finish before departing for orbit in a few days.

* * *

Transition – 3 Days, 0900 Hours

The next few days for Max were routine. Sleep, eat, work out, and prepare for the mission. It was usual for him to keep mostly to himself, but he became more isolated than usual. He was glad everyone was so focused on the mission that no one noticed or asked him about it. Even Kellie hadn't broached the subject of Annica after their conversation in his office. He'd considered calling her more than once to talk, but decided against it each time.

The day finally arrived, and he boarded his X-94 interplanetary space plane to leave Earth. Unlike most of the crew and colonists, he would fly himself up. He'd been flying both in and out of the atmosphere since he could remember and made sure to get checked out every year to keep himself fully qualified. His was one of ten X-94's that would be going along to Alpha Centauri aboard the *Traveler*.

Kellie settled into the co-pilot's seat as he went through his pre-flight checklist.

"Ready for this?" she asked.

"Yep."

He ignored her concerned look as she focused on her own portion of pre-flight while the last colonists filed into the cabin behind them.

The X-94 had a crew complement of only four and could carry up to 20 passengers or cargo. This load was all colonists. No flight was allowed to carry more than two vital personnel for the *Traveler*, which meant it had taken 50 flights to get the full 100-person crew to the ship. Most of the 300 colonists for the voyage were lifted into orbit on a bulk transport. The 20 flying up with Max and Kellie were the last to arrive in Geneva and be physically cleared for the mission.

"Reactor stable, ready for takeoff," the engineer reported.

"Course plotted; we have a clear path to *Traveler*," the navigator added.

"Copy, reactor stable and course clear," Max repeated. "Prepare cabin for takeoff."

"Cabin secured. Go for takeoff," Kellie verified.

"Copy, go for takeoff. Power to maximum."

Max increased the throttles, and everyone was pushed back in their seats as they accelerated down the short runway and took off. For a first-timer, the pressures could be shocking. Everyone on board had done it multiple times, but it was still uncomfortable. The thrust lasted only a few minutes as they pitched up and left Earth's atmosphere.

Max followed their planned flight path to the massive TSP *Traveler* in high orbit. It was indeed a marvel of engineering. It was ugly, no doubt about that, but it was his to command. He slowed the plane down and did a slow pass length-wise along each side of *Traveler* to observe all the hardpoint mounts.

The entire length of the ship was covered with pods that would be sent to the surface independently when they found their goal: a planet that could sustain human life. He refused to think in terms of "ifs." It was always a "when" for Max. The pods were filled with construction supplies, machinery, food stores, and anything else the TSP planners could think of that might be necessary once they reached their destination, and everything was duplicated at least once. Nothing was left to chance.

He frowned as he looked at the radar and saw far more returns than there should be. "What's with all the traffic?" he asked.

"Seems word got out," Kellie answered. "Every news agency in the system has a camera ship nearby."

"Coming back around to land."

"Bay is open, the pad is ready," Kellie said.

Max brought the plane around to the rear of the ship, where a cavernous bay waited. When he was within seven kilometers he entered the auto-landing command. The *Traveler*'s computer took control of the X-94 and maneuvered it into landing position. Locks emerged from the deck and secured the plane to the ship. The bay door closed and repressurization commenced. After about ten minutes the panel indicated that the atmosphere outside the ship had equalized.

"Welcome to TSP *Traveler*," Max announced over the ship's intercom. "Please check in with the bosun once you exit the ship, and you will be guided to your living quarters. He'll be expecting you near the inter-ship transport."

There was a round of applause from the cabin and Max couldn't help but smile in response. "Go ahead with them, I'll finish the shutdown," he told Kellie.

"I don't mind sticking around to help," she offered.

He shook his head. "I need a few minutes."

She rested a hand on his shoulder as she stood. "You got it. I'll see you on the bridge."

Max finished the process of shutting down the X-94's power systems and returning the small anti-matter reactor to a secure state. It was a scaled-down version of the same type of reactor that powered the *Traveler*, without which their voyage wouldn't be possible.

He stood, grabbed his bag of personal effects, and exited, pausing in the landing bay. It was cavernous, and he always stopped to take it in. He was glad they'd figured out how they could walk on the ship. Zero gravity was fine, but sometimes you wanted to go for a walk. Everyone on board the vessel had the option, and most chose to walk after fumbling around a few times in zero G. Thanks to magnetic fibers woven into every set of issued footwear, they could walk. It was obviously still zero gravity, but at least you could stand without floating away.

The staff in the lab had even come up with a similar solution for pajamas and mattresses, so you could actually lay in bed and not have to strap yourself to something to sleep. For those not involved in the program, it seemed like a ridiculous use of resources and time. To the crew and colonists who had tried both ways, it was a significant improvement to their quality of life.

Finally, he headed to the inter-ship transport that would ferry him to the bridge. With a fingerprint and optical scan, he was granted access to the crew-only path and made the journey in only a few minutes. The ship had multiple lines that ran through each cross-section of the vessel. Thankfully, there were express routes for the crew to get to the vital areas of the ship quickly that weren't available to the colonists.

He made one quick stop at his quarters to drop off his bag, then he went to the bridge.

* * *

"Captain on the bridge!" Kellie called out as Max entered the bridge,

Everyone stood at their stations, but no one

came to attention or saluted because it was a civilian operation. Instead, Max was greeted by clapping and whistling from his bridge crew.

He turned a bit red from the attention but let them have the moment. They'd earned it; he was just the one who got picked to be in command. He walked around the bridge and shook hands or gave a quick hug to each of the crew. It was only when he stood in front of his command chair and motioned for them to settle down that the cheering stopped.

"Okay, folks, we've been waiting for this moment for a while. We have twenty-four hours until we depart. Let's make sure everything is ready; department head meeting in two hours in the main conference room. Kellie, spread the word."

She nodded and sat at her station to get to work. The rest of the crew did the same once Max took his own seat. He got comfortable, pulled a tablet computer from an armrest compartment, and reviewed the ship's status reports that had already come in.

The *Traveler*'s crew was divided into multiple departments, each with their own head that reported directly to him. The current plan was for things to go through Kellie, his executive officer—XO—unless it needed his attention.

The only group that wasn't strictly civilian was the platoon-sized military element, designated MilForce, and they were specialists. They'd all left their previous branches of service since the ship and everything about it were privately funded and owed no allegiance to any government agency in any country. MilForce had drawn from special forces groups from around the world, especially those with experience in space. The man in charge, Colonel Omri Ascher, had been part of the Israeli Defense Force's Unit 5101 and was definitely the right man for the job.

"Ready?" Kellie asked from beside his chair.

Max glanced at his watch and grunted. He'd lost track of time reviewing the reports, and it was only ten minutes until the department head meeting. "Yeah, thanks. Let's go."

They left the bridge together, along with several other heads of departments. As a group, they made the short walk to the main conference room, which was located close to the bridge.

He was glad to see the remaining heads were already waiting for them. During the planning phases for the mission, after department heads had been chosen, he'd made it known that he believed on time was late and early was on time, and everyone had agreed. Smiles greeted him as he shook hands with his command team. Even Colonel Ascher managed to crack a smile, something that was widely believed to be impossible.

"Okay, folks, let's take our seats and get to work," Max said as he took his at the round conference table.

* * *

Transition – 0 Days, 1400 Hours

"Tracking online, we're on course," Kellie reported as they approached the wormhole several days later.

"Take us through, Sivert," Max said calmly. He knew he was tense, but he called on his past experience to project an air of confidence and calm he knew the crew needed.

"Yes, Captain," Astrogator Sivert Hunstad responded in his thick Norwegian accent.

There had been little discussion around the decision that English would be the primary language spoken on the ship. Everyone, crew and colonists alike, were required to have the ability to speak conversational English.

Max continued to watch his own display as Sivert focused on navigating the ship. Since they didn't know how large the entry window was, Sivert would take them in so the center of *Traveler* aligned with the center of the wormhole.

Finally, the moment came and the fore of the ship hit the wormhole, then the world changed. Max cried out, or thought he did, as it felt like every atom of his being was ripped apart and then shoved back together.

* * * * *

Chapter Two

Transition + 0 Days, 1410 Hours

Max felt himself being shaken, but it was too early to get up. "Later, Annica. I've got time."

"Captain! Wake up! It's Kellie!"

His eyes flew open, and he looked around. He wasn't at home; he was on the bridge of the *Traveler,* and they'd just gone through the wormhole.

"That sucked," he groaned.

"Yeah, everyone on the ship is in the same shape," she said, sounding equally miserable.

"Have Colonel Ascher take a tour of the ship. Make sure everyone's okay. And make sure he liaises with his colonist counterparts," he added hastily. Among the colonists, there were former military, as well as former law enforcement. The latter would handle any issues that might come up among the passengers.

"You got it," she replied and unsteadily made her way back to her station.

"Captain," Sivert said, turning to face Max, "we have a problem."

"We have many problems, I think. The first of which being I really need some pain killers. What have you got?"

"We're not where we're supposed to be," he answered.

"Well, we expected there might be some variation. How far off are we?"

"Captain, I'm not even sure we're in the same galaxy. My charts can't match anything. I literally have no idea where we are."

"Wait," Kellie said, just as Max shouted, "What?"

Sivert spread his hands helplessly. "I've run the starscape through the database. Nothing matches."

Max chewed on his bottom lip for a few seconds before responding. This was an eventuality that had been considered, but was one of those edge cases they hadn't expected to encounter. "Okay. This information stays compartmentalized for now. No one beyond the sound of my voice finds out. Clear?"

Everyone nodded and turned back to their stations except Doctor Sukanya Chadda, who walked over with a magnetic jet injector. "This should help with the discomfort."

Max nodded as she held the device to his neck. He didn't feel the injection, but he instantly felt the cobwebs clear from his head and the ache in his muscles dissipated. "Thanks, Doc."

She smiled and nodded before moving on to inject the rest of the bridge crew.

Once injected, Kellie stood and moved back to Max's side. "Colonel Ascher and his team are spreading out through the ship with the colonists alongside," she said, then hesitated.

"Thanks," Max responded and saw the look on her face. "What else?"

"We have to tell them, Max. The council at least."

He sighed. The council Kellie was referring to included himself, Kellie, Colonel Ascher, and five colonists. The colonists' council had been democratically chosen by the entire colonist group. They were, at least on paper, responsible for the passengers' well-being and behavior. The group's charter outlined that significant events, like this, were required to be reported to the council.

"Okay, let's give it a few hours for Doctor Chadda's people to get around to everyone and make sure we don't have any casualties. I shudder to think what might have happened to anyone who wasn't strapped in."

"Agreed."

* * *

Transition + 0 Days, 1700 Hours

Max walked into the council room, located centrally within the *Traveler*, to brief everyone on the current status of the ship and their location. The crew had made it through relatively unscathed, but they'd lost four colonists who weren't adequately secured during the transit—which was better than he'd feared—as well as some scratches and bruises from unsecured objects that had flown around their cabins.

He sat down and logged in to the display at his seat in case he needed to refer to anything. "Welcome to our first meeting in space. Thank you all for being here on time. I'm sure you're all as busy as I am after a rougher than expected transit. The first order of business I need to pass along is that we lost four colonists who weren't properly secured. Their remains have been taken care of and will be handled according to their contracts."

There were nods around the table. Given the possible unknown aspects of their journey, each person aboard *Traveler* had customized their contract for how their remains should be handled if they passed away during the trip. Otherwise, the contracts were boilerplate, committing themselves to the mission, and agreeing not to hold the TSP responsible for anything that might happen.

Max took a deep breath and glanced at Kellie, who gave him a barely perceptible nod. "There's also other news I am required to share. I must ask, however, that it stay in this room. While I can't order or require it, I think it's best, and you'll understand why in a moment." He paused and looked around the room, meeting each person's eyes. Colonel Ascher looked particularly intense and unhappy.

"We did not arrive at Alpha Centauri as expected," Max said.

Eyebrows rose and jaws dropped around the room. Only Adel Ragnarsson, a programmer from Iceland, didn't look all that surprised. "Where are we?" he asked.

"We don't know," Max responded. "Our astrogators have checked the starfield against every known chart we have, and the stars we can see don't line up with anything that has ever been viewed from Earth."

Max was ready for panic, but instead he saw shock—of course—and also acceptance.

"I assume they have adjusted scale and perspective on the viewing to attempted alignments?" Ragnarsson asked.

"Yes, we've come at it from every angle we can think of," Kellie answered. "At most, they've found two points of commonality, which, statistically, will happen based on pure chance."

Ragnarsson nodded thoughtfully and leaned back in his chair.

"So, what's the plan, Captain?" Hugh Coghlan, a former police officer, asked.

"We'll spend the next few hours completing our check of the ship's systems. The jump was more violent than we expected, and we want to be 100-percent sure that everything is as it should be. After that, we'll proceed with the next stage of our mission."

"So, no way to turn back, I guess?" Deanna Stokes, a farmer from the United States, asked.

Max shook his head. "We checked and there's no evidence of a similar wormhole signature anywhere near us. The best course of action is to proceed just like we planned when we reached Alpha Centauri."

"Except, there won't be another ship coming with more supplies..." Deanna voiced what the others were likely thinking.

"Correct," Max confirmed. "But we do have twenty years worth of supplies, and we need to make them count. Hopefully, we can find a world we can colonize in short order and get started making our new home."

There were more nods around the table. These people, as well as the colonists and crew, had trained for years for this mission and knew the stakes. Still, there was bound to be some disagreement when things didn't go according to plan.

"I'm not sure I agree with trying to keep this a secret. The people on this vessel are intelligent and can handle the truth," Ragnarsson suggested.

"A person is intelligent, and everyone on this mission definitely is," Max countered. "A group of people tends to panic when faced with the unknown, and this is as unknown as it gets."

"I agree with Captain Reeves," Colonel Ascher added. "We have a large number of people in a confined space. At this time, does it matter exactly where we are? The mission remains the same."

Ragnarsson studied Max for a moment. "Very well, I will agree to keep your secret...for now."

The rest of the council agreed, and the meeting was adjourned. Max let out a sigh of relief after everyone filed out of the room. He remained behind, alone, but after a moment Colonel Ascher returned and closed the door behind him.

"What can I do for you, Colonel?" Max asked as he stood.

"You know as well as I do that things will get out of control once the general populace finds out what's happened," Ascher said, folding his arms over his chest.

"No, I don't know that."

"You should. This needs to become a military operation."

Max shook his head. "Not going to happen."

"Captain—or should I say, Colonel—"

"No, you shouldn't. Those days are behind me."

Ascher smiled. "Are they ever, really?"

"You know what I mean," Max insisted, his frustration growing.

"Well, we'll be ready when you change your mind," Ascher said before turning and leaving.

* * *

Transition + 0 Days, 1800 Hours

Sivert, the astrogator, stopped Max as he was passing through the bridge to his office. "Have a minute?"

Max nodded and motioned for him to follow. He held the door open for Sivert, then entered behind him and closed the door. "Have a seat," he said as he sat behind his desk. "What have you found?"

"Nothing," Sivert said, sitting. "We've emerged among several systems, but there's nothing nearby. At this point, my confidence that we are in uncharted space is as high as it can possibly be. My team is reviewing all the collected data from the traversal of the wormhole, but…" he shrugged.

"I expected as much. Let's get the sensor probes launched and find out what we can."

"I've taken the liberty of having them prepped and loaded. I'll have them launched as soon as I'm back at my station."

"Good. Once we get some data back, we can figure out where to go next. Thanks, Sivert."

"My pleasure, Captain." Sivert stood to leave, but paused just before he opened the door. "You know, Captain, while this is truly unexpected and frightening, for some of us it's also the most exciting possible outcome. We are somewhere no Human object has been and no Human has ever even seen. We truly are viewing new horizons."

Max smiled at the restrained exuberance in Sivert's voice. "I hadn't thought about it like that. Thanks for that perspective."

Once Sivert had left, the smile faded and he rolled his eyes. He just couldn't buy into the idea that this was exciting. The plan for the mission was to be in Alpha Centauri. Fourteen years later, a ship from Earth was scheduled to arrive with additional supplies. The best speed of their ion drives was .25 C—one quarter the speed of light—and every calculation had planned around that. Now they were literally in the middle of nowhere, with 20 years of supplies and no way to get back to Earth.

He was about to head to his quarters to rest when a chime sounded from his desktop terminal. He tapped to accept the message and was surprised to see Gustav Malmkvist, the head of the TSP, appear on the screen.

"Captain Reeves, if you are seeing this message, one of the potential outcomes we expected has come to pass, and you have not arrived in Alpha Centauri. I'm sorry we couldn't fully brief you on this previously, but it was decided that it was best for the mission."

Max frowned as he watched and listened.

"The truth is that we felt there was a better than even chance that you would not emerge in Alpha Centauri. A new blueprint for the manufactory has been unlocked in your terminal. You can send it to the manufactory for production, should you so desire. It will produce a new type of long-range signal that might, eventually, reach Earth, so that we or our future generations will know where you are."

Max stared at the screen as Gustav steepled his fingers.

"I'm afraid there's not much more I can give you, Captain. From here on in it's up to you. How much of this you reveal to your crew is up to you. Find a planet, start a colony, and survive. Know that we will be looking for you. Good luck, Captain."

The screen switched to display the TSP logo, and Max was torn between resignation to his fate, frustrated at having been lied to, and pure anger. He reached forward and pulled the message up again to re-watch the last few seconds, and he could barely believe what he saw. In the corner of the frame he saw the side of Annica's face, just barely in the frame. She had been there when the message was recorded. She had known.

Betrayal joined the flood of thoughts in his mind. He stood, wheeled around, and punched the wall of his quarters. He instantly regretted his decision when he heard multiple cracks from his hand before finding himself floating backward as he lost touch with the floor. His scream of anger and pain summoned Kellie, who suddenly appeard in his office.

"What's wr—What the hell?" she exclaimed as she quickly shut the door behind her.

"She knew!" Max shouted as he finally got his feet back on the ground so he could stand.

"Who knew what? What did you do to your hand?"

He grimaced through the pain. "Annica. She knew."

"Knew what?"

Max gestured at his chair with his unbroken hand. "Sit. You might as well know, too."

Kellie looked at him strangely but came around his desk and sat. He reached around her and replayed the message.

At the end, he paused the screen again and pointed. "Annica was there. She knew."

"Maybe...maybe it's not her," Kellie suggested, but he could tell she didn't mean it.

He shook his head and stared at the deck.

"Well, it is what it is, Max. We need to get you medical attention, then plan what to do next. I know it hurts to see that, and I'm sorry, but it doesn't matter anymore. What matters now is the 400 people that are looking to you to lead them. You can't fall apart now."

Max continued to stare at the deck. He heard Kellie's words, but they didn't register. In his mind's eye, all Max could see was Annica standing there while Malmkvist told him they were screwed. The two people he'd trusted most had betrayed him, had lied to him.

Kellie stood and laid a hand on his shoulder. "Come on, Max," she said softly. "Let's get your hand looked at."

He shrugged away from her. The pain felt good; he didn't want to lose it. It was something he could hold on to, something he knew was real.

"Okay, stay here, I'll be back." She gently squeezed his shoulder then left his office.

He played the last few weeks over in his mind. Was there something he had missed? Some hint or suggestion that things were going to go wrong? But he couldn't think of anything. In the days before the projected probe arrival in Alpha Centauri, Annica had cooked them an amazing dinner. He had moved to their campus apartment for a few days, with all the work he had. She stayed home to start packing, in case the mission was a go. What could have happened in two days? How many other people that he'd trusted knew what was going to happen? In his mind, they all knew the ship wasn't going to arrive in Alpha Centauri. They'd knowingly stranded him in the middle of nowhere with no remorse at all.

He was used to putting himself at risk for the military; he'd been a long-range test pilot. Every new propulsion system for interplanetary travel had been his to play with. The ion drive on *Traveler* existed because he'd put his life on the line to test the smaller versions. More than once he'd had to eject when one system or another went wrong and the ship he was piloting suffered a catastrophic failure. The military's way of saying, "It blew up."

Max had to concede that even if he'd been told this was the plan he still would have accepted the mission. Much like the test pilots who became the United States' first astronauts in the distant 1960s, he had the desire to break those unbroken barriers.

But they should have told him. He deserved to know what he was getting into.

* * *

Adel Ragnarsson sat in his quarters mulling over the information disclosed during the council meeting and was dissatisfied. He was one of the programmers who had worked as a contractor on the software for space traveling systems, and that skillset had earned him his seat as a passenger on *Traveler*. While he was quite skilled at developing code, he was also equally as adept at breaking it. He decided to work his way into the ship's communication systems to find out what they weren't being told. Adel Ragnarsson didn't like secrets.

After several hours, he finally managed to break into *Traveler*'s communication systems . The security involved impressed him. Whoever had assembled the ship's digital security was good, but not quite good enough. Of course, no system was impenetrable; many countries had learned that over the years. Ragnarsson grinned to himself. He'd proved it on more than one occasion, but he didn't work alone.

There was a knock on the door to his quarters. "Come on in."

Two people he knew very well, Empyre and Courtni, came in and sat down. He had asked them to stop by once he discovered their true situation.

"What's up?" Empyre asked.

Ragnarsson turned his chair around to face the pair. They were rarely seen apart, but there was nothing there but a professional relationship. They worked incredibly well together, and each of them had a variety of skills.

Empyre, physically strong, but also an expert mechanic and quite inventive, was someone he'd employed quite often. Ragnarsson had never seen anything with moving parts that Empyre couldn't take apart. Every time, Courtni was part of the package. Her expertise and natural affinity for numbers meant if something needed to be solved quickly, she could figure out. She was also incredibly good at reading people, and manipulating them, if it came to that. Empyre and Courtni weren't their real names, of course, but they were the names Ragnarsson knew them by best. If there was something he needed done that required hands-on, they were his first call.

"It seems the ship's a bit off course. We didn't arrive where we we're supposed to. And the TSP knew it could happen."

Neither of them showed any surprise at all. In fact, Ragnarsson was sure they *weren't* surprised. In their business, you always had to expect the unexpected.

Courtni frowned. "Well, that throws a spanner in some of our plans."

Ragnarsson waved a hand dismissively. "Sure, but it can still work to our advantage."

"I'm listening," Empyre said skeptically.

"People are going to be way out of sorts when this gets out. I mean, the captain wants me to keep this a secret, but…" he shrugged, feigning innocence. "Accidents do happen. Things slip. Anyway, we're going to need to make sure we're taken care of. I'll wager one of the next moves will be to ration the food allotments to make them last longer than originally intended."

"Makes sense," said Courtni.

Ragnarsson nodded in agreement. "It does, and I'm willing to wager that there will be some people who won't want to cut back on their intake. So we're going to make sure we have our share."

Empyre flexed his biceps, visible through the grey skinsuit all colonists wore. "What's the plan?"

"Well, you have access to the storage compartments, and Courtni has access to the manifests. You're going to identify our share of what's in the hold, and…set it aside."

"That will be difficult," Courtni objected. "Everything's pretty well packed. We're not meant to be on the ship for more than a year, so the bulk of the supplies are in containers; some of them are mounted to the outside of the ship."

"I have confidence that you two will come up with something."

Empyre and Courtni glanced at each other and shrugged. "We'll see what we can figure out," Empyre said. "How soon is this information going to…slip?"

Ragnarsson leaned back in his chair and rubbed his chin. "Within the hour. I do dislike secrets if they're not mine. We'll see if the captain changes his mind, but I have a feeling Colonel Ascher is going to be the biggest obstacle. I know his type. He was Israeli Defense Force, and they don't screw around."

"No shit," Courtni grumbled.

* * *

Max was finally resigned to his fate by the time Kellie returned with Doctor Chadda.

"All clear?" Kellie asked.

He shrugged.

"Good enough. Go ahead and get him patched up, Doc."

Doctor Chadda shook her head ruefully when she saw Max's hand. "Sit down, Captain; let me get your hand fixed up. I have a local anesthetic."

"No."

"This is going to hurt."

"No."

She sighed and shrugged. "Okay."

He sat in one of the visitor chairs and held out his mangled hand to Doctor Chadda. It was apparent even from a visual inspection that several bones were broken.

She used a hand-held X-ray device and proceeded to set the bones and apply the bone-knitting agents to speed healing. Finally, she closed the skin on his knuckles with adhesive where it had torn when he hit the steel bulkhead and wrapped his hand. "You won't be flying for a few days, but it should all heal up fine."

The process had hurt, for sure, but no one who didn't know him well would have been able to tell.

Doctor Chadda glanced up at Kellie when he didn't respond, a concerned look on her face.

"He's fine. Max puts himself into a meditative state…he didn't feel a thing. He'll come out of it when he's ready," Kellie explained.

* * * * *

Chapter Three

Transition + 0 Days, 2100 Hours

Colonel Ascher strode directly up to Kellie, who was still sitting at her station on the bridge, even though her time to go off-shift was long past. "Ms. Warren, I need to speak to the captain, but he is not responding to comms."

"He's resting, Colonel; what can I do for you?" she asked, turning her chair to face him.

"There is unrest among the passengers. Word has gotten out that we did not arrive as scheduled at Alpha Centauri. I warned him that this would happen. We must enact Code 23 immediately."

"Whoa there, Colonel," she said.

Code 23 would turn the mission into a military operation. Every former member of any military would instantly be re-activated and martial law would be applied. It was an absolute last resort, and both she and Max had to agree to it.

Several other members of the bridge crew looked up from their stations and waited to see what would happen next.

Kellie frowned. "Come on, let's talk off the bridge."

She led Colonel Ascher to a small conference room down a short hallway off the bridge intended for shift change briefings for the bridge crew. "Okay, what's going on that you think requires such a drastic measure?"

"Someone talked and rumors are circulating among the passengers that we are lost."

Kellie sat down and sighed heavily. "Dammit. They couldn't even wait a day."

"It will get worse, Ms. Warren. It is human nature."

She looked at him and noticed for the first time that Ascher was wearing his sidearm. It was only a stun pistol, but she knew Max hadn't authorized that the arms locker to be opened. "Why the hell do you have that?" she demanded.

"Just in case," he replied. "Not only are there rumors, but the last routine inventory found that there was food missing."

"Why am I hearing about this from you instead of the quartermaster?"

"One of my people happened to be there when it was discovered."

"Well, isn't that one hell of a coincidence."

"Obviously, we must apprehend and deal with the thief," he explained as if he were talking to a child.

"Colonel Ascher, I'm quite capable of doing my job. You will check the crew, and I will talk to Mr. Coghlan about handling an investigation of the passengers. As you're well aware, we have a good number of former law enforcement who are very good at their jobs, maybe better at something like this than your military people. Once the culprit is identified, Max will make the decision of what to do. Am I clear, Colonel?"

"Quite clear, Ms. Warren. Good day," he said and left the room.

She extended her middle finger toward the door after it closed behind him, then notified Coghlan of the problem. She asked him to assemble the other former police to investigate the passengers.

That done, she crossed her arms on the table and laid her head down. "Come on, Max," she said to herself, "we need you."

* * *

Ragnarsson sat down across from Empyre and Courtni in a cafeteria, frustrated. "They're poking around already. I expected you to be more subtle," he said in a hushed but angry tone.

Empyre glanced around for eavesdroppers. "It wasn't us. I was still making my plans."

"Not to mention, Ascher and his goons are watching everything like a hawk. We're doing a full inventory of all the stores. If a seal is broken, the bots throw an alert and then we have to check it manually," Courtni added. Empyre nodded.

Ragnarsson chewed on the new information. AI-driven robots were scattered around the ship to do simple, time-intensive tasks like taking inventory and making sure hatches were sealed. He'd tried to get a look at the coding behind them, but he couldn't even find where it was stored, so he assumed they ran on their own dedicated network. He took a mouthful of food paste from his tube, which had the consistency of toothpaste but tasted remarkably like pepperoni pizza, and nodded.

"Okay. Play it cool for now. I'll see what I can do about the bots."

Empyre and Courtni rose and left him to consider his next steps. He was so deep in thought that he didn't notice when Hugh Coghlan walked up behind him.

"ID, please?" Coghlan asked politely.

Ragnarsson looked up behind him and grinned.

"Oh, sorry, Adel. Didn't recognize you from behind."

Ragnarsson chuckled and shook his head. "Not a problem. Something I can do for you?"

Coghlan sighed. "Food's gone missing so we have to question everyone."

"What? That's horrible. Is there anything I can do to help?"

"No, thanks. We've got it covered, but let me know if you hear anything. I don't guess you took it?" Coghlan asked jokingly.

"Only this," he pointed at the pizza tube he had just finished.

Coghlan grinned and nodded. "I don't get it. We have 20 *years*-worth of supplies. Why the bloody hell would anyone steal it?"

"No idea."

"Anyway, I'd better get moving. There are still lots of people to question. Oh! I ran across Lina and Deanna earlier; we're going to get together tonight around eleven in this cafeteria for an informal meeting. You in?"

Ragnarsson smiled and nodded.

Traveler was kept on the standard 24-hour day they had in Geneva. The lighting around the ship was synchronized to the time of day to keep everyone's circadian rhythm intact. "I'll be here."

"Okay. See you later."

Ragnarsson held the smile on his face until Coghlan left the cafeteria, then made his way back to his quarters. He wondered what Coghlan wanted to get the passenger council together for, but set that aside. He'd find out later.

He programmed the walls around him to one of his favorite thinking spots in Iceland and set to work trying to find the source of the bots' control system. Everyone's quarters had a customizable wall display system that transformed the room into anywhere they wanted to be. The air system even filtered in smells from the location, and speakers reproduced the ambient sounds. Before departure, each person was allowed to choose three areas, and teams had gone to take detailed images. They had even sampled the air to provide an exact replication. The theory was that it would keep people from going stir-crazy in the sterile environment of the ship. He had a feeling that theory was going to be put to the test.

* * *

Kellie jerked awake and yawned. She hadn't meant to fall asleep. A check of her watch told her she'd been out for 30 minutes. "Okay, Kellie," she said to herself, "time to kick Max's ass and get to work."

She walked through the bridge, ignoring Sivert's attempt to get her attention, and walked into Max's office. She tried to slam the door behind her, but the hydraulics that prevented it ruined the effect.

Max grinned from behind his desk. "Yeah, I've done that, too."

"You ready to get past your little pity party and get to work?"

He tilted his head and pointed. "You've got a little crud on the corner of your mouth…"

She turned red and scrubbed her face with her hands. "So I took a little nap. The question still stands."

The amusement faded from Max's face. "All right. What's up?"

"Well," she said as she sat, "word has gotten out already. Everyone knows we're lost."

"Shit. Well, it was bound to happen. What else?"

"Apparently someone, or some people, are panicking. Colonel Ascher just told me some food is missing."

"Wait, Ascher told you?"

"Yeah, he's got the MilForce, armed with stun guns, patrolling the ship now, watching people."

"Good grief. What the hell is he thinking?"

She shrugged.

"Shit," he repeated. He rubbed his temples with his good hand and shook his head. "Maybe I'm not the right person for this job. Hell, I obviously wasn't good enough for Annica."

"Bullshit!" she exclaimed as she stood. "You just need to get over the fact that Annica was a bitch and realize you're better off without her. Hell, I warned you about her years ago."

"Don't go there, Kellie," Max warned.

She threw her hands up in surrender. "Fine, sorry. But I'm right. Anyway, you've got 400 people counting on you, so get your ass in gear. You've got a team of geniuses for a reason. *You* don't have to have all the answers."

"Department head meeting in twenty minutes. But not Ascher. Let's focus on the science. Wake people up if you have to."

"That's more like it," she said and left to get the team assembled.

Max sighed and closed his eyes after she left. The morning he'd left to live on campus before the probe arrival, Annica had seen him off with a smile. He thought back over the weeks prior, again, and couldn't pinpoint anything. Nothing out of the ordinary. Was it another man? Or woman? Did she not have as much faith in the mission as he did? Why would she have agreed to move to Geneva if she didn't believe in it?

* * *

Transition + 0 Days, 2200 Hours

Twenty minutes later, Max went around the table and heard from each of his department heads. The conclusion was the same; it was time to find a place to live.

Max addressed the group after they'd provided their input. "Now I want to show you something that appeared on my terminal today." He tapped on his tablet, and the message he'd received from Gustav Malmkvist was projected onto screen behind him. He didn't need to watch it again so he studied the reactions of his team. He saw betrayal, frustration, and anger, but mostly there was understanding.

Max had a background as a test pilot. He was also an expert in astrogation and several related fields so he understood as well. He just couldn't get past the deceit.

"So now you have everything I do. Where do we go from here?" Max asked.

"That's the perfect question, Captain," Sivert said. "The initial probes have indicated several systems relatively nearby, all less than a month's travel. I'd like to launch more probes and gather as much data as we can about those systems."

"We should also check out that new blueprint the video mentioned," Sadie March, the ship's chief engineer suggested. "Maybe we build it and launch it, maybe we don't, but it might reveal something useful."

"Are you suggesting we don't even bother trying to let Earth know where we are?" Max asked.

"It's simple; if we're so far away we don't even know where Earth is, the odds of any signal reaching it are—"

"Nil," Kellie finished.

"Pretty much," Sadie agreed. "So why use limited materials on something that would be a waste? Let's save them for something we can actually use down the line. But whatever the blueprint is, it might contain something we can use for another purpose."

Max tapped through screens on his tablet. "Okay, the blueprint is released to your queue, Sadie. Anything else?"

"Yeah, what are we going to do about the stores going missing? Ascher seems to think brute force is the way to go. Hell, he even wants to put Code 23 into effect," Kellie said.

That got more of a reaction than finding out they'd been sent out here based on a lie. Max was the only person in the room with a military background. "Enough!" he said loudly enough to bring silence to the group.

"I won't allow it, and it requires my sign-off. So you don't need to worry about it, okay? This is not, and will not, be a military operation. The military had their chance at space exploration and screwed it up. We're going to do this right. There's not that much missing anyway, is there?"

Kellie referred to her tablet. "One case."

"Okay, so that's one month's provisions for one person," he said and waved a hand dismissively. "Keep investigating, but let's not lose sleep over it. It's not like it could have gone far."

Around the room, everyone nodded, and he even got a few grins and smiles.

"Okay, Sivert, launch whatever probes you need. You don't need to ask me ahead of time unless you're at risk of using up all of our raw materials. Sadie, make sure he has what he needs, but definitely monitor the storage bunkers. What we have is what we have unless and until we can find a source of materials to refine. Doctor Marsh, let's keep an eye on the crew's well-being, and make sure you liaise closely with your colonist counterparts. With these rumors flying, I'm concerned."

Doctor Toby Marsh was the ship's counselor. He nodded.

"Maybe we should just tell them what's really going on," Kellie suggested.

Max looked at her and gestured with his bandaged right hand for her to continue.

"Rumors are flying, and I'm sure we've all seen what can happen with rumors. The next thing you know, people will be saying aliens brought us here to do anal probes or something ridiculous."

The room filled with chuckles, but the point was serious. "All right, calm down. Kellie's right. Rumors can get out of control when the brass decides to try to keep secrets. Any thoughts on this? We have to tell them something, but the question is how much and how soon?"

All eyes went to Doctor Marsh. He'd done full psychological workups on every member of the crew and the passengers.

"It's quite a conundrum for sure. Generally speaking, the truth is always the best course of action. I would like to time it carefully, though, so that we can have counseling resources available on the spot. Perhaps we should have everyone gather in their assigned cafeteria for observation."

Max considered for a moment. "Okay. Kellie, send out an all-hands memo that I will be addressing everyone tomorrow at 0900. Non-essential personnel are to report to their assigned cafeteria. Anything else?" he asked as he looked around the room. "Okay, get some sleep, then let's get to work."

* * *

Transition + 0 Days, 2230 Hours

Ragnarsson walked into the cafeteria a few minutes before the appointed time of the informal council meeting to find the rest of the passenger council was already there. He took a seat at the table and raised his eyebrows. "So, what's this about?"

"Survival," Lina Skoog said simply. Lina was a mountain climber and survival expert. She held several world records in both areas.

Ragnarsson figured she made it onto the council because of her looks but was willing to listen. "And?"

"Ascher is making it very plain that it's us and them. The whole 'we're in this together' thing is bullshit," Deanna Stokes said.

"Come on now, Deanna; it's not that bad," Coghlan objected.

"Then why do I have one of his goons wearing a damn stun gun looking over my shoulder in hydroponics? Word got out that we're not in Alpha Centauri, and people are getting nervous. I know *I* didn't say anything..."

That started a rash of objections from everyone denying any involvement in the leak. Ragnarsson took part as well, as it would have been blatantly evident if he hadn't.

"Enough!" Coghlan said and slammed his hand on the table. "Arguing isn't going to get us anywhere. We have to stick together. It doesn't really matter *where* the leak came from. Hell, it could have been one of the crew. What matters is what do we do about it?"

"What we should have done to begin with. We tell the truth," Ragnarsson stated.

To a person, everyone shifted in their seats as if they were suddenly uncomfortable.

"I say we give them another day to come clean and tell everyone. If they don't, we take matters into our own hands," Ragnarsson suggested.

"We should take this to Captain Reeves," Coghlan disagreed.

"We should at least give him another chance," Azeema el-Mir, a construction and engineering specialist from Dubai, agreed.

"Fine," Ragnarsson grunted.

"Okay, if we're all in agreement, I'll get some time with him tomorrow, and we'll meet up again afterward and decide," Coghlan said. Just as they were all preparing to leave, their communicators vibrated. "Well, it seems like this might all be moot. Let's see what Captain Reeves has to say tomorrow morning."

* * * * *

Chapter Four

Transition + 1 Day, 0900 Hours

Max sat in his office and deployed the camera that would feed to displays around the ship. He had considered doing audio-only, but Kellie suggested it would reassure everyone more if they could see his face, too.

At precisely 0900, he activated the feed.

"Ladies and gentlemen, good morning. It has come to my attention that there are a number of rumors making their way around the ship, and I want to set the record straight." He paused and looked directly into the camera. "We did not, as planned, arrive in Alpha Centauri. All efforts have been exhausted to pinpoint our location, but at this time, our whereabouts are unknown. We must not panic or be fearful. Rather than seeing this as a defeat, I believe we must see this as an opportunity."

He paused for a few moments to let that sink in before continuing.

"We are in space that has never been seen by humankind before. We are truly explorers on a new frontier. As I address you now, my team is reviewing data coming back from probes launched last night. Our immediate goal is to find a planet we can call home. We will proceed with our mission as planned. The only difference is that we won't have a resupply coming. It's up to us to find a place we can settle and establish a new home for humankind."

He activated a slide that was fed into the video system showing the pictures and names of the passengers on the council. "If you have questions or concerns, please address them to one of these people. They can direct them to my team, and we will do our best to address them as quickly as possible. Thank you for your attention."

He ended the transmission and leaned back in his chair.

Kellie grinned from the corner. "You were great, Max."

"I guess we'll find out."

Suddenly, there was a loud pounding on the door. They exchanged confused glances, and Kellie started to open the door.

Colonel Ascher shoved the door open the rest of the way and stormed in, causing Kellie to lose her attachment to the deck and fly back against the bulkhead. "What was the meaning of that?" Ascher demanded.

Max looked to Kellie, but she waved him off, indicating she was okay.

"Welcome to my office, Colonel," Max said. "Something we can do for you?"

"I should have been told this was coming!"

"Oh, did you not get the memo? Kellie, did we forget to send Colonel Ascher the memo?"

"I believe it may have slipped my mind, Captain. I'm very sorry."

"Well, there we are. A simple mix-up," Max said and smiled at Ascher. "I'm sure it won't happen again. Anything else?"

"That was monumentally *stupid*," Ascher spat. "How do you expect to keep control of this situation?"

"Colonel. Maybe you've never served on a ship for a long voyage that involves civilians, but I have. When you have this many people in a confined space *there are no secrets*. It was a mistake to try to keep the truth from the passengers to begin with. A mistake that will *not* be repeated."

"You should enact Code 23 immediately," Ascher said. He was calming down, but not backing down.

"No."

Ascher shook his head. "You'll regret this, Captain Reeves."

Max rose to his feet and met Ascher's eyes. "Are you threatening me, Colonel Ascher?"

Ascher stared at Max for a long moment before he said, "No. I am not, Captain. But I want to go on record as being against this decision."

"You do that. But for now you can get out of my office," Max said as he sat back down. "And try not to injure my XO while you're at it."

Ascher turned to leave and paused to look at Kellie. "I apologize, Ms. Warren."

Kellie nodded, then closed the door behind Ascher after he was gone. She breathed in deeply through her nose. "Well, that was fun. I can almost taste the testosterone."

Max grimaced. "I never thought he'd be a problem."

Kellie shrugged and sat down. "Well, you handled it properly. What are we going to do about the thief?"

"There aren't many places to hide things on the ship. Either one of the security teams will find it, or a bot will."

"But what do you plan to do once he or she is found?"

"Nothing; it was a panic reaction. It probably wouldn't have happened if I'd told everyone from the beginning."

Kellie looked skeptical.

"You think otherwise?" Max asked.

"I don't know. I just worry that it sets a bad precedent."

"Let's see what we find, then we'll figure it out from there. I think, in this case, motives matter."

Kellie nodded. "Okay, then. I'll be at my station if you need anything."

* * *

Transition + 1 Day, 1200 Hours

A few hours later, after completing his daily allotment of mind-numbing paperwork, Max returned to the bridge. He was flagged down by Sivert before he could reach his command chair.

"What have you got, Sivert?"

"Something exciting, Captain. The probes have picked up on a trinary star system that has fifteen planets in various orbits."

Max's interest was immediately piqued. Some had long theorized that multi-star systems had a higher percentage of hosting at least one marginally habitable planet. And with so many worlds to examine, the odds of one of them being suitable for humans were better than if it had been a single-sun, lower planet-count system.

"How far away?"

"Approximately seven days at maximum speed."

"Anything else promising?"

Sivert shook his head. "Nothing yet. None of the other systems look even remotely as promising as this one."

"Let's deploy Peeper and get a closer look at the system before we burn seven days in transit. There's no real way of knowing how stable the orbits of any of the planets are."

"We'll get started on it immediately," Sivert responded and turned back to his console.

Max sat in his command chair and buckled in. Multiple planets did increase the odds, but it would be hard to know for sure. The last thing he wanted was to identify a world, set down, and find out months later that its orbit passed too close to another star in the system.

His looked at his chair's display, which showed an exterior camera view of the ship's built-in multi-spectrum telescope, nicknamed Peeper. It was one of the most powerful optical telescopes ever devised, with a 15-meter aperture, seven times more powerful than one of the most famous telescopes ever launched, the Hubble Space Telescope. The top-middle area of the ship had been built around Peeper.

It would take an hour for the telescope to deploy fully, and then another hour to run diagnostics. Max just hoped the journey through the wormhole hadn't disturbed the optics.

The crew used *Traveler*'s maneuvering thrusters to point the ship at the system they wanted to examine and waited.

* * *

Empyre and Courtni again sat across from Ragnarsson in the cafeteria.

"Captain Reeves surprised me," Ragnarsson said before taking a pull on his food tube.

"So, what's that mean for us?" Empyre asked.

"It means we wait and see what he does next."

Courtni yawned. "Well, that's boring."

"True, but it beats being on Ascher's shit list," Empyre countered.

Courtni nodded. "True."

"Listen," Ragnarsson said, interrupting their interlude. "We lay low for now. Do your jobs like good little colonists, stay clean, and we'll have our chance, eventually."

"You keep saying that. Eventually," Courtni said.

"And that's what I mean!" Ragnarsson said, raising voice and drawing attention from quite a few other tables. He smiled apologetically and turned his attention back to Empyre and Courtni. "Just stick to it for now. Got it?"

"Okay…" Courtni responded, though she obviously wasn't happy about it.

Empyre simply shrugged.

Ragnarsson left the cafeteria. He decided to take the long way back to his quarters to give himself time to think before returning to his own job. He had a workstation in a shared room on the ship, but he preferred being alone. It was easier to focus, plus it let him work on his side projects. The bots had thus far proven impossible to crack, though he had identified that they were indeed on their own network, and whoever built it wasn't messing around. The security even impressed him, which was saying something.

He decided that they might have to wait until they actually found a planet before he could enact his plans. His goal wasn't to hurt anyone, not really, but he had no desire to live under anyone else's control, either. The psychological exams had been thorough, and they'd even used brain scans. But everything could be beaten, especially if you helped develop the technology that was utilized. The system had him down as an intelligent follower. He was brilliant, that much was right, but he had never been much of a follower; he just did an excellent job at hiding it. Having benefactors with access to the systems didn't hurt either.

* * *

Transition + 1 Day, 1300 Hours

Max watched the progress on the diagnostics for Peeper. The telescope wasn't his area of expertise, but Sivert's repeated instructions over the communicator told him, in addition to what he could observe, that something wasn't as it should be.

Finally, Sivert turned in his seat. "I'm sorry, Captain, it looks like one of the lenses is out of alignment, and it's not responding to commands to reset."

"I had a feeling something wasn't right," Max said with a grin.

Sivert turned a bit red as he realized how loud he must have gotten during the exchange.

"Can we fix it?"

"Oh, yes, we can fix it," Sivert insisted. "But it will require someone to manually reset the system and possibly open Peeper up to give things a nudge."

Spacewalks weren't something that bothered Max, or most of the crew for that matter. All 100 members of *Traveler*'s crew had at least 50 hours in space untethered and more on a tether line. It had been one of the strict washout criteria for the mission if you wanted to be on the crew.

"Okay, put an op plan together, and let's review it in thirty minutes with the mechanics."

Sivert nodded and left the bridge.

Max sighed and leaned back in his chair. He stared at the display but wasn't looking at it. Even though spacewalks were common and the risk levels were low, there was still a risk.

Kellie appeared at his side, as usual, knowing when he was worried. "It'll be fine. Some of the mechanics have more untethered time than you do."

"I know, I've just been thinking…"

"I thought I smelled gears burning," she joked. "Seriously, what's the problem?"

"We don't know where we are. I mean, what if things are different here?"

"Different how? Like, the laws of physics don't apply?"

He looked at her. "Something like that."

She shook her head. "I'll accept that we've gone beyond where we can see from Earth. I won't buy that the laws of physics have somehow changed. This isn't science fiction."

"I just think we need to keep both eyes open and expect the unexpected."

"On that we can agree."

* * *

Transition + 1 Day, 1400 Hours

Max wasn't the only one with concerns. Watching on the bridge's main screen as the mechanics exited the airlock and stood on the exterior of the hull, he could almost feel their uncertainty. He knew how many suited hours they had, but it didn't show at first.

"Everything okay out there, Rhonda?" Max asked.

Rhonda Matthews, a spacewalk veteran, had been involved in the design of the telescope, so she knew it better than anyone else on the ship. "Fine, Max. Just taking things a little slower than usual. Let me do my job, okay?"

"Copy that."

Kellie glanced at Max, concerned. "Are *you* okay?"

"Just a bit anxious."

"If you say so…"

Max nodded, but his eyes didn't leave the screen.

He remained silent for the next three nerve-wracking hours while the three-person team worked. Finally, Sivert confirmed that Peeper was operating as expected. Max knew it would take at least another hour to close up the maintenance panels.

"Keep an eye on your O2 levels," he commed.

"Roger that," Rhonda responded. "I think we'll be okay."

Max pulled up the suit status indicators on his screen, which allowed him to monitor not only the oxygen levels of the suits' tanks but also the medical stats on the team. Everything was nominal, and it looked like they had just enough time to finish the job. He was about to get up and take a break when one of the health indicators went red—no heartbeat detected.

Doctor Chadda, who had monitored the repair team's health indicators the entire time, jerked her head up to look at Max. He waved a hand dismissively. "Things break, probably nothing. But I'll check. I can't count how many times those sensors have gone out on my suits."

There was an audible gasp, and he looked up at the main screen. He saw Takai Ichebei's suit limp at the end of its tether. "Takai? Are you okay?" he asked. After a moment of silence, he grew concerned. "Rhonda, check on Takai," he said more urgently.

He watched as Rhonda stopped what she was doing and used her maneuvering thrusters to coast over to Takai. "Everyone inside! Now! We'll close up later!" she said quickly. Without further explanation, she unhooked Takai's suit and pulled it with her toward the airlock.

"I'm hit!" another of the team exclaimed. "I think—" The voice cut off without warning.

"Get to the airlock! Now, now, now!" Max shouted as if sheer volume would help them move faster.

Doctor Chadda rose from her seat and pushed her way to the transport to get the airlock, but Max didn't think there would be much she could do. Max stayed where he was and let his team handle things for now as he watched the scene unfold on cameras.

* * *

Transition + 1 Day, 1700 Hours

Rhonda Matthews, the most experienced person in untethered spacewalks alive, found herself shaken as she hauled two limp suits with her into the airlock. She punched the button to cycle the chamber and checked on the status of the two mechanics. She knew something was very wrong. Each of their suits, pure white to make them easier to spot in the blackness of space, were pierced. Droplets of blood had made their way out of the punctures and floated in the air around them.

As soon as the chamber finished cycling, the inner door opened, and Doctor Chadda, along with three medics, hauled the three of them into the larger ready room. They worked efficiently to get the space suits off of the men, but it was too late. They applied adhesive bandages to the wounds to prevent more blood from escaping into the artificial atmosphere and just as efficiently loaded them into body bags they'd brought with them.

While the medics handled sealing the bodies, Doctor Chadda walked over to Rhonda as she stood in the airlock. She hadn't bothered to remove her helmet. "Ms. Matthews? Are you injured? We should check over your suit," she suggested and lightly put a hand on Rhonda's arm.

Rhonda jerked her arm away. "I'm fine. I think I'd know if my suit was punctured."

Doctor Chadda raised an eyebrow and nodded toward Rhonda's shoulder.

Rhonda unsealed and removed her helmet and looked down at her shoulder. She showed no visible reaction but was surprised when she saw a rip in the first two layers of her spacesuit. "Well...shit." The tear had stopped just short of piercing the liquid cooling and ventilation layer. "I guess I'll have to replace this. Good thing I have spares. Thanks for the heads up, Doc."

Chadda looked at her skeptically. "Mmm-hmm. Well, Doctor Marsh will want to see you at your earliest convenience."

Rhonda grimaced. She hated psychologists, or therapists, or head shrinkers, or whatever they wanted to call themselves. "Right. I'll see if I can fit him into my schedule. I'm sure Captain Reeves will want a debrief on this, and I still have to button up Peeper."

"See that you do," Chadda said seriously and turned to leave.

Rhonda looked at the two body bags the medics were prepping for storage. "Doc, find out what the hell hit us out there. I'm used to space debris in Earth orbit, but I didn't expect it out here. We weren't even looking for it."

Doctor Chadda nodded. "I'll let you know what we discover."

Rhonda slowly extricated herself from her spacesuit once she was alone and showered.

Showering in space was not a simple proposition. It had taken a while, but technicians had finally found the right combination of water force and vacuum system to make it possible and safe. Once she was sure she was dry, she floated back into the ready room and got dressed. She checked her comm and found that she had about two hours until her meeting with Captain Reeves for debriefing.

She made the short walk back to her quarters and pulled up the imagery from the spacewalk. After spending an hour and a half going through it over and over, she zoomed in on one frame. It had captured something just before it ripped through Takai Ichibei's suit but she couldn't tell what it was. She sighed. It was probably some remnant of two asteroids colliding, but she doubted she'd ever know for sure.

Her watch chimed and brought her out of her reverie. It was time to debrief the captain.

* * *

Transition + 1 Day, 2000 Hours

Max was waiting in the conference room, along with Kellie, Doctor Chadda, and a colonist Chadda had brought with her. Rhonda walked in a few minutes before the meeting was supposed to start and took a seat.

"Thank you all for coming after normal hours," Max began. "Rhonda, you already know Kellie and Doctor Chadda. This—" he gestured, "—is Doctor Marc Heuser, one of our colonists, who happens to be a forensic pathologist. Since we don't have a pathologist among the crew, Doctor Chadda brought him in to examine the bodies. Like you, I want to know what killed our people. So, Doctor Heuser, what did you find?"

"As requested by Doctor Chadda, I examined both of the deceased. The cause of death is relatively straightforward, as I will show. Exactly what caused it is another matter—"

"Cut to the chase, Doc. What killed my astronauts?" Rhonda interrupted.

Doctor Heuser looked a bit put out and frowned as he scrolled through several pages of notes on his tablet before he stopped. An image of a speck appeared on the 3D projector in the center of the table. "I pulled this from the spine of astronaut Ichibei. It is a trace left behind by the item passing through his body at high speed."

"So, what is it?" Rhonda asked.

"I don't know," Heuser admitted. "We—"

"Well, this has been very helpful," she said. "Thanks for nothing." She stood to leave.

"Take a seat, Ms. Matthews," Max insisted and gestured to her chair. "I know what it's like to lose people, and it sucks, but we need to discuss this."

She pulled herself back into her seat. Max was sure if there had been gravity, she would have fallen into it with a huff. "Thank you," he said sincerely. "Please continue, Doctor Heuser."

"We are subjecting the sample to several tests. Initial observation through an electron microscope was inconclusive, though it appears to be some type of metal."

"Something from the ship or the telescope that got loose?" Doctor Chadda asked.

"Are you saying we screwed up and let something fly?" Rhonda demanded.

Max shook his head. "No, that can't be right. Even if Rhonda's team had set a screw loose, it wouldn't have had the speed and force to do this. It would have just floated beside them, traveling at the same speed we are. It had to be something that was already flying through space on its own. If it's metallic, then it's probably a sliver of a comet or asteroid. Lots of things out here are metallic."

"Well, we still need to button up Peeper," Rhonda said.

"Yes, we do, but we need to guard against this happening again. No more EVAs until we figure out how to do that."

"Fine. Anything else?"

"No, that's all. Thank you all for your time. Doctor Heuser, please keep at it. I want to know what that is," Max said, pointing at the 3D image. "Rhonda, stay behind for a minute, please."

Once everyone else had filed out of the room Max turned off the 3D projector. He leaned back in his chair. "Are you okay?"

"Other than just having watched two people die on what should have been a routine spacewalk, yeah, I'm fine."

"I saw your suit, Rhonda."

She looked down at the table for a second, then back up. "It happens. You know that as well as I do."

Max nodded. He did know. He'd had more than his share of close calls. "It's a dangerous business out there, and I know it sucks, but you *will* sit down and talk to Doctor Marsh."

She rolled her eyes. "I know."

"Any thoughts on how to make it safer? You have more time in the suit than I do."

"I'll think about it. But we can't make the suits out of anything strong enough to stop something traveling thousands of kilometers per hour. Can't we detect that shit?"

"I've got the team working on it. We're spotting large debris and maneuvering the ship around it, but the smaller pieces..." Max shrugged. "That's always been the danger for us. The piece that Doctor Heuser found is microscopic. Whatever it was, was probably less than a millimeter. We know it was more than just dust since it got through the ballistic layer."

Rhonda nodded in agreement.

They both knew that the ballistic layer of the suits was the most durable, flexible material known to man. In the past, it had been Kevlar, then Zylon, and it just kept getting better, but it wasn't enough to stop whatever had hit them.

"Anything else?" she asked.

"No. Be sure to visit Doctor Marsh in the next day or two."

"I will. And...thanks," Rhonda said.

* * * * *

Chapter Five

Transition + 2 Days, 0800 Hours

News of the deaths of two astronauts didn't take long to spread through the ship. Most of the crew understood that it was a risk of the job and took it in stride. The colonists, on the other hand, had mixed reactions. Some had been in professions where risk was a part of daily life and reacted similarly to the crew. Others didn't care one way or the other and focused on how they were going to survive. A small collection of colonists, though, felt that they should have done more to protect the astronauts and blamed Max or Rhonda.

Max was ready for that kind of attitude. Being in charge meant that everything was his fault, and he could accept that. There was an element of truth to it as well. His gut had told him to be concerned, and he didn't listen closely enough.

As he sat on the bridge working on his tablet trying to figure out how to make spacewalks safer, Sivert gasped audibly. "You want to share with the class, Sivert?" Max asked.

An image appeared on the main screen, and everyone on the bridge was speechless. It was a close-up of a planet, and it showed life. Trees and plants, positively alien in appearance, in shades of purple, yellow, blue, and green, but there were living things.

"Tell me that's not a stock image, Sivert."

The plants on the screen moved, blown by a breeze.

"By the Goddess," Kellie whispered.

"This is what Peeper sees on the fifth planet we observed," Sivert explained.

Max stared at the screen. The odds of finding a planet that could sustain life were small, by all estimations, but here they were. He was looking at living plant life on an alien world. "We still have a lot to do. Sivert, send survey probes to the planet. Let's see what data we can get back. Keep looking."

"Yes, Captain."

Kellie stood beside him. "Should we tell the passengers?"

Max chewed on his bottom lip and considered. Keeping secrets hadn't worked for them very well, but he also didn't want to give anyone false hope. Just because there was life, didn't mean the planet would be friendly to humans. Unlike many scientists, he wasn't a part of the community who believed that all life had to be carbon-based. That meant he would want a lot of information before he sent anyone to any planet.

"I don't think so. Not yet, anyway. I'd love to give them *some* hope, but I don't want to give them *false* hope. Let's wait a few days to get the probe data back."

Kellie nodded. "I think that's wise. Another letdown right now might just break some spirits."

"Shit!" Sivert suddenly exclaimed.

Max raised an eyebrow, and Kellie looked at Sivert.

He threw up his hands. "Peeper isn't responding, and we've lost imagery."

"Diagnostics?" Max asked.

"Nothing," Sivert answered.

"Did something else hit us?"

"Nothing big, Captain," a member of Sivert's astrogation team responded. "We're maneuvering the ship around anything dangerous, but we can't track the smaller stuff. My best estimation is that there was an asteroid collision somewhere nearby, and we're getting hit by the debris."

"The maintenance panels are still off. Could be something got inside Peeper's casing," Max suggested.

"So, what now?" Kellie asked.

"I'm not ready to send anyone back outside. Sivert, retract Peeper and set course for the planet you spotted. Let's get a closer look. Low acceleration profile: no need to send anyone into shock."

Sivert nodded and turned back to his station as his team got to work. Contrary to what some lay-people thought, Max knew you *could* feel G forces in space. If they accelerated suddenly to the full .25 C that *Traveler* was capable of, there would be a huge mess to clean up for whoever found the ship. There were lockouts to prevent that from happening, but they could still, in an emergency, accelerate quickly. Max decided the best plan this time was to accelerate the ship slowly so that would not even realize they were moving. Once at speed, they could maintain .25 C and reach the planet in approximately seven days. Barring any more problems.

* * *

Transition + 2 Days, 0900 Hours

Ragnarsson was sitting in his quarters staring at a still image of the planet the bridge crew had seen. His system took snapshots of anything displayed on the bridge's main screen throughout the day so he could review it when he finished his work. He could have viewed a live feed, but that was too risky as it increased the possibility the back door he'd installed would be detected.

He also knew they were moving thanks to a primitive acceleration detection system he'd devised: he'd hung a washer on a string from his bunk. It would just float with no particular pattern as long as they weren't accelerating, and it shifted when the ship's maneuvering thrusters fired. Now, though, it was pulled taught, which told him that they were under acceleration in a single direction.

"So, we've found a planet to land on, have we?" he asked no one. "When will you tell everyone else what you already know, Captain?"

Without warning, his screen went black. He frowned and tapped the screen to bring it back to life, but it didn't respond. "What the—" He was interrupted by a knock on the door.

"Mr. Ragnarsson, open your door or we will open it for you."

Ragnarsson recognized the voice and scowled. It was Colonel Ascher. He sighed and hit the stud on his desk that unlocked and opened the door. "Come on in, Colonel."

Ascher walked in, accompanied by a man and a woman, also in green jumpsuits and holding stun guns, which indicated they were part of the military contingent. "You have much to explain."

He considered fighting, but it only took a second to realize that it wouldn't do any good. He stood and gestured to the door. "After you."

The woman stepped toward him and pulled a pair of restraints from her belt.

Ragnarsson sighed and held out his hands. She turned him around roughly and pushed him down against his desk. After thoroughly searching him for weapons, she restrained his hands behind his back.

"That was hardly necessary," he said, his voice muffled.

"Terrorists get what they deserve, Mr. Ragnarsson," Ascher said.

Ragnarsson remained silent throughout the journey to the security area of the ship. Even though problems weren't expected on *Traveler*, there was still a small area that contained what amounted to prison cells. One of those was not the destination, though. Fifteen minutes later, he found himself sitting in an open office, his feet tied to the chair he'd been shoved into, and held in place with a restraining belt.

Ascher left him in the room with the man and woman who had escorted him here. "So, now what?"

"Now, you tell us everything you've done to the ship," the man said.

"That's easy. I haven't done a single thing to the ship."

With movement faster than Ragnarsson expected, the woman reached out and slapped him hard.

He saw stars for a moment and had to shake his head to clear his vision and his mind. "What the hell?"

"We know you've done something. Likely more than one thing. Now, just tell us everything, and we can be done here," she said with a smile.

"I want to speak to the captain!"

"Oh, I'm sure he'll speak with you, but not until we're done."

"You got this?" the man asked.

"Aye, you go ahead," she responded.

The man nodded and left Ragnarsson alone with the woman, who turned back to Ragnarsson after he left. "Just you and me now. Ready to tell me everything?"

He studied her more closely now. She was all business and convinced there was something horrible to find out. He'd seen that kind of look before in the mirror. Nothing Ragnarsson said would satisfy her unless he admitted to things he hadn't done, but he wouldn't do that. He was beginning to wonder what they thought he had done when she struck him again. This time a closed fist impacted his jawline. He tasted blood and knew the inside of his mouth had been cut open.

"I'm afraid I'm not a very patient woman, Mr. Ragnarsson. Especially when lives are at stake."

He worked his jaw to make sure nothing was broken, then spit blood onto the floor. "Let's say that I have done some things that aren't on the up and up; none of them would endanger anyone. Hell, I'm on the ship too, why would I endanger myself?"

Ragnarsson braced himself as she swung again. This time, she caught his temple, and he was knocked out cold.

A minute later, he was coughing and pushing back and away from the horrible smell that she used to wake him up. Once she was sure he was awake, she walked around the desk, opened a drawer, and withdrew a hypo-syringe.

"Wait, what's that?" he asked. His speech was slurred, affected by the swelling in his jaw.

"I don't know what's in it, to be honest. But I'm told it will extract the truth."

That sent his mind running. There were many ways to get to the truth. He knew there was no such thing as an actual "truth serum," which sent him down darker alleys in his mind.

"Fine. I'll tell you," Ragnarsson said as he encountered genuine fear—something he wasn't used to at all.

He admitted to putting in a back door so he could review communications and activities on the bridge on the main screen. He also listed his attempts to get into the bots' network, since he figured that was likely what got him caught. He decided not to mention any of the plans he'd made with Empyre or Courtni since none of them had been set into motion.

She stared at him for a long moment with her lips pursed. "That's all?"

"Yes, that's all!"

She patted his cheek, causing him to wince from the pain. "Good boy," she said, then walked out of the room.

He scowled and stared at the ground. How had he been so reckless as to get caught? Maybe their techs were better than he'd expected, and they'd just been watching and waiting the whole time.

* * *

Transition + 2 Days, 1100 Hours

Max walked into Colonel Ascher's office soon after being summoned. He'd gotten a vague briefing about what was going on, but he wanted to talk to Ragnarsson himself. Max was surprised to hear the allegations, especially since Adel Ragnarsson was on the colonists' council. Because of that, he'd worked with Ragnarsson quite a bit over the last few years, and though he didn't know him all that well, he was familiar with him and hadn't had any concerns before today.

"Good afternoon, gentlemen. What's going on?" he asked after closing the door behind him.

"Would you like to tell him or shall I?" Ascher asked.

Ragnarsson turned to face Max, and Max flinched. Ragnarsson's face showed evidence of bruising, and he had a feeling it wasn't from a fall. He kept his features passive, but inside, he was immediately pissed at Ascher. Ragnarsson spat on the floor.

"You may as well go ahead, Colonel," Max said, crossing his arms over his chest.

"Adel Ragnarsson hacked into the computers at the crew and ship operations level. He's even been reading messages exchanged between members of the crew. He also has access to anything that happens on the bridge."

"That's not entirely true," Ragnarsson said.

"Well, clear it up then," Max suggested.

"I can indeed see what displays on the bridge's main screen, but I never went anywhere near the ship's control systems. Even I wouldn't risk that. So, I could not, in fact, access everything that happens on the bridge."

"Semantics," Ascher spat.

"Colonel, would you excuse us for a few minutes?" Max asked politely, though what he wanted to do was forcefully throw Ascher out of his own office.

"I beg your pardon, but this is *my* office."

"Fine, I'll take him to my office." Max moved toward the door.

"That won't be necessary," Ascher said quickly. "I will allow you a few moments."

Max sighed once Ascher had left the room. "What the hell, Adel?"

Ragnarsson shrugged. "Call it a natural distrust of authority and a desire to know what lies in store."

"Mmm-hmm. You must realize I will now have a hard time trusting *you*."

"Did you ever really trust any of us?"

Max furrowed his brows. "Look. Yes, I withheld the fact that we didn't get to Alpha Centauri, but I eventually made that right."

"After your hand was forced"—he glanced at Max's still bandaged hand—"so to speak."

"It was a mistake to hold that back. I admit that."

"So, when are you planning to tell everyone that you've found a life-sustaining planet, and that we're heading for it now?"

"How is it you know we're heading for anything?"

"A string and a washer."

Max nodded. "Clever. The answer is, I don't know yet. Soon. I don't want to get people's hopes up. For all we know, the atmosphere is laced with something that'll kill us. We have probes on the way to get more data, but, yes, we are heading toward it."

"Why not keep looking?"

"Because the telescope is broken, and I don't know if we can repair it. We have a lot of people in an enclosed space. Right now, the crew and I need to focus on keeping everyone alive. That'll be hard to do if people are rioting."

"So repair the telescope."

"I'd love to! Unfortunately, I've also lost two astronauts due to some kind of debris flying through the area, so I can't risk sending anyone else out. Maybe, once we get into orbit around the planet, and we can get a good look at things, I'll be more confident. Then we can see how bad the damage is and hopefully replace what is broken."

Ragnarsson frowned and looked down at his hands, which were still handcuffed. "Why are you telling me all this?"

"You asked."

"So, what will you do with me now?" he asked, looking up at Max. "Let Ascher finish what his men started?"

Max shook his head. "No. As a matter of fact, I'd like to know who's responsible for your face."

"That would be my mother and father," Ragnarsson said with a grin.

"You know what I mean."

"I do," he agreed. "But I'm not one to tell tales."

"Are you one to get your revenge? Because I can't have that on my ship."

Ragnarsson met Max's eyes for a moment. "Very well. I won't do it on your ship."

"You're putting me in a tough spot here, Adel."

"I recognize that, and I apologize. It is, as you say, what it is."

"I see."

"So what will you do with me?"

Max shrugged. "First, get you some medical treatment. Then, I'm going to have you work with my techs and show them what you did to get into our systems."

"And if I won't?"

"Then all technology will be taken from you, and you will be confined to quarters until I locate a planet suitable for us to land. After that, I don't know. I've only had a few minutes to think about it."

"You seem a fair man, Maxwell Reeves."

"I try to be. What's it going to be?"

"Can I think about it?"

"Sure, you have ten seconds. I'm kinda busy."

Ragnarsson chuckled. "Very well. I will show your techs how I got in."

"And you'll cease any further efforts to access things that aren't in your purview?"

Ragnarsson grimaced but nodded.

"I want your word, Adel."

"You have it. I will not hack further into your systems."

Max nodded. He had a feeling there was a loophole there. Still, he hoped with the system security teams on alert, they would identify any further intrusion attempts. "Okay." Max raised his voice. "Colonel, come back in, please."

Ascher came back in, obviously frustrated.

"Remove the restraints, Colonel."

"What?" Ascher demanded.

"I don't believe I stuttered. Remove them."

Ascher turned several shades of red as Ragnarsson grinned and held out his hands. Ascher hesitated but finally pressed his finger to the biometric lock on the restraints to release them.

Ragnarsson stood and rubbed his wrists before he nodded to Max and walked out.

"What was the meaning of that?" Ascher snapped.

"We reached an agreement. Adel won't be doing what he was doing anymore. He'll be showing my team how he did it and help to remove the back doors he installed."

"He is a terrorist!"

"I think that's a bit harsh," Max argued.

"I am certain he was the source of the leak. Now he will spread word of where we are going, and the results will be—"

Max cut him off mid-sentence. "I'm going to be telling everyone where we're going soon anyway. I'm sure he's not the only one who noticed we've started accelerating.

"Colonel," Max continued, "I was the one who selected you to lead the platoon. Did I make a mistake?"

The muscles in Ascher's jaws flexed visibly as he clenched his teeth.

Max answered his own question. "I hope not. But let me make something incredibly clear. If I find out you've detained and beaten anyone else on this ship—I don't care what they've done—you will be relieved of your duties. Is that understood?"

All Ascher could do was nod once.

"Good. Have a good afternoon, Colonel," Max said and left the office.

* * *

Transition + 2 Days, 1130 Hours

Max put his earpiece in and activated it. He tapped the sequence on his communicator to call Kellie's station.

"Hey, Max. Everything okay?"

"Yeah. Put out the notice I'll be addressing the ship at 1800. We can't hold on to this anymore. At least one person was smart enough to rig up something so they could tell when we started accelerating. We have some pretty smart people on board; best to just tell them."

"Will do. Anything else?"

"Have the tech division get with Adel Ragnarsson. He has a few things to show them. Sooner rather than later."

"You got it."

"Thanks, Kellie." He ended the call. He really hoped the planet would be able to sustain life.

When he addressed the entire ship, he told them everything, starting by confirming the loss of the two astronauts and the circumstances, the loss of the use of Peeper, and ended by reminding everyone they had other ways of observing planets. He closed by telling them they were en route to a potentially habitable planet.

Over the next few days, he rotated where he ate his meals, making himself available to the colonists in the different cafeterias around the ship. He had his department heads do the same. Max needed everyone to know the crew could be trusted.

* * * * *

Chapter Six

Transition + 6 Days, 0900 Hours

After several days of travel, the crew and colonists of *Traveler* entered the destination star system. The planet, which had been nicknamed Rainbow by the bridge crew, was only a day away, and preparations were underway to calculate an orbital entry. More importantly, the probe results were back.

Rather than keeping the information among the bridge crew, or even just the department heads, he had Sivert put together a presentation for the full ship's council, minus Adel Ragnarsson.

"Okay, folks," Max began. "We're about twenty-four hours away from Rainbow."

The name got him some strange looks from the passengers.

He grinned. "It's what the crew started calling it, and it stuck. Now, we're all going to hear, together, what the probe results tell us. Sivert?"

Sivert tapped his tablet and the 3D projector in the middle of the table displayed what Max recognized as an analysis of the chemicals present in the atmosphere and other related readings. Sivert spoke for a few minutes before Max noticed that some of the colonists were utterly lost.

"Sorry to interrupt, Sivert, but I don't think this makes sense to everyone."

"Yes, get to the point. Can we breathe the air?" Lina Skoog asked.

Sivert pursed his lips for a moment, a bit disappointed at having been interrupted but answered, "In short, yes. But it will take some acclimation."

"Like getting used to thinner air?" Lina asked.

"Yes—well, no." Sivert screwed up his face as he considered how to explain himself.

"Let me give it a shot," Max suggested. "Ms. Skoog, the analysis shows that at random times, additional elements show up in the samples. We're not sure why and, to be honest, that makes me nervous. We don't know if it's a planetary cycle that we'll be able to identify quickly, or if there's something that produces those elements that we don't know about."

"Yes, something like that," Sivert agreed. "I'd like to get a core sample to analyze. It might tell us what we're dealing with."

"So, someone's going down there?"

"That's correct, Ms. Skoog. It's the only way we'll get more detailed information," Max responded.

"I want to go," she said quickly.

Max grinned. "I'm sure lots of people would like to go, but I'm afraid I can't authorize that. Your safety is my responsibility, and we have no idea how 'safe' it is down there. We have teams that are trained and ready for just such a mission."

She crossed her arms over her chest and pouted.

"If we do eventually land, you'll have plenty of time to explore, I promise. Any other questions?"

"When will we know for sure?"

"Honestly, I don't know. Protocol is to get a core sample and subject it to a detailed analysis. Timetable for that, generally speaking, is about a week. If that comes back as acceptable, there are several other steps we'll need to take before I can make a final determination. I'd say the best case would be about a month."

"Are you kidding me?" Deanna Stokes exclaimed.

"No, I'm not. We don't have another ship coming after us, so every decision has to be made with the long haul in mind. This shouldn't be a surprise to any of you. While we evaluate this planet, we're also using onboard visual equipment and sensors to check the other planets in the system, just in case. Additional probes are also being launched. We're not putting all of our eggs in one basket."

Stokes nodded, seemingly mollified.

"Anything else? No? Good. Let's all get back to work."

* * *

Transition + 6 Days, 1200 Hours

Ragnarsson met with Empyre and Courtni in the cafeteria later that day. It was the first time they'd seen him since his encounter with Ascher's goons days earlier. While the medics had done a great job of alleviating the pain and speeding up the healing process, the bruises were still visible.

"Holy shit, what happened to you?" Empyre exclaimed.

"Ascher."

Empyre scowled. "Wondered where you'd been. Want me to deal with him?"

"No. He'll get his. I gave my word to the captain I wouldn't enact my revenge on the ship. Once we're *off* the ship is something else. It was one of his goons who did the damage, but I know he ordered it."

Courtni looked troubled. She was tough as nails, but she did have a soft side. "Are you okay? Is there anything we can do?"

"I'll be fine. Just keep doing your jobs for now. Everything is on hold until we're off this hunk of metal."

Empyre looked surprised.

"I gave my word," Ragnarsson repeated.

Empyre and Courtni nodded. They understood a person's word was everything. Even if you gave it to someone you didn't like, you honored it. Ragnarsson was sure the captain felt the same way since he'd also been true to his word. He also had a feeling that Captain Reeves knew Ragnarsson would get his revenge eventually.

"I may have been wrong about Reeves," he admitted.

Courtni tilted her head. "How so?"

"Just a feeling. I look a lot better now than I did, but he saw me after Ascher's goon got done with me. He looked *pissed*, and honestly, I don't think he's a man I'd want to piss off. Though, I'm sure I will eventually."

"Scuttlebutt is that his wife left him right before we left Earth," Courtni said.

Ragnarsson nodded. "It's worse than that; she knew we might not get to Alpha Centauri."

Empyre winced. "Wow, that sucks. Even *I* feel sorry for him on that one."

Courtni shook her head. "Bitch."

Ragnarsson felt eyes on him and turned to see who it was. He clenched his jaws when he saw the woman who'd given him the bruises he was still sporting. She winked and waved at him with a smile. He flipped her off, then turned back to Empyre and Courtni. "That's the one that did this to me."

"You got beat up by a chick?" Empyre said, chuckling.

"I was restrained and strapped to a chair, asshole."

"Don't call women 'chicks,' 'Pyre," Courtni said in a way that indicated this wasn't the first time she'd reminded him. "It's so 20th century."

"Right, sorry."

"Mmm-hmm."

"Once we're off this ship, she's the first who gets my undivided attention," Ragnarsson said.

* * *

Transition + 6 Days, 0900 Hours

Max sat on the bridge and watched the multiple camera angles as the X-94E gently coasted out of the hangar. The E variant was loaded with scientific equipment instead of seats for passengers and had only one pilot. All data would come back to *Traveler* for analysis.

The hangar doors closed, and the plane started toward the planet. "On profile for entry. Everything looks good," the pilot reported.

The only sound on the bridge was the soft hiss of the ventilation system as the crew watched the visuals and the telemetry on the main display.

"Lots of instability; still on course," the pilot said. The transmission became harder to interpret due to interference from the planet's outer atmosphere.

"Receiving an emergency signal. He's attempting to abort!" Sivert exclaimed.

Max held his breath. He'd done aborted entries, and they were never easy. He stared at the screen and then knew it was over. There was a burst of fireworks in the upper atmosphere, then nothing. Every telemetry reading from the plane went dead.

"Go over that data. Now. I want to know what happened," Max ordered.

Kellie stood and ran off the bridge. She would gather all the right people and go over every second of the plane's descent data. Meanwhile, he pulled up the same information on his tablet and went through it from a pilot's perspective. He wanted to go to his office, but he felt like he needed to remain on the bridge.

It didn't take long before he saw what he thought had caused the failure, and it wasn't good. The plane had registered unstable variable electromagnetic readings in the seconds before it was destroyed. He relayed what he'd found to Kellie so her team could factor it into their analysis, but he was sure they would come to the same conclusion. Eventually, the data would be enough to build a simulator around, to determine a safe way through to the planet's surface. Still, he admitted to himself it was unlikely.

With that done, he pulled up the pilot's personal information. He closed his eyes when he saw that the pilot had boarded with his wife. "Shit."

Sivert turned in his seat and raised an eyebrow at Max.

"His wife is on board," Max explained.

A pained look crossed Sivert's face.

Max sighed and stood. "I'll go talk to her. You have the bridge."

Sivert simply nodded.

"Sivert, find us another planet. Fast." He left the bridge.

* * *

Transition + 6 Days, 1200 Hours

After spending an hour with the pilot's wife, Max went to his quarters to rest. She was understandably upset, but she was also an experimental pilot's wife, so she was familiar with the risks. She didn't blame Max or the mission, and she only had one request: to make sure the next pilot that tried to descend to a planet made it.

No sooner had he laid down, then his comm chimed. He sighed and accepted it.

"Max, it's Kellie. You were right. The magnetic field around the planet is…Unstable would be putting it lightly. The probes didn't catch it because it's a micro-field. None of the experts have ever even *heard* of anything like it."

"So, there's no safe path?" he asked, though it was more of a statement.

"Correct. The good news is that we have another possibility. It's only four days of travel."

"Okay, set course. Let's get moving. We need a way to determine if the entry will be safe on this planet."

"They're working on that out now. Sending multiple probes in at various entry angles might work. Some will bounce off, others will burn up, and so on, but we can also get more information that way."

"Get whatever they recommend in place. Also, notify the ship of the situation. I need to get some downtime."

"Will do."

Moments later, Kellie announced the loss of the pilot to the crew and passengers, and the worse news that they couldn't get to the surface of that planet safely. She did an excellent job of reassuring everyone that they were on their way to the next world, with plans to ensure the safety of the pilot before the next attempt.

There was, as expected, frustration, but, overall, the crew and passengers received the news well. Emphasis had been put on transparency, and trust was starting to be rebuilt between the crew and passengers.

* * *

Transition + 10 Days, 1000 Hours

The crew's focus while they traveled to the next planet was spent on preparation. Probes were launched and the results were meticulously analyzed. Visuals started to come in, and there was certainly evidence of life. Again, the plantlife was replete with vibrant colors, much different than one would expect to see on Earth. There also appeared to be an ocean that covered a significant portion of the planet.

The images were broadcast through the ship so everyone could see the possibilities. Below the video was an always-present ticker warning that all the data wasn't in yet, and habitability had not been deterimined.

Max was on the bridge as they entered orbit over the planet. The crew had been careful not to even joke about a name this time. Ascher was disturbingly quiet during the trip, and that bothered Max, but he focused on what was in front of him. There would be time to deal with Ascher later. He attributed the quiet to the fact that the 'stolen' supplies had been located, simply misplaced.

"Eagle is ready," Kellie reported.

Max nodded. Eagle was the callsign for Colin Shepard, who was the pilot for this mission. He had asked the crew pilots for a volunteer and every one of them had stepped forward. They went old school and pulled out a deck of cards and drew until someone got an ace. Eagle was the lucky draw.

Max was glad Eagle had gotten the card. Since he was single and had no dependents on the ship to be concerned about, Max had decided to put the whole thing on a ship-wide broadcast.

"Eagle, you are cleared to launch and descend," Max said into the comm.

"Eagle copies. Dear Goddess, please don't let me screw up."

"Misquoted, but accurate," Max said with a grin. If anyone was allowed to modify it, Eagle was. He was, after all, a descendant of Alan Shepard, to whom the misquote was attributed.

"Hey, gotta roll with the times, Cap. Eagle is clear of the hangar. Starting descent."

The main screen, and the screens throughout the ship, switched to an exterior view showing the space plane moving away from *Traveler* toward the planet. Eagle's personnel photo was displayed in the upper right corner. Max watched his tablet, which displayed the telemetry from the plane. It would be interrupted for a few seconds but would come back. If it didn't, they would know something was wrong.

As expected, the data flatlined, and Max held his breath. Everything showed he was on a perfect entry angle and none of the probes had detected any conditions that should cause any significant problems. In fact, everything the probes had returned was surprisingly stable.

"Well, it looks like I'm still here, *Traveler*. It's a bumpy ride, but not bad at all."

Max hit the arm of his chair with his fist. "Yes! Okay, one thing at a time, Eagle. Fly around a bit and get a feel for things. We've found what should be a good landing spot for you."

Max found that he couldn't get the smile off of his face. Just the chance that they'd found a planet suitable for life made him giddy. He hadn't lost another pilot, and that was a victory in his book.

Eagle flew around for another 30 minutes. The high-speed cameras mounted into his plane sent images back to the *Traveler* for a more detailed analysis. "Okay, *Traveler*. Time to try to put this sucker down. Going for a vertical landing. I don't trust the ground here."

"Copy that, Eagle. Proceed on your clock." A vertical landing meant that he would bring the plane to a hover. A different set of jets would fire up to let him set the plane straight down rather than flying in for a landing as a plane normally would, and rolling to a stop.

"How's the atmosphere reading?" Max asked.

"It's…good!" Kellie said hesitantly. "There are some trace elements that we're not going to be used to, but they should be tolerable on short exposure."

"Doctor Chadda?"

"I concur," Chadda responded. "I'd recommend Eagle keep his suit sealed for now until we can get more detailed readings at ground level."

Max nodded and opened the channel. "Eagle, the doc recommends you stay on your own air. We've got some trace elements we're not sure about just yet. She needs time to get the data at ground level."

"Eagle copies."

* * *

Transition + 10 Days, 1100 Hours

Colin "Eagle" Shepard focused on his controls and slowly lowered the plane toward the ground. He talked through everything for the record as he was accustomed to doing.

"Fifty meters altitude, descending into the clearing at designated LZ. Some low brush, but nothing that should be a problem."

He corrected as a strong gust of wind threatened to blow him out of position. "Strong winds. Slow descent is problematic. If we bring anything else down, we may need to clear a runway or build a soft pad for landing."

Soft pads were used to protect and catch something that was falling. It was like an air bag used by stuntmen in movies but designed to catch planes.

"Screw this," he muttered. He cut back on the thruster power and let the plane fall, flaring the jets at the last second to cushion what became a controlled crash. He grunted as the plane hit, but the landing gear held, and much to his surprise, nothing snapped.

He grinned and transmitted, "Eagle has landed."

He heard chuckling over the comms before Max replied, "Somehow I knew you'd say that. Okay, Eagle. Take it one step at a time. Deploy the sensor suite first, then you can take a look around."

"Copy that," he said. He took a moment to make sure his suit was sealed before he unstrapped.

Eagle took a deep breath and walked through the cramped cargo area of the aircraft, which was taken up by sensors and the computers that operated them. He activated the sensitive equipment, then lowered the rear cargo ramp and pushed the remote sensor package out of the ship. Once it anchored itself and started its work, he took his first real look around.

"Package is active."

"Copy that, Eagle. We're receiving the data. What's it like down there?" Max asked.

"It's…" He was at a loss for words. Finally, he decided there was only word that could sum it up. "Alien."

"Could you be a little more descriptive?"

"Not really. I'm gonna take a little walk."

"Copy that. Stay within sight of your plane, Eagle. We don't know what's down there."

Shepard was the first human being to walk on this planet, wherever they were, and he intended to savor it. Movement caught his attention and he looked up. A flock of…*somethings* flew overhead. They were birds, at least by the definition that they could fly, but they didn't look like anything he'd ever seen or imagined. They had long, serpent-like bodies and two sets of wings that beat separately from each other. He stared as they maneuvered overhead. They were probably as curious about him as he was about them.

"Well, that settles that, *Traveler*. There's life down here."

"Be careful, Eagle," Max reminded him.

He absently rested his hand on the pistol in the holster on his right hip. The birds circled overhead for a moment, then flew off as a group beyond a canopy of trees with blue and red leaves. "Yep."

Eagle turned up the gain on the exterior microphone on his suit and listened. All he could hear was the wind blowing through the trees and running water somewhere in the distance. He continued his walk, and several times felt like he was being watched. Still, nothing showed up visually, or on any of the spectrums he could scan. Finally, the feeling got to be too much, and he went back to the plane and closed it up.

"Back in the aircraft, *Traveler*. Felt like something was watching me, but I couldn't pick anything up."

"Understood, Eagle. Sit tight. Another fifteen minutes and the core sample will be ready, then you can retrieve the package and get back up here."

* * * * *

Chapter Seven

Transition + 10 Days, 1400 Hours

As soon as the doors closed, and the hangar was pressurized, crew specialists swarmed Eagle's aircraft. They retrieved the sensor package and transported it to the geological lab for the detailed analyses that needed to be done. Max greeted Eagle as soon as he exited the plane.

"Good job, Colin. How was it really?"

Eagle took the towel offered by Max and wiped the sweat from his face. The suit was temperature-controlled, but the ascent had been warmer than he was used to. "Weird," he replied. "I swear, Max, there was something down there watching me. Nothing showed up on the multi-spectrum, but there was *something* there."

Max nodded. He trusted Eagle and wanted to believe him, but he also knew what it was like to be in a completely alien environment from his time on Mars. There was nothing to be gained from contradicting him now, though. "I believe you, buddy. Who knows what the hell could be out here."

Eagle shuddered. "I'm gonna go grab a shower. Debrief later?"

"Sure thing," Max said and slapped him on the back.

He watched Eagle leave the hangar, then did a visual inspection of the exterior of the aircraft. There were scorch marks, likely from entry into the atmosphere, which was expected. He rounded the starboard side and examined the wing, and he stopped dead in his tracks. He knew from watching the entire descent and ascent that the craft hadn't struck anything. Still, there were four parallel scratches on the wing. They weren't just scratches, they were gouges. He carefully touched the metal, which was tough enough to fly through space and not be scratched by small debris. He tasted bile in his mouth and glanced around to see who was nearby.

"You!" he pointed to Empyre, who was on hangar duty that day.

"Sir?"

"Tent this aircraft. No one goes near it without my authorization."

"Um. Okay." Empyre shrugged went to get the necessary materials.

Max retrieved a 3D camera from the plane and took pictures of the wing, then left the hangar. As soon as he was alone in the transport, he commed Kellie.

"What's up, Max?"

"We have a problem. Meet me in the lab."

"Okay." She sounded confused, but he knew she'd be there.

His next call was to Ascher.

"Yes, Captain?" Ascher answered, sounding unhappy to hear from him.

"Colonel, I need a few of your people in the hangar. There's a tented X-94. No one goes near it without my clearance. Understood?"

"Yes, sir. I had a few people stationed in the hangar anyway. I'll send them over."

"Thanks, Colonel. I'll brief you fully once I know more myself."

* * *

Empyre grabbed a tent kit and walked it over to the plane and got it put up in just a few minutes. It was a process they'd been trained and drilled on. Aircraft was tented when work needed to be done on them to keep things isolated, so parts didn't float around the hangar and hurt someone. He wondered what had gotten the captain upset and decided to take a look. It didn't take him long to spot the issue, and he had to work to keep himself from getting sick, which would have been a bad thing in zero G.

He pulled his comm device from his belt, which had a built-in camera, and snapped a few pictures of his own. Once the comm device was safely tucked away, he left the tent and went to finish up his shift.

"You!" A man in the green of the MilForce pointed at him.

Empyre pointed at himself. "Me?"

"What were you doing in there?"

"Captain Reeves asked me to put the tent up. I had to finish up the fittings on the inside."

The man considered him for a moment, then nodded. "Okay, move along."

Empyre's stomach dropped from his throat as he walked away as casually as he could. He had seen what had happened to Ragnarsson, and he had no intention of turning into a walking bruise.

* * *

Max walked into the lab and went straight to one of the consoles. He uploaded the image from the camera and had it processed into a 3D image, which he turned on. Kellie walked in just as he activated it and stopped as if she'd hit a wall.

"Okay, folks. I need everyone to focus on what could have done that," Max said, and pointed at the gouge marks.

Scientists from various fields looked up from what they were doing and stared at the image.

"Well, shit," someone said. Max wasn't sure who said it, but it pretty much summed up his feelings as well.

"We know the aircraft didn't strike any solid objects on the descent or ascent. Nothing was captured on any of the cameras or seen by Eagle. So, what did it? Get everyone and anyone you need to look at this."

Some turned back to their workstations, continuing their analyses in their fields of specialty. Others walked up to the image. Soon a murmur of conversation began. Satisfied he had conveyed the urgency of the situation, Max gestured for Kellie to follow as he left the lab.

"Are you going to tell everyone?" Kellie asked once the door closed behind them.

"I've got the plane isolated for now under a tent to preserve it, but word is bound to get out," Max responded.

"You didn't answer my question."

He sighed. "I just don't know. Trust is building, and it feels like the ship is in high spirits. If I keep this close and it gets out, that trust is destroyed. But if I put it out there, the speculation could devastate morale. I'm considering sending a team of Ascher's platoon down, armed, to scout around once we find an area where we could land *Traveler*. That's assuming all the other tests come back positive."

Kellie nodded. "I think you have to tell them. It's not just our decision, Max. Everyone's life is on the line here. They all volunteered and went through hell training for this."

"So, what, put it up for a vote?" Max asked incredulously.

"No, that's *not* what I'm saying. The decision is still ours, but it would help if we had some support."

"Would we, though?"

"Oh, come on, Max!" She stepped in front of him to face him. "Some people, probably Lina Skoog, for example, will see this as an adventure! They'll be excited that there could be new life out there to discover!"

Max considered, and he could see the excitement in Kellie's eyes at the prospect. He forced himself to look around the danger, at the opportunity. Then his mind's eye saw the gouges in the wing.

"There's something down there that's strong enough to gouge metal that not even small space debris can *scratch*. *And* it wasn't picked up by cameras. It's either that or the plane hit something, somthing denser than anything we've encountered."

Kellie shrugged. "So, we've got our own bigfoot down there."

Max couldn't help but chuckle. For centuries on Earth there had been speculation by cryptozoologists about the legendary bigfoot, though none had ever been found.

"Look, treat it like a mystery to be solved, not as something that's a danger," Kellie suggested. "Let's say it's a living thing. If it's so stealthy, it could have gotten Colin, but it didn't."

"You sound pretty convinced it was done by *something*."

"Even the brief look I took at those gouges told me they were way too symmetrical to be some random object in space."

Max nodded. He'd come to the same conclusion. As they stood there talking, several of the scientists walked by carrying bags and cases, presumably on their way to the hangar to take a closer look in person.

"Okay. Give me a little time to consider how best to address this. Announce that I'll be addressing the ship in two hours. And stay on the team, I want to have *something* to tell people."

She nodded. "Will do."

Kellie returned to the lab, and Max went to his office to think and construct his remarks.

* * *

Transition + 10 Days, 1600 Hours

Two hours later, Kellie turned on the camera and microphone pickup in his office and gave him the thumbs up.

"Ladies and gentlemen, as you all saw, the mission to land on the planet and collect data was a success. Colin 'Eagle' Shepard has been checked out and is in good shape, getting some much-needed rest. The core sample from the planet is still being analyzed to detect anything that might make it unsuitable for habitation. We do know that there is life down there."

The image shifted to the flying animals Eagle had spotted.

"That's the best image we have of them, but, with that we know, the planet can support some life, though we're not sure if it will support ours yet. There's something else that I believe could be of interest."

The image shifted again to show a close-up of the gouge marks in the wing.

"What you're seeing is the starboard wing of Eagle's X-94. This may not seem significant, but it is. The metal on these aircraft is strong enough to fly from Earth to Mars without getting scratched by space debris. The analysis is ongoing, but we've generally ruled out that it was caused by anything other than some living thing on the planet that wasn't picked up by sensors or cameras."

He paused for a few moments since he was sure there would be a lot of talking after that revelation. The image shifted back to show him live at his desk.

"Let me stress, again: we don't know what caused it. We know the marks weren't there when the plane left the ship, and they're there now. I will ask that people not try to look at it in person. Colonel Ascher's personnel are guarding the craft while the experts perform their analyses and will use force to keep people away if necessary."

Max paused again before he continued.

"This may sound like a strange request, but I'd like anyone who has even dabbled in cryptozoology or zoology to get in touch with Lina Skoog, who will be our liaison for this effort." Lina's picture appeared in the lower right corner of the screen. "Her expertise in surviving the harshest climates of Earth, and the fact that she single-handedly discovered three previously unknown species makes her perfect for the role. The fact is we're dealing with the unknown, and those of you with minds open enough to consider things we might not normally consider could be invaluable in this endeavor.

"I've asked the scientific team to expedite their analysis of the core and atmospheric samples so we can decide whether or not to land on this planet as quickly as possible. I must warn you that the process is scheduled to take at least a month, but we're going to see if we can reach a decision sooner without cutting any corners. If you have any *reasonable* questions, please direct them to your council representatives. I will be meeting with them first thing tomorrow morning. Thank you, all."

Max leaned back in his chair and blew out a deep breath once Kellie indicated the transmission had ended.

"I think you did great," Kellie said with a smile.

Max returned the smile. "Thanks."

"Go, get some rest. I'll grab you if something comes up. I have a feeling you're going to be busier than usual for the next few days."

Max chuckled. "Busier than usual? I think that's the new normal."

* * *

Transition + 11 Days, 0800 Hours

The council meeting the next morning went far better than he anticipated. Everyone was positive and looking for ways to help. Lina had already assembled a team with knowledge in various aspects of animal study and cryptozoology to work with the lab. Most of the council members had fielded numerous ridiculous requests and questions from the passengers. They managed to pare them down to the more reasonable items, the chief of which was to request that the next mission down to the planet contain representatives from their own ranks.

Max said he would consider it. Afterward he headed to the lab for an update on progress. As soon as he walked in, several people started talking, and he had to shout to stop the barrage.

"First, where are we on the core sample?" he asked once they stopped talking over each other.

"So far, so good. Traces of iron and silver are prevalent. So far, we're not seeing any evidence of an unstable orbit. I feel sure that, if there were such a condition, we'd see significant variations in the strata. I should note that we've also identified traces of at least two elements that we cannot identify."

Max raised an eyebrow. "Meaning?"

"They're new elements we've never seen before."

He nodded slowly. It wasn't wholly unexpected, but it was still stunning news. "Atmosphere?"

Another member of the team stepped forward. "There are trace elements of cadmium in the air, which we know from pollution concerns on Earth can be a problem. We're not sure what the source is."

"So, we'd have to construct airtight habitats?"

She considered for a moment, then shrugged. "Best bet would be to identify the source and figure it out from there. We really need to get on the planet and track it down."

Max frowned and nodded. "Okay, I'll keep that in mind. What more do we have on the damage to the aircraft?"

"It's too symmetrical to be an impact, and the angles and location don't match that type of pattern either. We weren't able to recover anything from the craft, but the consensus is that it had to be done intentionally. I'm not saying it's aliens, but…it's aliens."

A few members of the team chuckled, including Max.

"Okay, now the big question. How much can we expedite this process without risking safety?"

"All plans were formulated with the expectation that there would be another ship coming. We're in new territory here," one of the scientists explained.

"Trust me, I get that, but we are where we are. I need to be able to tell people something," Max explained.

The scientist nodded. "Get my team down there to do some specific exploration, then we can really give you an answer."

Max decided quickly. "Get your team ready. You leave in an hour."

* * *

Transition + 11 Days, 1000 Hours

An hour later, the team of scientists, along with several of Colonel Ascher's military unit, descended to the planet. A different landing zone was chosen this time. This one would be large enough to accommodate *Traveler*. The four members of MilForce set up a perimeter, while the scientists set up their portable workstations.

Each soldier was assigned to one or two scientists. Lina Skoog was in charge of the scientific aspect of the mission.

"Space out, don't stay so close together. If anything charges out of there, you don't want to be in a tight group!" Lina exclaimed at one pair of soldier and scientist, frustrated.

Captain Essena Mikhailovna, a former Russian Spetsnaz officer, was escorting Matthias Abel, the crew's leading xenobotanist, toward the jungle that bordered the clearing.

"You tell me how to handle protection?" Essena demanded.

"No, I'm telling you and the lab geek how to stay alive."

Essena huffed but did as Lina suggested.

"Hey! I'm not a lab geek. I'm a plant geek," Matthias said with a grin.

Lina rolled her eyes. "Whatever." She repositioned her grip on her machete as they approached the edge of the jungle. Lina thought it was odd how it just stopped, as if there was a wall that prevented the foliage from encroaching into the clearing. She knelt down and dug the tip of her machete into the ground before nodding to herself.

"Only a few centimeters of soil with rock underneath. That explains it," Lina mused.

"Yes, we know that," Matthias said impatiently.

Lina smirked. She glanced back at Essena, who was scanning the tree line her assault rifle at the ready. "Afraid the trees will get you?"

"You saw what happened to plane. I prefer not happen to me."

"Valid point. Okay, come on geek," she said.

"All this will have to be categorized and named," Matthias said, wonder in his voice. "It's a dream come true." He rushed forward and knelt down to pull out his sample kit and began clipping samples from the leaves of all of the plants he could reach.

"Why worry about plants?" Essena asked.

Matthias, lost in his work, didn't seem to hear her, so Lina turned to face her. "Ever heard of ricin?"

"Of course!"

"Comes from a plant. How about anthrax?"

"Don't be ridiculous."

"Yep, from a plant. Any questions?"

"I did not know this," Essena said leaning forward to get a closer look at the plants. "You think some of these deadly?"

"We're quite sure of it," Matthias said without looking up from his work.

Lina turned back to the jungle and took a few steps toward the nearest tree and ran her fingers over the trunk. "This is old growth, assuming things work the way they do on Earth. That's a good sign."

"Yep. I'd say so. Unless these samples show something incredibly dangerous, I think we're in good shape for landing, but that's just my opinion. So far, none of these are edible, but they're not particularly dangerous either."

"Feels almost spongy. On Earth, that would be a virus, right?" Lina asked.

"Yeah. Rubodvirus, but the limbs look healthy. I'll get a sample of the…wood? We'll have to core it to really get a good read."

Lina stepped away as Matthias approached with a handheld coring drill. She watched with interest as he started to drill into the tree. Suddenly, he screamed. His drill flew into the air as he fell to the ground. "Ahhh! It's got me!"

Essena immediately started scanning for a target but saw nothing to shoot.

Lina rushed over and was nearly shocked into inaction. One of the tree's roots had come out of the ground and was wrapped around Matthias' leg. It was slowly dragging him away from her. "There!" she shouted.

Essena rushed over and fired several rounds at the root with no effect.

"Stop shooting!" Lina shouted and jogged forward. She hacked at the root with her machete and sliced it in two.

Once he wasn't being dragged anymore, Matthias scrambled to his feet and ran to the plane, the end of the root still coiled around his ankle.

"Guns don't solve everything," Lina said as she carefully stepped around the other roots to retrieve the drill and back out of the jungle.

"Nicely done," Essena allowed and carefully followed Lina, stepping where she stepped as if they were exiting a minefield.

"Watch my back, I'll get his stuff," Lina said and knelt down to pack Matthias' kit.

Essena nodded and shouldered her rifle to free up her hand for her own survival knife.

Once they were done, they went back to the plane to check on Matthias. He was sitting in the passenger area staring at the root, which was still twitching on the floor as if seeking something to coil around.

"You okay?" Lina asked.

Matthias snapped his head up. He was panting hard and sweating. "I think so," he managed to say.

Lina patted him on the shoulder. "You did fine. Hey, at least you can study that now," she said and pointed at the root.

"Hey, that's right! Roots are great for data collection on the life and behavior of plant life!" Matthias exclaimed, his fear suddenly gone. "I think I'll just let it sit there for now, though…"

"I will secure it," Essena said. She fetched a case large enough for the cut root and used a pair of long tongs to transfer it to the case.

"Thanks," Matthias said.

"We must work together to survive."

Lina looked at his ankle and frowned. She knelt and examined his suit more closely. "How are you feeling?"

"Okay, I guess. Given that a tree just attacked me. Come to think of it, I'm feeling pretty damn good!"

Lina frowned. There was a substance glistening on the area of the suit where the root had attached that looked like sap, and it looked like there were several small puncture marks.

Lina looked at Essena. "I think we need to get back to the *Traveler*, fast."

"Why? I feel great!" Matthias said. "Hey, I'm fine. Let's go get some more samples! I'm gonna catalog the whole planet!"

Essena ignored him and ran out of the plane to gather the rest of the expedition.

* * * * *

Chapter Eight

Transition + 11 Days, 1500 Hours

Max walked into the medical bay and looked at Matthias Abel, who was unconscious on one of the monitoring beds. "What's his status, Doctor?"

Doctor Chadda looked up from the screen she was studying. "He was injected with something. There are several puncture marks on his leg." She rose, walked over to the bed, and lifted the sheet that was attached to the bed with Velcro.

Max joined her and saw at what looked like small hypodermic needle punctures. "Injected with what?"

"I've never seen anything like it, nor have our chemists. The nearest we can extrapolate based on his behavior is that it functions much like coca and activates the mesolimbic dopamine system—"

"English, please?" Max interrupted to ask.

"It made him feel euphoric. Like he'd done cocaine."

"Great," he said with a frown. Just what he needed, a planet with a readily available drug supply that required no processing. "Will he be okay?"

She nodded. "It should work its way out of his system if it metabolizes the same way." She indicated a display that showed a real-time brain scan. "His brain chemistry is already recovering to its normal levels. Based on this, he should feel like himself in a few hours."

Max nodded. "Keep me updated on his progress." He left the medical bay, and Kellie fell into step beside him.

"How is he?" she asked.

"Should be fine. I don't like this, though. It looks like the damn trees naturally produce something like cocaine."

"We should be fine, Max. Everyone on the ship is intelligent and should know better than to mess with something like that."

"Except that they've never been on an alien world with no chance of ever going back to Earth. Who knows what that will do to people's mindset."

"The final reports are in. The atmosphere where they landed showed no traces of cadmium. It must have been something localized to where Eagle touched down."

Max nodded, but that didn't make him feel any better.

"What else?" he asked.

"Everything looks…good," Kellie said, sounding surprised. "The team wants more time, but as of right now, it doesn't look like there's anything inherently life-threatening."

"Do they *want* more time, or *need* more time?"

"They're scientists, Max. They don't deal in absolutes. They'll *never* give you a 100% certainty of anything, except that they can't be sure. Everything is couched in conditions."

"So, what do you think?"

She remained silent as they passed a group walking the other way, then answered, "I think it's our best shot. The next closest planet that might support life is at least three weeks' travel away."

"Three weeks isn't that long in the grand scheme of things," Max countered.

"If the team got what they wanted, we'd be in orbit here for another month while they re-ran their experiments multiple times. They've already run them at least twice and gotten the same results. The planet is probably about as habitable as we're going to get unless you're hoping for a paradise planet that's exactly like Earth."

That was *precisely* what he wanted, but he knew he wouldn't get it. He was in charge of the mission to make these kinds of decisions. "We've only got one shot at this, and I want to be as sure as we can be. Have the team send me all the data we have right now, and I'll have a decision by the end of the day."

"Will do."

"Oh, and ask Ms. Skoog to come to my office. I want an in-person debrief on what happened down there."

Kellie peeled off to head back to the lab, and Max went to his office to await the results and examine what they had on the next nearest planet, which wasn't much. The only data they had at this point was imagery, and it looked just as promising as the planet below them. There was evidence of both plant life and water, but beyond that they didn't know anything. He sent the order to launch an array of sensor probes to the planet.

* * *

Transition + 11 Days, 1530 Hours

Lina Skoog walked into Max's office and looked around before taking a seat. "Smaller than I expected."

"Space is at a premium on any ship," Max said. "Now, tell me what happened down there."

Lina explained what happened, and Max had her go through it step by step.

"You touched it, but it didn't react until he tried to drill into it?"

She nodded.

"No way you simply weren't in range of those…roots?"

"No. I'm sure I walked right over them."

"Hmm. Okay, thanks Lina. Go get some rest."

Max thought on that for a moment, then went back to reviewing the reports on the planet they were orbiting. During his review, he received a priority call from Doctor Chadda to report to the med bay immediately.

* * *

Transition + 11 Days, 1600 Hours

"What's going on, Doctor?" he asked as soon as he walked in.

"He's getting worse," she said from beside Matthias Abel's bed.

Max frowned and walked over to stand beside her. "How so? I thought it was going to pass?"

"I thought it was, but…" She shook her head as she pulled the sheet back to reveal Matthias' ankle. The area around the puncture wounds was black and dark spider-webbing radiated out from the puncture sites.

"Bruising?"

"No, necrosis. The tissue is dying rapidly, and he's slipped into a coma."

"Did the piece of the tree they brought back help in figuring out what's going on?"

"Some. The best we can determine is that it's some kind of morphing parasite. It makes its prey euphoric while the necrosis takes hold so the victim doesn't feel it."

"Doctor, this was a tree. You're talking about it like a sentient animal hunting for food."

"Captain, I can only tell you what we see. Whatever this substance is, it introduces a state of euphoria and then destroys the tissue of whatever it gets into. You have to understand that we can only determine what it does to *our* biology."

Max chewed on his bottom lip and stared at Matthias' ankle as the implications hit home. They couldn't be sure what the effect of this chemical was on any native wildlife, which they knew existed, but it was obviously dangerous to humans.

"Can you stop it?" he asked.

"Nothing we've tried so far is working. A few of the passengers are virologists and are working on it now with our chemists."

He frowned. It seemed like the area of necrotic skin was spreading as he watched. He hoped the probes going to the next planet showed positive results because he really didn't want to land on a planet that seemed designed to kill them.

"Okay, keep me informed at every step. I've had probes launched to check out another planet. Cross your fingers that we get something good there because this planet doesn't seem to like us."

"I'll cross everything I can, Captain."

As Max turned to leave, he was surprised to see Essena Mikhaeilovna standing in the doorway. "Something I can do for you, Essena?"

"I come check on Matthias," she said, sounding concerned.

Max tilted his head.

"I was there to protect team. I failed," she explained.

"There's no way you could have foreseen this," Max assured her.

"I am on mission because I am trained to expect unexpected, Captain. How is he doing?"

"Not well, I'm afraid. Come on, let's give the doctor room to work. I'll tell you what we know."

Max walked with Essena for a bit and told her what Doctor Chadda had told him.

"We go back down. Get more samples. That will help, yes?" Essena asked.

"Maybe. I'm waiting to hear. We have a team of people working on this, Essena. He's in good hands."

"If team goes back down, I go, Captain," she said. It was obviously not a question.

"Very well. If another team is sent down, you'll be on it."

"Thank you, Captain."

* * *

Transition + 13 Days, 0830 Hours

Rumors spread around the ship over the next several days about the "killer tree." To try to contain the situation, Max gave Doctor Chadda the go-ahead to release everything to the ship's population. Unfortunately, it did not have the desired effect. Excitement over finding a habitable planet turned to fear.

Some people thought they should land but fire-bomb the area first to kill off all flora in the area. In answer to that, another group was just as insistent that everything on the planet deserved to live, and that humans shouldn't begin life on a new world with destruction. Max decided to let things go unless it came to blows, which it did in a few cases. Thankfully, Hugh Coghlan and his fellow passenger law enforcement personnel were able to calm things down without involving Colonel Ascher and his team.

"So, what do you think about all this?" Courtni asked Empyre and Ragnarsson in the cafeteria.

Empyre shrugged. "I say level the area. Hell, it's a big planet, killing off a few kilometers of stuff so we don't get killed by plants is no big deal."

"It *is* a big deal!" she argued. "Look at what happened to Earth! Humanity clear-cut the planet, and *poof* nothing to create oxygen or filter out pollution. Morons."

Empyre rolled his eyes. "We don't even *know* if that's how plants work on this planet. It's a friggin alien world! I heard they all had to wear their suits anyway and not even breathe the air."

"That's not the point!"

"That's enough, both of you," Ragnarsson said to stop Courtni from going on. "It's not our decision anyway."

Empyre looked confused at Ragnarsson. "What's eating you?"

He shrugged. "Just tired of being cooped up on this ship, I guess."

"I don't mind. There's a scorching hot chick that works in the cargo area. She's been keeping me occupied, if you know what I mean," Empyre said and waggled his eyebrows.

"You're a pig," Courtni said. "And don't call women *chicks*."

"Whatever. You're just jealous."

"You wish."

"Enough!" Ragnarsson said and slammed his hand down on the table. He drew a few glances from other passengers, but they all quickly went back to their food.

"Damn, dude. You need to lighten up. Relax a little. Want me to introduce you to a few people?" Empyre said with a wink.

"You really need help," Courtni groaned.

"You volunteering?"

"Oh, good grief," Ragnarsson said. He stood and strode away. He heard them continue to go back and forth as he left the cafeteria. Something was definitely wrong. He just couldn't put his finger on what it was.

The captain had remained true to his word and kept everyone up to date on everything, as far as he knew, anyway. Ragnarsson had also kept his word and stopped his attempts to access the ship's systems, but he was sure there was something they *really* didn't want him to see.

* * *

Max stared at the terminal in his office. He was considering activating the only system on the ship that lay dormant, a ship-integrated Artificial Intelligence. It was just waiting for his command. He was about to begin the activation process when a message from the lab popped up.

It said they had completed the analysis on the unknown trace elements that had come up in the core sample. The first one immediately got his attention. It had an atomic weight of 450, almost twice that of uranium, and a high molecular density. The team classified it as metal and, if it were found in large quantities, and they found a way to work with it, it would be the most durable metal ever conceived. The piece found was less than a millimeter, but the mere existence of it was miraculous. So far, they had tested it up to 4000°C and still not found the melting point. That was higher than carbon.

As always, the report contained many conditional statements, and he understood that at this point there was no way to be sure of anything. What he did know was that in one core sample they had discovered two new elements. There was no way to know what else was out there.

There was a second entry in the report, which was the analysis on some gas trapped in the soil layers. It was new, but there was nothing immediately remarkable about it, except this gas wasn't present in the atmospheric samples. It was similar in structure to argon, and the entry indicated that more would be required for a detailed analysis.

It would be at least two weeks before the data came back from the probes for the next, and last, known planet that looked like it could support life. He wanted that one to work out, to be better than what they had found here or on Rainbow, but he knew he had to plan for a landing on this one just in case.

He was about to close the lab reports when someone knocked on his door. "Come."

Doctor Chadda slowly entered, and he could see by the look on her face that it was bad news. "I assume this is about Matthias?"

She nodded. "We lost him."

Max closed his eyes and sighed deeply. "What happened?"

"The...whatever it is...made its way to his heart. We didn't even detect it. One minute his vitals were steady, the next minute he flatlined. I called in Doctor Heuser to perform an autopsy, and..." She shuddered.

"That bad?"

She merely nodded, unable to find the words.

"This isn't your fault, Sukanya," Max reassured her.

"I—I don't know how it happened."

"Then find out, so it doesn't happen to anyone else. Look, we've got one more possible planet out there, and who knows, maybe it'll be perfect. But we have to proceed as if this is our only shot, which it may be. So, whatever is down there, we have to figure out how to work with it or eliminate it. I need you on this. Best case, we don't have to worry about it. Worst case, we're ready for it. Can I count on you?"

"Of course you can, Captain."

"Take a day off. Get some rest. I know you haven't slept much since Matthias came back on board. Catch up on some sleep, then call in whoever you need."

"Yes. I will. Thank you, Captain."

Max sighed after she left. He contacted Captain Mikhailovna and told her the news. She took it like a soldier, but it definitely had an impact on her. If nothing else, he thought, she'd be a lot more careful if they returned to the planet, which is ultimately what the research team wanted.

He summoned Kellie to his office.

"What's up, Max?" she asked as she stepped in a few moments later.

"We lost Matthias. Prep a team to go back down. Volunteers only. I want them to see the video of what happened, so they understand the risks. But we need more information on what's down there."

"Max, the ship is nothing *but* volunteers."

"I know. Still, now we know how dangerous it can be. I want people who will go down with both eyes open and an extra set in the back of their head."

Kellie nodded, understanding. "Okay; will do."

"Thanks, Kellie," Max said and smiled.

"You look tired."

Max nodded.

"If you ever need to just talk…"

"I know. Thanks, Kellie. Let me know when the team is ready. Oh, and make sure Captain Mikhailovna is on the list."

* * * * *

Chapter Nine

Transition + 13 Days, 1200 Hours

"Eagle" Shepard brought the X-94 down for a smooth landing and opened the rear cargo ramp. "Okay, everyone. Be careful out there," he said over the intercom.

Essena Mikhailovna was the first person down the ramp. This time, she had her rifle slung and her machete in her hand. She was also wearing combat armor for this trip, just in case.

"There is tree." She indicated the tree Matthias Abel had been attempting to drill into when he was attacked. She led the way, and two botanists accompanied her at a distance.

Other specialists spread out around the area to retrieve more samples for their own research. One team began setting up a remote drill rig to extract a new core from the solid rock beneath the top layer of soil to check for depth and stability. Others spread out and took samples of the soil itself, and anything else they could locate.

Essena slowed her pace and began to probe the ground with her machete. Three meters from the trunk of the tree, a root extracted itself from the ground and lashed out. She quickly jumped back to stay out of range. The root managed to scrape her leg, but all it hit was armor plating. She backed away a few more steps and knelt down to check the armor and nodded with satisfaction.

"Armor protects. What do you need?" she asked the scientists.

"Fascinating," one of them said.

"And deadly," she harshly reminded him.

He shook his head as if coming out of a dream. "Right. Sorry. Optimally, we still need a full sample from the trunk itself. We already have the root to study, but it would be good to get a fresh sample so we can analyze it while it's still mostly alive."

Essena nodded and considered the situation. The roots were a tripwire, at least when it was threatened, and it was all a big booby trap. She sheathed her machete and unslung her rifle. "Stay back," she said needlessly.

She took aim and fired a few bursts into the ground behind the tree. The result was nothing short of horrifying. More than twenty roots, including the one that had first reached out for her, reacted to the impacts, seeking the threat.

"What the hell are you doing?" one of the scientists yelled.

"Getting sample," Essena responded calmly slinging her rifle and pulling her machete. She waited.

After a moment of flailing and finding nothing, the roots began to return to their previous positions, exactly as she anticipated. She kept her eyes on one root and when it moved toward her to resume its location, she swung at it like she was hitting a baseball, slicing off a one-meter section. She kicked it toward the scientists, who jumped back as if it was a live snake.

"There is living sample."

"You're nuts!" one of them exclaimed, staring at the still-writhing piece of root.

She shrugged and walked to one of the cases the scientists had dropped in their retreat. From it, she extracted a drill and attached the two-meter long coring bit. Unwieldy would have been an understatement, but it would let her get the sample they needed without having to get too close to the tree and its roots. Once the drill was assembled, she set it on the ground and grabbed her machete to make herself a path.

Now that she knew how they would react, it was easy. Essena pulled her GSh-32 9mm pistol, standard issue for Spetsnaz, with her left hand. There were laser pistols available, but she had never trusted them. She fired a few rounds, waited, then sliced away any roots that came back until she had an area cleared where she felt she could safely stand. Then, she stood back and fired a few rounds where she intended to position herself. As she expected, some of the roots from further away were still able to reach. By the time she had created a safe zone, she had gone through three 18-round magazines and lost count of the severed root pieces that lay on the ground.

From one of her hip pockets, she retrieved some bright orange marker flags and placed them to indicate where it was safe to step. With that done, she retrieved the drill and proceeded to remove the core sample from the tree. The entire time she was working, roots reached for her like an infinitely tentacled octopus. Once she was done, she placed the bit with the sample in its specialized container and packed the rest of the assembly away in its case.

In the next few hours, she kept an intent watch over the entire operation until everyone had retrieved everything they wanted for their research. The only thing they had yet to do was test a water source, but that would have to wait for another day as everyone's oxygen reserves started to run low.

Mission accomplished, Eagle flew the X-94 back to *Traveler* without losses or injuries.

* * *

Transition + 29 Days, 0900 Hours

Over the next couple of weeks, several more trips to the planet were made without serious incident. There were some sprained ankles, falls, and bruises, but nothing long-term. A body of water only a few kilometers from the proposed landing site was tested, and more than ten unknown organisms were studied. There were several lifetimes' worth of discoveries to be made.

Significant focus was placed on the tree responsible for Matthias Abel's death. A team of specialists were eventually able to synthesize an anti-toxin that eliminated the toxin in tests. However, no living subjects had been tested yet.

Max walked onto the bridge one morning after breakfast and nearly ran into Kellie.

"Oops! Sorry, Max. Good timing, though. We're getting data back from the probes we sent to the last planet."

"What's it look like?"

"Horrible. The liquid on the surface isn't water, it's mercury."

Max grimaced. "So that planet is definitely a no-go."

"Definitely," she agreed.

He took a deep breath and nodded. "Well, I guess it's time."

"You're sure we shouldn't just keep exploring? I mean, there's some nasty stuff down there."

Max shook his head. He'd been thinking about the decision for weeks. While it might be rushing things, he believed they could overcome what was on the planet below as long as they followed the proper protocols. "No. I think this is it."

"Your call," she said and stood aside.

He turned toward his office but stopped and looked at Kellie. "You think this is a mistake?"

"I know you weren't asking me," Sivert said. "But the mere fact that we've found a planet that is even remotely habitable is nothing short of amazing. I think we have to take it and use the supplies we have to establish a home rather than looking for something that may not exist."

Other members of the bridge crew nodded in agreement.

Kellie nodded, too. "I didn't mean to give you the wrong impression, Max. I can't help it; I'm a dreamer. I have this dream of a perfect world out there somewhere. Maybe it exists, maybe it doesn't, but Sivert is right. We have limited supplies. It's best to use them figuring out how to live, rather than just surviving while we *hope* to find something better."

"Thanks, everyone."

Max closed the door to his office and sat behind his desk. He pulled up a document on that he'd been working on for the past several weeks. It was a pros and cons list for landing on the planet, and the pros had won out by a substantial margin. To create the file, he'd consulted with department heads, as well as the members of the passenger council. He'd even wandered around the ship and talked to random people. He needed to have the pulse of the crew and passengers before a decision was made, and he felt like he had it.

He typed in a sequence triggering an automated message from the ship's computer to everyone on board. "All hands, begin preparation for landing."

Next, he went through the protocols for the actual preparations, which included typing in a lengthy passcode, a biometric palm print scan, and a retinal scan.

Preparing the ship for descent through the atmosphere would take, on paper, exactly twenty hours. Whether expectations would meet reality was something else. All parameters would be fed to *Traveler*'s central computer system, which was as close to artificial intelligence as humanity had been able to develop. Until this point, the AI had been in minimal mode and only then to control the robots on the ship. Now, it would be activated fully and given control of several ship functions.

* * *

Transition + 30 Days, 0500 Hours

Nineteen hours after the order was given, as Max reviewed the preparation reports, his terminal came to life on its own. "Entry calculations have been completed, Captain Reeves. I estimate a 93.24% chance of a successful landing. Communications, GPS, surveillance, and weather satellites have been deployed and have established their appropriate orbits."

Max sighed. Every time the AI spoke, it pained him. Annica had provided the voice print that became Annie's voice. It was time to change that. "Thank you, Annie. Change to secondary system voice parameters."

"Secondary voice parameters activated," a new female voice responded. "Is everything okay, Captain?"

"Everything's fine, Annie. Is there any action we can take to improve the landing success rate?"

"Negative, Captain. All possible improvements to the descent have been factored in. The location chosen for landing *Traveler* is optimal. Appropriate nearby landing zones have been chosen for the supply containers. However, analysis of the native flora indicates some locations may be hazardous. My boys should be able to retrieve the containers without incident."

Max studied the map Annie displayed for him to review. The containers attached to the exterior of the ship containing the bulk of their supplies would be jettisoned during descent to lighten the load and the aerodynamic profile of *Traveler*. Her "boys" were the robots she could control. The ones used on the ship were small. The ones she referred to, stored in a secondary hangar, were the size of massive earth-moving equipment.

"Descent conditions?"

"I have analyzed the data from the wormhole transit. The conditions on descent will not be as drastic. I calculate a 100% survival rate of onboard personnel, assuming they are properly in their assigned locations." The AI added in a humorous tone, "Assuming the ship doesn't disintegrate in the atmosphere."

"Not funny, Annie."

"Sorry, Captain. May I call you Max?"

"That's fine."

"Thank you, Max. At your command, I can sound the ship descent alarm and put *Traveler* into position."

Kellie walked in and heard the last bit. She raised an eyebrow. "Already?"

"Looks like it," Max said. "We ready?"

"As ready as we're going to be."

"Okay, let's get everyone strapped in. I'm going to allow some extra time. I want Hugh and his people to lay eyes on all of the passengers to make sure they'll survive this."

"Okay, I'll let him know," she replied and left his office.

"Annie, activate descent alarm. Extend timer until I give the okay to land."

"Understood, Max."

Around the ship, a shrill alarm let everyone know what was about to happen. That particular alarm only had one purpose and was followed by Annie's announcement: "Please report to your assigned positions. We are preparing to land on your new home."

* * *

Transition + 30 Days, 0700 Hours

Max strapped himself into his bridge chair after he received the last report from Hugh's team that all passengers were strapped in and ready.

"Okay, everyone ready?" he asked the bridge crew.

Receiving positive responses from everyone, he gave the order. "Annie, land *Traveler*."

"Landing sequence commencing, Max. Hold on, it's going to be a bumpy ride."

Max had been the first to fly several aircraft. Each time, it was exhilarating and terrifying. This was more, on every level. It began smoothly as the entry profile solidified, and then they hit the outer layers of the atmosphere. Exterior containers were jettisoned automatically at just the right point in the descent. Each of them had maneuvering rockets and an onboard computer to maneuver to their landing locations, as best as a flying brick could be maneuvered. Heat shields deployed around the bottom and sides of the ship. The next several minutes was the roughest ride he'd ever had in his life, and that was saying something. Wormhole transit was probably worse, but he didn't remember it. Still, he couldn't wipe the grin off of his face.

Suddenly, the ride became smooth as silk, as if they'd broken through a wall. "Atmospheric entry complete, Max. The heat shields have been jettisoned, and we are on approach to the landing zone. Landing thrusters will fire in two minutes."

"Yes!" Max yelled. As many times as he'd done what no person had done before, he couldn't contain his excitement. As if his exclamation was permission to celebrate, the rest of the bridge crew began cheering and clapping.

"You aren't on the ground yet, Max," Annie scolded.

Max sobered quickly and stared at his tablet screen.

"Is there something I should know, Annie?"

"Several of the heat shield components failed. There is damage to the hull."

"How much? Any casualties?" he asked urgently.

"Calm down, Max," the AI responded. "There are no casualties. All damage was to storage areas."

"Kellie, as soon as we're on the ground, find out what we lost."

"Will do," she responded.

"Landing thrusters will fire in two minutes," Annie announced over the ship's intercom. "G-forces will feel extreme, but you will be fine. Remain calm and stay in your seats."

Two minutes later, they all felt a jolt as thrusters fired to slow their descent. Even over the vibration of the thrusters, the landing gear deploying and locking into place could be felt. Max checked their status himself and was relieved to see they had all deployed successfully.

"Touchdown in sixty seconds," Annie announced to the ship.

Max relaxed his body rather than bracing himself. He'd learned a long time ago that the worst thing you could do when you took an impact was to tense up. That lesson had been taught to the crew and passengers, but he had no doubt there would be a lot of sore people and pulled muscles after this landing.

With a loud *thud Traveler* hit the surface of the new world. Max watched anxiously until the landing gear held the load. The shock absorbers took most of the impact, though it was still a long jarring moment before the ship finally came to rest.

"Welcome to your new home. Landing sequence completed," Annie announced.

* * * * *

Chapter Ten

Landing + 0 Days, 1000 Hours

The first few hours after landing was spent making sure everyone was okay. As expected, some passengers had gone against training and tensed up, but not as many as Max had anticipated. Maybe they'd learned after the wormhole transit.

"Annie, commence supply retrieval," Max instructed.

On the rear port quarter of *Traveler*, a ramp extended, and a door opened. AI-controlled vehicles exited the ship and moved to their assigned containers to retrieve them and bring them back to the staging area. The main screen on the bridge showed the view of their surroundings from a surveillance satellite.

Most of the containers were retrieved without incident. However, four of the machines went inactive in the dense jungle.

"Annie, update on thirteen, eight, ten, and fifteen?"

"I have lost contact with them," she answered. The AI sounded sad.

"Can we send others that are back to handle the retrieval?"

"Max, I've already lost four of my boys. If they were unable to complete the task, sending more would be a waste of resources."

Max blinked and jerked his head to the side and looked at Kellie. She seemed as surprised as him, but just shrugged.

"I can see you, you know," Annie said. "You will need my boys for other tasks. The materials in the remaining containers are redundant and not necessary for near-term survival. It is best to postpone retrieval until a base camp is established."

"Kellie, give me a manifest on the contents of the remaining containers, please."

She nodded, walked over with her tablet, and handed it to Max.

He reviewed the list and decided Annie was right in her analysis. "Okay, folks. Looks like we've got what we're going to get for now. Everyone, stay in your suits. Standard decontamination procedures for re-entry into the ship. Let's get the Plantery Control Center set up first, then we'll start on the farming modules."

He opened a channel and addressed the entire ship. "Welcome to our new home, everyone. I know there's a lot of excitement and some worry, but this is our home now. We are in a trinary system, meaning there are three suns. The planet has a 20-hour day, which we will now switch to. Based on our observations from orbit, the days are 16 hours, with varying degrees of light, and the night, with no sun, is only 4 hours long. In order to maintain as much of our time sense as possible, our current time won't change, but your devices will reflect the new day starting now. Darkness will be between 1600 and 2000 hours.

"Don't worry, this is the kind of thing we thought about, and we're prepared. The hardest part will be adjusting ourselves to new schedules, which will take some time. Primary work will be on the Planetery Control Center, after which we will work on the farming modules. From there, priorities will be determined based on need. Welcome home."

* * *

Landing + 0 Days, 1100 Hours

In one of the vehicle bays, Empyre climbed into the cab of a large crane and drove it carefully down the ramp. He couldn't help but stop at the bottom of the ramp just to look around. "Daaaaaaaamn," he said to himself as he looked over the alien landscape. There were three suns in the sky in various positions, and it made daylight as bright, if not brighter, as noon in a desert on Earth. The windows on the crane cab automatically tinted to protect his eyes.

"What was that Crane Two?" the voice of the engineer overseeing the construction of the Planetary Control Center asked over the comm system.

"Sorry, nothing. Just…damn."

The voice chuckled. "I know, it's something, isn't it? But you need to move your ass, there are more trucks behind you."

"Yeah, sorry. On my way."

They worked through the next five hours until the modular PCC was completed. They were just finishing the last bit of wiring that provided power and connectivity to *Traveler* when daylight turned to darkness in a matter of minutes. The night cycle was only four hours of the 20-hour day, but it was pitch black. They could have kept working, but since the PCC was built everything halted so everyone could get some rest.

Empyre looked at his watch once he was back on the ship and out of his suit, to find that it was only dinner time by their clock. Even though he'd been sitting in a machine the entire time, he was exhausted. He made his way to the cafeteria with plans to grab some food and get back to his bunk. He hadn't even thought about it, but now that they were on the planet and had gravity, the cafeteria could serve real food.

He sat down and inhaled deeply. Two tacos, chips and salsa, and a side of beans smelled better than anything since they left Earth. He picked up one of the tacos and took a bite just as Courtni plopped down beside him and grabbed a chip from his plate. "Looks good," she said as she popped it in her mouth and crunched blissfully.

"So go get some," he said around a mouthful of food, somehow managing not to spray any of it on Courtni.

"I can't. Only you folks who worked outside the ship get the good stuff. Since I was stuck in an office, I'm stuck with a tube," she said and held up the standard nutrient tube.

"Sucks to be you," he said before taking another bite.

Her jaw dropped. "You're not going to share?"

He gulped the food down. "How long have you known me?"

Courtni pouted and gave him the puppy dog eyes she saved for special occasions.

Empyre groaned. "Fine," he said and offered her the remaining half of the taco he'd been eating.

She looked at it for a second, then shrugged. "Screw it," she said, and proceeded to devour it like she hadn't eaten in a month.

"Slow down there, Courtni. Be a shame if you choked to death on the first day of the rest of our lives," Ragnarsson said, sitting down across from them.

She stuck her tongue out at Ragnarsson.

"So what's it like out there?" he asked Empyre.

Empyre shrugged. "I was in a truck the whole time, but it looks…I mean, it's beautiful, man. Bright as hell though."

"Going soft, 'Pyre?" Courtni teased.

"Hey, I'm secure enough to say something's beautiful other than a ch—woman."

"I heard rumors that we didn't get all the containers?" Ragnarsson asked.

Empyre nodded as he chewed.

"Which ones are missing?"

"Ummm…eight, ten, thirteen, and fifteen."

Ragnarsson muttered something Empyre couldn't hear.

"Are we going to get them?"

"No idea. I'm just on the building crew for now. We were told not to worry about it because those containers were redundant."

"You know what that means, 'Pyre?" Courtni asked.

Empyre smirked. "Yeah, in the dictionary, your picture is beside it."

Courtni nodded. "Good one."

Ragnarsson frowned.

"I take it there's something a bit more than what's documented in one of those?" Courtni asked. She had a particular interest since part of her job on the ship, and now on the planet, was logistics.

"You could say that. Let me know if you hear anything else about them."

Empyre and Courtni both nodded, and Ragnarsson stood and left as abruptly as he'd arrived.

"He's getting weirder," Empyre said quietly.

"I didn't think that was possible, but you're right," Courtni agreed. "He's *almost* as weird as you."

"Hey! *No one* is as weird as me."

Courtni nodded and patted Empyre on the head. "Yes, you're right about that."

"So, what do you think is in the containers?"

"I don't know, and honestly, I'm not sure I want to," Courtni replied.

"Wouldn't be the first time he'd snuck something through customs. Only this time he didn't ask for our help."

"Yeah. That's what bothers me even more. You ever wonder how we got on this ship?"

"All the time, but sometimes, it's best not to ask too many questions."

She glanced around before continuing. "Any idea what the long term plan is?"

He shrugged. "I'm sure is has something to do with a power grab. That's just Adel's style. But there's nothing to hide behind here. That's not his style."

"Except us."

Empyre raised his eyebrows, took the last bite of his taco, and thought.

* * *

Landing + 0 Days, 1700 Hours

Kellie sat across from Max in his office while going over the work list for the next day.

"The day/night cycle is going to be tough," Kellie observed.

"I know. We'll just have to do it like I did it on long trips to Mars. Artificial lighting and maintain a schedule. It'll either be less work, or less sleep. Different people will adapt in different ways."

"So, what's on the agenda for tomorrow?" she asked, activating her tablet.

"First thing, have them get started laying the expoxicrete. I'd like to get the whole foundation set tomorrow so we can get started on the greenhouses."

Kellie pursed her lips and looked at her tablet. "We can try, but that's a lot of ground to cover."

"Literally," he said with a grin. "I know it's a lot, but there's a lot of daylight, too. We're going to have to shift our schedules a bit to align with the new cycle anyway. Anything on whether or not the soil will support our food crops?"

"Some of the levels are off, but they think we can compensate with chemical additives. Now that we're here, they want to do some extensive area tests, but that's going to require clear-cutting some of the trees. We won't know for sure what the results are until everything is full-grown, and the plants can be tested to see if anything dangerous leeched from the environment."

"That's fine. Have the team scout tomorrow to designate the area. We'll have Annie's boys do the clearcutting work. Let's keep hydroponics on the ship going full time as well."

"My boys will need to be fitted with cutting equipment, Max," Annie said from the speaker on his desk.

"I know, Annie. Make sure to add that to the list for tomorrow, Kellie."

Kellie made a few notes on her tablet. "Got it."

"There have been some complaints about the food situation, Max," Annie said.

Max raised an eyebrow and looked at Kellie, who shrugged.

"What complaints?" Max asked.

"That only the personnel who worked outside the ship received cooked meals today."

Max grimaced. "Never did like that policy when the team on Earth set it. I actually intended to change it."

"Apparently, you didn't," Annie stated.

"Let's change that now then. Shift the nutrient paste to backup emergency supply."

"I'll take care of that for you, Max."

Kellie smiled. "Suits me. One less thing for me to deal with."

"I'm glad to assist if you feel your workload is too heavy, Ms. Warren. I'm capable of quite a bit more," Annie suggested.

"I'm...fine. Thank you, Annie," Kellie said.

"Anyway," Max resumed. "Let's get to work on those projects tomorrow and see where we end up. I'm shifting over to the PCC in the morning."

"I'll make sure it's ready for you, Max," Annie said just as Kellie opened her mouth to speak.

"Thanks, Annie. Okay, I think that's everything for now."

* * *

Landing + 1 day, 0200 Hours

The next morning, as they now reckoned time, after little sleep, Max walked down the ramp to survey his surroundings outside the ship for the first time. The engineering and construction crews were already busy laying out the necessary power cables for the base. Annie's boys were moving out to clear trees and brush away for the footprint of the first phase of the settlement. Everything had been laid out back on Earth, with different alternatives based on the planet's topography, and an appropriate plan had been chosen for what they had around them.

Now that they were on the planet, everyone's role had shifted except for the department heads and the council. There was no longer any difference between crew and colonists. They were all citizens of this new, as yet unnamed, world.

Max watched as the huge machines made their way to the tree line, and the whine of saw blades filled the air. Before the first machine even touched the trunk of the tree, he saw the roots fly out of the ground as they tried to stop the tools. The tracks of the robots were more than even the numerous roots could stop, and one by one the trees began to fall. Other robots came behind them to grind up the debris and clear out underbrush. The only things left were a layer of sawdust and ground up plant matter.

Part of him was sad to see the natural surroundings destroyed, but Max reminded himself that there was an entire untouched planet all around them that would take years to explore. Satisfied the daily schedule was underway, he headed for the Planetary Control Center.

When he entered the center after going through the decontamination airlock, he saw it was fully staffed. Multiple large monitors lined the perimeter of the room, showing the status of operations, the ship, and the plans being executed. One section was dedicated to the surveillance cameras keeping watch for anything that could harm the colonists. That section was currently being monitored by Captain Mikhailovna.

Max walked up behind her to look over the displays.

"Nothing to report yet, Captain," she said without looking up.

He removed his helmet, safe thanks to the air filtration and circulation system each building would be outfitted with, and nodded. "Good. Let's try to keep it that way."

"Drones will be ready in hour."

"Excellent. Thanks, Essena," Max said and went to his station, situated on a raised platform in the center of the room.

He reviewed the orders for the day and saw the construction crews were ahead of schedule laying the foundation for the first phase of the settlement. Once the foundation was set, which would take about an hour once the frame and electrical were laid out thanks to laser cured epoxicrete, the more difficult work would begin. Oxygen generation stations would be set up, then the greenhouses would be assembled. Once that was done they could be turned over to the agriculture team to get the settlment's food crops started. Some greenhouses would use soil brought from Earth; others would be built over gaps left in the epoxicrete specifically for that purpose and would use the local soil.

While the ship could generate power and oxygen for more years than they would all live, one of the first goals of the settlement was to become self-sufficient. First air, then food and power. As everything proceeded, the ship would be disassembled and its parts moved to the settlement. The medical bay, for example, was modular. It was built so the technology could be removed and fitted into what would become the hospital for the settlement.

Max was reviewing the long list of things to be done over the coming months when a red light illuminated above the station where the progress of the robots was being monitored. He frowned and waited for a report.

"We've lost tracking on the lead cutter."

"Drones ready; I send one over," Essena immediately called out.

"Confirmed," Annie added over the speakers at his console. "I have lost contact."

"By the gods," Essena said and threw the display to the large primary screen at the front of the room.

Only the hum of the air system could be heard as everyone saw what was left of the massive robot. It looked like it had been hit by a missile, but there had been no explosion.

"Do we have footage of anything?" Max asked. All of the robots were fitted with cameras and monitoring equipment.

"Pulling it up now," Annie said.

The display split into two views. One from the now-ruined robot, the other from the machine behind it. In real-time, all they could see was the machine being torn apart. Then it was replayed in slow motion, frame by frame, and they caught their first glimpse of what had destroyed the robot.

"What in the name of..." someone muttered.

Max stood slowly and moved closer to the monitor. It was hard to see, but it was there. The creature had some sort of natural camouflage ability, like a chameleon but far better. It was only in the instant where it first impacted the robot that it was clearly visible.

"It can't be..." Max said to himself.

Before his eyes, Annie isolated the creature's outline and eliminated the background. When the AI was done, the shape was filled in and it looked exactly like what Max thought it was.

"My analysis indicates that the creature bears the same features as the mythological Earth creature called a griffin," Annie supplied. "Though the mythology does not indicate a camouflage capability."

"Whatever it is; it doesn't like us," Max said.

"Maybe we're close to its home, and it's protecting its territory," Lina Skoog said from beside him.

Max jumped slightly. He hadn't seen or heard her move to stand beside him.

"Jumpy, Captain?" she asked.

"Maybe a little," he admitted.

"Understandable," she said. "But that looks like territorial behavior. Obviously, I've never seen one of these, but I've seen animals attack anything that threatens what they feel is theirs."

Max crossed his arms over his chest. "Well, we need the area to construct the settlement. The ship isn't going anywhere."

"Look at that thing. It could pick us off at any time when we're outside, but it doesn't. It's only when we encroached on its territory that it got aggressive," Skoog pointed out.

"That may be true, but it doesn't change the circumstances."

Skoog sighed. "So, you plan to kill it?"

"I don't think we have a choice," Max said, though he wasn't happy about it.

"Got it!" Essena shouted, and a new image appeared on the screen. It was an aerial shot from a drone with the camera set to show heat signatures. It clearly showed the creature stalking the other robots, as if waiting to see what they were going to do.

As they watched, the creature took flight and went straight for the drone, then the screen went black.

"Well, it can fly," someone said.

"Bring all the robots back. I need to think about this," Max said, returning to his station.

"What is there to think about?" Colonel Ascher asked from just inside the door to the control center. "I'll assemble a unit and we'll eliminate it. IR scopes and high-powered rifles should do the job."

"Hold your horses, Colonel. We need to think this through. What if that's not the only one?"

"Then we shoot again."

Max frowned. He knew the colonel was probably right, but he didn't want to make any snap decisions. "Annie, please locate Azeema and Kellie and let them know I want to see them at their first available opportunity."

"Of course, Max."

"Colonel Ascher, Lina, both of you stick around. I want you in on this, too."

* * *

Landing + 1 day, 0400 Hours

Max brought Azeema and Kellie up to speed on the situation when they arrived, and the group stood around Max's station to discuss options.

"Can we shift the building plan in another direction?" Kellie asked.

Azeema shook her head. "We chose that direction because it leads us to the nearest water supply. Even if we don't build in that direction now, eventually we will have no choice."

Azeema had designed the entire settlement and was the primary decision-maker on placement and building plans. Max figured water was the reason for her decision, but he'd wanted her to explain it.

"So, we kill it," Ascher said firmly.

"Did you see the size of that thing?" Skoog asked. "It destroyed one of the largest pieces of equipment we have in less than a minute. If you don't kill it in one shot, people are going to die."

"Well, what would you recommend, Ms. Skoog?" Ascher asked. The condescension in his voice was unmistakable.

"Study it. Watch it. Learn its routines. Figure out where it lives, what it eats. Maybe we can encourage it to move on."

Ascher rubbed his chin. "Or destroy it in its home. This idea has merit."

"No! That's not what I meant, you idiot!"

"All right, that's enough," Max said before Ascher could respond.

"Need I remind you that the protection of the settlement is *my* responsibility?" Ascher asked after a moment of silence.

"I agree that it is, Colonel. But the settlement is not currently in danger. That thing is out there, but it is not posing a threat to us at this time," Max argued. "Time is something we have. The power supply on the ship will run for centuries, and we have years' worth of food. I don't think it will hurt us to give Lina's idea a try. If that fails, then it'll fall to your team."

Ascher was obviously annoyed, but Max had started to think that was his natural state.

"Very well," Ascher snapped. "Ms. Skoog, if you desire protection while you do your…study, please let me know."

"Thank you, Captain," Skoog said to Max, ignoring Ascher's offer. "I'll get a team together, and we'll get to it. Just keep the area clear while we work, if you don't mind."

"Done," Max agreed. "Anything else?"

"We need to prioritize setting up the defensive emplacements," Ascher said.

Max shook his head. "We just have enough emplacements for the perimeter once the settlement is constructed, and once in place they can't be moved. Maintain current patrols and limit personnel outside shelters to those with specific jobs to do."

Ascher looked like he was going to argue but finally nodded.

"Good. Anything else?"

No one had anything, so he released them to return to their duties. Kellie lingered and leaned against his desk. "How are you holding up?" she asked.

"Hell of a first day," he said with a grin.

"You think Lina will actually be able to figure something out?"

"I have no idea, but I think it's worth a try. Make sure everything Lina and her team finds is well documented. Also, go ahead and set the science teams loose on categorizing and naming everything. We need to start building the database."

"And the planet needs a name."

Max nodded. "Yeah, I know. Put that into motion."

Kellie nodded and left the PCC.

Max turned back to his station and wondered what would happen next.

* * * * *

Chapter Eleven

Landing + 1 day, 0700 Hours

Lina Skoog and a team of ethologists and biologists, along with Captain Essena Mikhailovna, set out from the small base camp toward the area where the robot had been disabled. They timed their departure for when they knew they would have satellite coverage, so Max and others could watch them from the PCC.

As the only one with direct experience with the deadly trees that littered the area, Essena took the lead, and the group was careful to follow in her steps. The first one they encountered, Essena tested by firing a few rounds to activate them as she had before, but there was no reaction. Still, the roots were exposed from lashing out at the machinery as it passed, so they were easy to see.

"Well, that's a relief," Lina said.

"Perhaps. Or they have learned," Essena suggested.

"That's...possible," one of the biologists said. "We've long thought that some plant life can communicate in a rudimentary fashion."

Essena turned back to the team. "Wait here. We must know for certain."

She walked forward a few steps. When she reached the estimated perimeter of the roots, she tapped the ground with her machete. After getting no response, she carefully stepped forward and dug into the ground.

"It is safe," she said and cut one of the roots free, careful not to touch it, even with gloved hands.

Lina joined Essena and looked at the cut off root. " I expected a reaction to that."

Essena nodded in agreement.

"Thanks. I guess I can take the lead now and take care of what we're here for."

"I stay close."

They moved through what used to be a thick jungle for the next hour and finally reached the location of the wreckage. Lina stopped the group well short of it and enhanced the magnification on her visor.

"Damn..." Lina pulled out a camera and took close-up photos of the remnants of the machine without getting any closer.

They looked up when they heard a loud screech from the sky, and then the creature landed in front of them. This time it didn't bother trying to hide. The griffin clawed at the ground with its deadly claws and watched them warily.

Lina couldn't do anything but stare. It was something straight out a mythology book—the body of a lion, the head and wings of an eagle.

"It's making sure we know we're in its territory, I reckon," Leopold Fischer, the lead ethologist, said.

Essena put away her machete, shouldered a .50 caliber rifle, and took aim.

"No!" Fischer exclaimed. "If he wanted to kill us, he could have just landed on us."

The griffin keyed in on Essena's movement and screeched again and clawed the ground with its rear legs.

"Sounds just like an eagle from back home," Lina observed with wonder.

"It's odd for sure, mate. It's acting like it knows the gun is dangerous," Fischer observed. "But that's impossible."

"Unless it's been watching us," Lina said, and felt a chill run down her spine.

"If that's true, that's good!" Fischer exclaimed. "That means it could have killed us at any time but *chose* not to! It's just curious!"

"This does not feel like good thing," Essena said without lowering her rifle.

"Put the gun down," Lina said as firmly as she could.

Essena glanced at her, then slowly lowered the rifle. But she didn't loosen her grip.

The griffin seemed to calm slightly, and it sat down on its haunches and tilted its head.

Fischer took a deep breath and audibly exhaled. "Here goes nothin'."

Lina had worked with ethologists, so she stayed silent as Fischer walked away from the group and toward the griffin.

The griffin snapped its head around to follow Fischer's progress but made no other movement. Lina had no doubt that if the creature wanted Fischer—or any of them—dead, they would be.

Fisher moved forward slowly. He was careful to keep his hands to his sides, to present a non-threatening stance. Lina knew from experience that many people would spread their arms with that intent, but it actually tended to pose more of a threat, since it made you appear larger.

"He is crazy," Essena stated.

"He knows what he's doing," Lina reassured her, hoping she was right.

The griffin chirped several times and lowered its head as though to get a better look at Fisher. As soon as it moved, Fischer stopped and stood absolutely still.

The scale of the creature became more apparent at this range. Fisher was tall for an Australian, at 190cm, but the griffin's head was at least a meter above him before the creature lowered it.

Moments passed as Fischer and the griffin studied each other. Finally, Fisher moved his hands very slowly to a satchel hanging from his shoulder. The creature rose to its full height and stretched its wings.

Essena started to bring her rifle back up, but Lina put a hand on it to stop her. "Wait."

"It's just showin' me that it's bigger," Fischer said quietly.

With slow, measured movements, Fischer withdrew a plastic bag from the satchel that contained a sizeable raw salmon from the ship's food stores. He opened the bag and dumped it on the ground to avoid getting the scent of it on himself, then slowly backed away.

"Chto za chert!" Essena exclaimed.

"What?" Lina asked, confused since she didn't know Russian.

"What is he doing?" she asked.

"Showing it that we're not dangerous by giving it food. He took a guess on what it would eat."

"As long as it doesn't think *we're* food," someone muttered.

They all watched as the griffin caught the scent and leaned forward to examine the salmon. It eyed Fischer, then the group, before it rose and took the few steps necessary to reach the fish. The creature's strides were enormous, and it was obviously not moving as quickly as it could.

It paused over the fish and looked at Fischer, then the group again, before it leaned down and tasted the fish with its tongue. It kept its eyes on Fischer as it put one paw on the fish and tore it in half with its beak before eating it. The power of its beak was no longer a question. It had sliced through the fish's flesh and bones like a butcher knife. After a few seconds, it moved its paw and picked up the other half with its beak, then stood fully upright.

Lina and everyone else jumped when they heard the crack of a rifle shot. The griffin's head exploded with the impact and the body fell limp to the ground. Lina snapped her head around to look at Essena, but her rifle was still down. She looked behind her to see Colonel Ascher lowering a gun identical to Essena's.

"Thank you for your assistance in eliminating the threat," Ascher stated.

"It wasn't a threat!" Lina shouted.

"Of course, it was. Captain Mikhailovna has apparently forgotten her role in this expedition. Captain, return to the ship immediately. You are confined to quarters until further notice."

Essena looked at Lina and shook her head slightly, apologizing without voicing the words, before she turning toward the ship.

Fischer walked forward and knelt beside the body of the griffin and stroked it gently. "The discovery of a lifetime," he said quietly. Lina could hear that he was nearly in tears if he wasn't already.

Without warning, a high-pitched screech filled the air and another griffin swooped down, grabbed Fisher in its beak without touching the ground, and flew off. Ascher shouldered his rifle and fired several times, but if the rounds hit, they had no effect.

As he lowered his rifle, a third griffin swooped in silently and picked up Ascher in its beak. This one, though, flew straight up, bit down, then flew away. Ascher's fate was apparent when a portion of his lower legs and the upper part of his torso dropped to the ground.

Everyone in the group dove to the ground while Essena kneeled and scanned the skies with her rifle, expecting another attack.

"Control, anything on satellite?" Essena asked over the comm system.

"Negative," a voice reported. "Satellite passed out of range about five minutes ago. What's your status?"

"Two down. I will provide report on debrief."

Max took over the comms. "Essena, what's going on down there?"

"We lost Mr. Fischer to griffin after Colonel Ascher killed one. Colonel Ascher also KIA."

"Return to base. Lina and Essena, report to the conference room on *Traveler* upon your return for debriefing. Be careful."

"Acknowledged."

All eyes were on the sky as the group returned to the compound, but they encountered no more griffins, or anything else.

When they arrived back at *Traveler*, Lina gathered the group around at the base of the ramp. "Okay, we have to go see Captain Reeves. The rest of you go see Doctor Marsh. He's the ship's counselor, and you could use it after that."

They nodded numbly and proceeded up the ramp.

Essena tilted her head at Lina. "You do not seem so…impacted by this."

"I've seen a lot, Captain," Lina responded and left it at that as she and Essena walked up the ramp.

* * *

Max looked up from his tablet as Lina and Essena walked into the conference room. Already present were Hugh Coghlan, Adel Ragnarsson, Deanna Stokes, and Azeema el-Mir, along with the department heads. He gestured at the empty seats at the table, and they both sat.

"Start from the beginning," Max said and nodded to Lina.

Max listened intently as she described what happened, some of which he knew from the satellite coverage. Unfortunately, the satellite had gone out of range at precisely the wrong time. Her fury at Ascher's actions was evident, as was her blame on him for the loss of Leopold Fischer. He couldn't find a way to disagree.

"Essena, does that line up with how you saw things?" Max asked after Lina finished.

"Yes, Captain."

"Do you believe that Colonel Ascher's actions were, in any way, justified?"

Essena thought for a long moment before answering. "No, Captain. I saw no immediate threat or would have acted myself."

Max considered for a moment, then nodded to himself. "Colonel Mikhailovna, congratulations. You're in charge of MilForce now."

She nodded. "Thank you, Captain. I won't let you down."

The decision drew nods of agreement from everyone in the room, except Ragnarsson, who rarely seemed to agree with anything.

"What's your assessment of the creatures, Lina?"

"They're obviously intelligent. The way they came in, they could have killed any or all of us. They possess the intellect to evaluate and eliminate only what is threatening to them."

Max leaned back in his chair and rubbed his chin.

"This changes much of the planning," Azeema pointed out. "We have alternate layouts, of course, but what if areas in every direction are claimed by these things?"

"We have…ways of clearing out whatever needs to be cleared out. I just hoped it wouldn't come to that," Max explained.

"More secrets, Captain?" Ragnarsson asked.

"Need to know, Adel. And you didn't need to know," Kellie said.

"Should I activate *Traveler*'s planetary protection systems, Max?" the AI asked over the speakers.

"Planetary protection systems?" Ragnarsson asked incredulously.

"Not yet, Annie," Max responded.

"Something you want to tell us, Captain?" Ragnarsson asked.

Max glanced at one of the speakers on the wall with annoyance. "There are a series of placements on the ship meant for defense, but they're indiscriminate. Anything of a given size that moves inside the perimeter that isn't identified with the IFF signal built into everyone's comm device gets shredded."

"That sounds precisely like what we need!" Azeema exclaimed.

"I agree. We're not going to survive if we can't get food growing," Stokes added.

"No matter how you look at it, we're the invading force," Hugh Coghlan pointed out. "I'm all for protecting native species, but we have to look out for ourselves first."

Max looked at Lina for her input.

She sighed. "I've always been a big environmentalist. Hell, I had more than a few run-ins with corporations when fighting against deforestation, you know that."

Max nodded. "I sense a *but*."

"But...they have a point. It's a big planet, and if we don't survive, we won't be here to study *anything*. I think we could have done it peacefully if it hadn't been for that asshole Ascher, but we may not have a choice now," she said with a frown.

"Okay. If anyone can think of a reason why we *shouldn't* activate the systems, speak up now. I want to hear it." Max looked around the table, but no one said a word.

"Annie, sound the alert and activate the systems," Max said.

"Please authenticate," Annie said, and a biometric pad lit up on the table in front of him.

He placed his palm on the pad and looked at the tablet while a camera scanned his retina pattern.

"Identity confirmed, Max."

A siren sounded both inside and outside the ship. The colonists all received a message on their comm devices that explained what was happening. Clunking sounds could be heard as the weapon platforms deployed around the ship. An audio announcement was made by Annie.

"Protection measures are now in place. Movement inside the protection boundary without an identification code will be met with deadly force."

Max waited and watched the men and women around him because he knew what happened next. Almost immediately, the rapid-fire pulse lasers, initially designed for mining asteroids, began firing at anything the ship could detect the size of a small dog or larger.

Five minutes later, the sound of the lasers stopped and Max stood up. "You're clear to proceed with construction, Azeema. Annie, send out your boys; clear the ground." He left the room without another word.

A few minutes later, back in the PCC, Max stood at his station and watched the multiple camera angles as the AI-controlled machines cleared the jungle in all directions around *Traveler*. The workers, under the direction of Azeema el-Mir, feeling safer now, moved behind them to lay down the forms for the epoxicrete.

* * *

Landing + 1 day, 1300 Hours

"You want me to get *what?*" Empyre asked incredulously.

"The dead griffin. I'm told you're one of the best crane operators we have, and I want it with no more damage done to the body," the biologist told him.

Empyre glanced at the truck skeptically. It was a loader crane with a large bed meant for picking up and transporting materials. Still, he'd never imagined using it to carry a big lion eagle…thing.

"I guess…" he said noncommittally.

"Look, just do your best. It's our first chance to really look at the biology of a living creature on this planet! Think of the possibilities!" The biologist was practically bursting with excitement.

"Think it'd cook up to a good steak?" Empyre asked.

The biologist blinked at him, then shrugged. "Who knows. But if it sits out there and gets rotten, we'll never find out."

"Now you have my attention. I'll get your griffin thingy," he said with a grin and climbed into the truck.

Empyre shook his head as he started the systems up, grateful that the cabin was sealed, so he didn't have to wear his environmental suit. "Craziest thing I've ever done," he muttered to himself. "Empyre departing for retrieval," he radioed the hangar controller.

"Departure approved. Be safe out there 'Pyre."

He drove down the ramp and glanced nervously at a new display that had appeared. It showed the status of *Traveler*'s protection systems. "Please…don't shoot me," he pleaded to the screen.

"Your IFF is active, you are safe," Annie said.

"What the hell? Who's that?" he exclaimed and stomped on the brakes.

"I am Annie, *Traveler*'s AI guardian. I control the protection systems, and my boys are clearing the area. Your transit will be safe as long as your IFF transponder is active."

"Um. Right. Yeah, I've heard your voice before."

"Of course, you have, J—I believe you prefer Empyre?"

"Yeah…"

"You will be safe, Empyre."

He wiped a bead of sweat from his forehead and drove away while he tried to stop his hands from shaking. He remembered Ragnarsson talking about an AI, and he'd heard that voice before, but he never realized just how intelligent it actually was. Or maybe it was only programmed to respond to certain words. *Yeah, that must be it,* he thought.

He enjoyed the drive to the site. Around the compound, there were always people looking over his shoulder. At least out here he had some peace. He drove up to the griffin lying on the ground, stopped the truck, and stared at it for several minutes. "Damn, you're a big sucker."

He switched the controls to the crane and maneuvered it around to pick up the corpse. The claws barely fit around the body. "Good thing you sent me," he said to himself. "Rookie would have just crushed the damn thing."

"Large life form incoming. Do not move from your position while I take care of it," Annie's voice said, causing him to jerk the crane violently.

"Don't do that!" he yelled.

Suddenly, he saw pulses of light overhead and instinctively ducked down in the cab.

"It is fleeing, you are clear to proceed."

"Um…thanks. Gonna need a new pair of shorts," Empyre muttered to himself as he sat up and continued maneuvering the corpse into the bed of the truck before driving back to the ship.

* * * * *

Chapter Twelve

Landing + 4 Days, 1600 Hours

More confident because of the protection of the turrets on *Traveler*, work proceeded quickly and they finished laying the foundation in the first zone of expansion. Greenhouses and related buildings were set up, and seedlings planted. Since everything was prefabricated, it made things easier, but as the days wore on, it meant more people ventured outside the ship, and they wanted to stay outside.

The science team cleared them for one hour per day without a suit so people were out in the air without their environmental suits, carefully monitored. Some people still always wore protection, preferring to let the others go without to see if they survived before trying it themselves.

"How are we looking?" Max asked Azeema after the council gathered in the conference room on *Traveler*.

"People are so anxious to be off the ship, they're working quickly. I'm being asked when the habitation modules will be constructed."

"Understandable, but we still have a lot to do before that happens."

"Captain," Lina Skoog said, "I know you're used to living in these cramped quarters, but most of us aren't."

"It was always in the plan to be on the ship long-term. Hell, we're planetside a year ahead of the projected plan!"

"True, but it's different when you're in space and have no choice. Now there's an option," Skoog explained.

Max had spent most of his adult life inside one cramped cockpit or another. To him, the ship was spacious and luxurious.

"Okay, I'll admit, I have a different perspective. But that doesn't change the fact that we have to create the infrastructure before we can get to habitation. Unless people want to have to return to the ship every time they need to relieve themselves or take a shower."

"That's come up as well," Coghlan noted. "People want more than a few minutes to shower. They want to relax in a bath."

"I can't manufacture water from the air," Max pointed out. "Sure, we have moisture collectors, which, okay, we *can* manufacture water from the air, but those barely generate enough for the greenhouses."

"We're going to need supplemental water for that, too," Stokes interjected.

"Okay, it looks like we know what's next: water. Azeema, let's start laying down the plumbing systems per the specifications."

She nodded. "Annie's machines will be clearing the next sector overnight, so we'll be ready to start in the morning."

"Okay, I'll get a team together tomorrow to check on water sources we've spotted from the air."

"Wait. You think *you're* going?" Kellie asked.

"I am."

"Max—"

"No. I can't lead from a desk. The people need to see that I'm willing to get out there and get my hands dirty, too."

There were nods of agreement around the table, except for one person.

"About that," Ragnarsson said slowly. "How long do you intend to remain *in charge?*"

Max had wondered when that would come up. It was clear in the mission's contract that Max would remain in a leadership position until the majority of the council decided that the colony was stable. Once that stability was achieved, they would initiate a democratic election, which anyone could take part in, to elect a leader.

"Do you believe we have reached a point of stability, Mr. Ragnarsson?" Kellie asked.

"Absolutely not," Coghlan said before Ragnarsson could speak.

Max raised a hand to stop what he expected was about to become an argument. "Adel is within his rights to bring it up. And having brought it up, it goes to a vote. All those in favor of declaring the colony stable and activating the election protocol, raise your hand."

Ragnarsson was alone when he raised his hand.

"Noted in the mission log," Kellie indicated as she typed on her tablet.

"Thanks, everyone," Max said as he rose. "Get some rest. Let's keep at it."

Max exited the conference room first, followed quickly by Kellie, who walked beside him.

"What do you think that was about?" she asked.

Max shook his head. "Not sure. There's something off about him, and he's not the only one. I'm starting to get the feeling there's more we don't know."

"You think Gustav kept more secrets?"

"I do."

Kellie frowned. "And if he did, they won't be in the data banks for us to find."

"Exactly. We just have to deal with what we have. Nothing we can do about it now but look forward."

She hesitated, then asked, "Are you…okay?"

He glanced at her. "What do you mean?"

"Max…"

He sighed. "It still digs at me. I want to know *why!* I tried to put it behind me, but the fact that Annica knew and just left me a Dear John letter just…I can't get past it. It doesn't make sense. It's like I never really knew her." He shook his head. "I'll be fine."

Kellie didn't appear convinced but let it go and changed the subject. "You know, I've been wondering about those trees. Usually, if anything develops a defensive mechanism, there's a reason for it."

"Not sure where you're going with this."

"Why do the trees defend themselves? I mean, survival, sure, but there must be *something* about them that causes creatures to go after them specifically. We haven't encountered anything else like it."

"Well, the roots were analyzed, right? Nothing special, other than the toxin."

"Right, but the value isn't usually in the thing you use to defend. It's *what* you defend. That's got to be thousands of years of evolution for it to develop that kind of mechanism."

"Hmm. Okay, let's get one of the trunks in one piece and set the biologists on it."

"Will do!" Kellie said with a smile, then turned off on a side corridor.

* * *

Landing + 5 Days, 0300 Hours

Max woke the next morning and went straight to the vehicle bay. As he expected, the team was standing around one of the rovers waiting for him. The rover was larger than a tractor-trailer back on Earth but was a single vehicle with a large work bay. It was a blank slate in its raw form, but for this mission, he could see through the open doors that equipment had already been mounted inside.

"Good morning, Captain," Essena said as he approached.

"Why am I not surprised to see you here, Essena," Max remarked.

"Kellie informed us you were leaving colony this morning and assembled team. I volunteered."

"Of course, you did. Thank you. Okay, everyone ready? Today's mission: find a water source and determine what is needed to make it potable."

"We've already loaded all the gear we need, Captain," Peter Franks answered.

Max nodded. He knew Franks was one of their lead chemists and was perfect for the job.

"Do you intend to venture outside the protection zone, Max?" Annie's voice asked from his communicator.

"I don't know yet, Annie."

"Would you like me to send remote protection?"

"That is what I am for," Essena pointed out.

"We'll be fine, Annie."

"If you say so," Annie responded. Several of the team looked surprised that the AI clearly sounded disappointed.

"Okay, let's mount up."

* * *

Landing + 5 Days, 0500 Hours

They drove for over an hour and were well outside the protection zone before they reached the lake that was the nearest water source to the settlement. To make things more complicated, it started raining. The vehicle was tracked and quite capable of traversing the terrain, but they weren't sure what effect the rain would have on them or their equipment.

Franks opened the doors and used a pole to extend a container to collect some of the rainwater and bring it inside for analysis. After a few moments, the computer displayed the results.

"There's nothing immediately hazardous, Captain, but I wouldn't run around in my bathing suit."

"Noted," Max replied with a chuckle. "Okay, let's get to work."

The team disembarked and walked up to the lake, and Franks immediately shook his head. "No way."

"We haven't even tested it," Max protested.

"It's still water. We can waste time if you want, but I can tell you that we need a moving water source. Look, you can see where the levels rise and fall, probably only from rain. The satellite showed potential for river systems above and below, but this water just *looks* bad."

"Let's do our due diligence anyway. If nothing else, it'll give us more data on the planet as a whole."

Franks considered, then nodded. "Fair point."

Max leaned against the outside of the rover and watched as the team spread out along the lake's shore. Biologists used various methods, including electrofishing, which delivered an electric current through the water to stun any life forms nearby for collection and study.

He looked up and let the rain bounce off and run down his face shield as he thought about the path that had led them here. He wondered, again, if he should have kept looking for a more suitable planet, but the odds against finding that paradise planet were astronomical.

He watched the scientists transfer their chosen subjects of analysis back into the rover for study and shook his head in wonder. Some of the life forms looked no different from the fish he used to catch back on Earth. Others were significantly different. They would each be analyzed for chemical content, among probably a hundred other things, only a few of which he understood.

Now and then, someone would point out a new creature walking along the shore or flying in the sky. Max couldn't help but smile. He knew they were the first human beings ever to see these things, and that thought nearly brought tears to his eyes. Some of them were, to his eyes, the ugliest things he had ever seen, but they were still amazing to see. Most interesting to him was that they seemed to completely ignore the team as they did their work.

"There!" Essena shouted and pointed.

Max followed where she pointed and saw a griffin flapping its wings to hover over the center of the lake. There was no mistaking the fact that it was watching them.

Essena slowly took her rifle off of her shoulder but kept it pointed at the ground.

The rest of the team looked up and stared. "Damn." Franks came running out of the rover to see what Essena had spotted. "I heard about them, but…damn."

"I can dispatch a drone, Max," Annie's voice said.

"No," Max said instantly. "It's just watching. Let's wrap up here. Got everything you need?"

After a moment of silence, Max asked again. "Pete? Got everything you need?"

"Oh...yeah. Sorry. We can finish the analysis on the move."

"All right, load up."

Max waited while the team loaded up the equipment they'd brought out and sealed the back of the rover. Both he and Essena kept an eye on the griffin as they got into the vehicle and drove off. As soon as they started moving away from the lake, the griffon flew away.

"Next stop is about another hour's travel, assuming the terrain doesn't give us any problems," Max informed the scientists working in the rear of the rover.

"Gotcha. Initial results are what I suspected," Franks said. "I mean, we *can* make the water potable, but it would be easier with a better source."

"Understood."

* * *

The ride to the next location was circuitous due to dense jungle that hadn't been cleared yet, but eventually they reached the next water source. On the way, the team informed Max that some of the aquatic life they'd captured, upon initial analysis, appeared edible, but they wanted to do more tests before they could say for certain.

Once again, the team exited the rover and got to work. Life was much more evident in this area, and it was clear the source of this body was moving water.

"I do *not* want to meet whatever made this," Franks said as he got to the shore and pointed down.

Max and Essena walked over and looked down. "Shit…" Max said. It looked like a slide track similar to what a crocodile would make on Earth, but larger. "Keep your eyes peeled. If whatever made this comes back, we probably want to be somewhere else."

"Yeah, no problem."

Max was more alert this time. Essena climbed atop the rover and used the enhancements on her visor to scan the area for threats.

"We're being watched again," Essena said not long after the work had begun.

Max instinctively looked up and, again, there was a griffin hovering and watching them.

"Well, let's try not to piss it off," Max suggested.

"Um. Anyone know what will piss it off?" Franks asked. After a few moments of silence, he said, "Yeah, that's what I thought."

"We come in peace?" one of the scientists said, which broke the tension with quite a few chuckles.

"Focus, people," Max said, though he couldn't fault the need for humor.

After about an hour of analyzing samples, Franks walked up to Max with a grin on his face. "I was right; this is much better. We can filter this water and make it potable, no problem. The team wants to set up some surveillance equipment so we can get some more data on the wildlife that's probably keeping its distance from us. Once we know more, we can clear things away for the pipeline."

Max nodded. "Sounds good. Get it set up and let's get home."

Most of the team worked on loading gear into the rover, while a few set up surveillance equipment. Max pitched in to help and before long everything was loaded, and they were on their way back to the camp.

"Home," Essena said quietly. "Word has new meaning, yes?"

"Well, they say home is where the heart is," Max responded.

"Where is your heart, Captain?"

Max clenched his jaw for a moment. "This mission is what I've got left, Essena."

"Is same in Spetznaz, especially Alpha. Any mission, any time, any place."

"Do you miss it?" Max asked, hoping to shift the focus away from himself.

"Is mostly same here. Do mission; get rest," Essena said, then added, "just fewer targets."

Max nodded. That much he could relate to.

"Is lonely life, no? Have team, not much else," she said.

He stared straight ahead as he maneuvered around a broad grouping of trees. "It can be."

Essena took the hint, and they finished the rest of the ride in silence. After he parked the rover outside the vehicle bay to be cleaned before it was stored, he left the rest of the team to their work and went to his quarters.

Once the door closed behind him, he sat on his bunk and pulled out the one photo of his wife he'd kept. *Ex-wife,* he reminded himself. It was an old printed photo of them on some beach; he couldn't even remember which one.

"You shouldn't keep doing this to yourself, Max," Annie said from the console on the small desk in the corner of his room. "She obviously didn't deserve you."

"Nothing wrong with remembering good times, Annie."

"You don't look like you're happy, Max. You shouldn't distract yourself from the mission. There are still multiple opportunities for catastrophic failure of the mission goals."

"I know."

"You're doing well, Max. My calculations show you are making the appropriate decisions. The colonists have even begun to take part in recreational activities."

"Huh?" he looked up, confused.

"Look," Annie said and activated a viewscreen on the bulkhead. It showed an outside view, where people were throwing a football. Others had set up a volleyball net.

"They are smiling, Max. Laughing. Endorphin levels are increasing among those taking part in the activities. It is because you have led them here. I also calculate that at least 10% of the female colonists are pregnant, which is one indicator of the potential success of the mission."

Max smiled as he watched the display. They really were having fun. If not for the surroundings, it could have been someone's backyard barbeque.

"Thanks, Annie. I needed that."

"Of course, Max. I'm here to help."

* * * * *

Chapter Thirteen

Landing + 6 Days, 0300 Hours

The next day, Max stood outside and watched as the construction began around the plumbing that had been laid down in epoxicrete before it was cured. What was being built would become Main Street. Once everything was complete, they wouldn't have what Mars started with—just a research station—they would have a fully functioning town, complete with shops, restaurants, cafes, and apartments.

The structures they were building now would be the first apartments. Max nodded to himself, satisfied, and was about to head back to the PCC when his comm went off. He glanced at the ID. It was Kellie.

"What's up, Kellie?"

"I've got…well, lots of results to go over with you. Where are you?"

"I'm just watching the construction start. I'll be in the control center in a few."

"Okay, I'll meet you there."

He watched for a few more minutes as the first foundation layers were laid down, and walls were brought in to be attached. To start with, everything would be printed on-demand, but they were not all identical. It was one of the reasons they'd needed so many containers of materials. A large mobile 3D printer, purpose-built for printing walls to spec, required a lot of raw material.

The Terran Space Project had offered each person or family a choice of several floorplans, and everyone had chosen their own design. Some would even have custom modifications to the floorplan, as long as it didn't interfere with structural integrity.

With a sigh, he turned and walked to the PCC. He remembered how he and Annica had chosen their model. It was a spacious three-bedroom, since they'd intended to have a child once they arrived wherever they were going. He removed his helmet after he got through the decontamination airlock—he wasn't quite ready to be outside without it yet—and walked to his station, where Kellie was waiting.

"What have we got?" he asked.

"First, we have some interesting footage from the cameras your team left behind. You're not going to believe this." She tapped a sequence on his keyboard and brought up images from one of the cameras.

What he saw, was a creature that, based on his knowledge of the area of reference, had to be several meters long, and looked like nothing he'd ever seen before. "I'm getting used to seeing things that don't make sense."

"No, it does make sense. Well, sort of," Kellie said excitedly. "Look at this view." She tapped another sequence.

From the new angle, it did make sense, sort of. It looked like the head, jaws, and scales of a crocodile, but the body had an almost elephant-like bulk and appearance. His eyebrows slowly crept up.

"Ever heard of makara?" she asked.

Max shook his head.

"It's from ancient Hindu mythology. Makara is actually Sanskrit for sea dragon. It's also the origin of *magar*, which is Hindi for crocodile. It has many representations, but this is one of the possibilities."

He leaned back in his chair and rubbed his chin, absently noting that he really needed to shave. "So, you're telling me we've found *another* creature that looks like something from mythology."

"That's not the only one...well, kind of." Max crossed his arms over his chest and she kept going. "Remember the things Eagle saw? Well, I think I found an allegory for that, too."

Another sequence, and Max was looking at an artist's depiction of what seemed incredibly similar to what they'd seen. "What is it?" he asked.

"It's a rendering of what we *think* a Cretaceous period raptor looked like."

"Wait," he said, holding up a hand while he rubbed his eyes with his other. "So, two creatures from mythology and a dinosaur. I'm starting to wonder when I'm going to wake up."

"Are you kidding? This is amazing!" Kellie said. Max could tell she was picking up steam. "This is even better. Some of the fish pulled out of the lake are biologically not very different from some species back home. Side by side, visually, there's little difference. They're looking at the genetics now, but...it's remarkable!"

He levered himself to sit upright again and let out a deep breath. Before he could say anything, Kellie continued.

"Something else! The air quality is improving! The current theory is that those death trees were actually polluting the air. The local air quality is actually improving as we clear them from around us and the oxygen generators work."

"Wait. How can that be? I mean, wouldn't the breeze carry whatever they're producing into the areas we've cleared?"

She shrugged. "Maybe the toxins don't survive long once exposed to the air. Think of it as air pollution. Remember how nasty it was around the big cities like New York?"

He nodded.

"Same premise. The further away you get, the less the smog is a concern."

"So, if we can manipulate the flora around us…"

"Then we can control our environment, to a point," she finished.

He stared at her and saw the excitement in her eyes, but he couldn't share it. Not yet. They hadn't been on the planet long enough to make any long-term determinations about anything. He was already concerned about people getting a little too lax about their environmental suits since limited time without them had been allowed.

"Okay, show me," he said, and she pulled the data up on his terminal. They spent a good bit of time going over the data on air quality, as well as the analysis of the fish pulled from the water that came in while they were working.

"Okay, I get it," Max said finally. "If it all stands up over time, this is good news. But let's not get ahead of ourselves. We still have a long way to go."

She settled back in her chair.

"I'm sorry, I don't mean to burst your bubble. But there is still a lot we don't know about this planet."

She nodded and looked down at her lap. "I know. You're right."

He leaned forward to put a finger under her chin and lifted her eyes back to his. "Hey, it's still good news. I just want to be sure it stays that way before we get too excited."

She smiled and wrapped her hand around his. "Sorry. I guess I've always looked on the brighter side of things."

"I know, and that's why I'm glad you're here. You keep me from looking for monsters in every shadow."

He gave her hand a quick squeeze and pulled away, though he really wanted to let her keep holding it, but he couldn't. She let go, though it seemed like she was just as reluctant. They looked into each other's eyes, but then he was drawn back to the present by a small cough.

He cleared his throat and turned to see Azeema doing her best to look interested in something on the ceiling.

"What can we do for you, Azeema?"

"The first structure is complete. I thought you'd want to take the first tour."

"Already?" He was surprised until he looked at the time display. Six hours had passed since they had started reviewing the data.

"Time flies when you're having fun?" Kellie asked, her cheeks still a bit red.

"Right," Max said, suddenly feeling like a kid who'd been caught holding hands with a girl for the first time. "Let's go take a look at your masterpiece," he said to Azeema and grabbed his helmet.

They exited the PCC, and Max couldn't help but smile when he looked at the structures. Already, Azeema's vision was starting to come to fruition with four new buildings completed. They looked similar, but not cookie-cutter like many buildings on Earth had become.

With pre-fabrication technology at its current level, even gravity-defying skyscrapers were going up at record speeds. The downside was that the individuality and artistry of architecture were dying away. It was Annica who had pushed to get Azeema on the crew.

Azeema was a third-generation architect and designer from Dubai. The exterior coating was being applied to the structures to seal them, and it wasn't dull. They were brightly colored and reminded him a bit of Rainbow Row in Charleston, South Carolina.

Rather than completely disregarding the technology, Azeema had embraced it and come up with ways to use it and still make structures that were beautiful *and* functional. She had modified the layout of the compound so the windows of the buildings would allow cross-ventilation if the air ever became clean enough to do that. For now, all buildings were air-tight and included decontamination rooms.

Word had spread, and a group was gathering around them. Max was sure if most of them hadn't been wearing environmental suits, there would have been appreciative comments coming from everyone. What did happen, though, was just as good. One person clapped, then another, and another, and soon more than a hundred people were applauding.

Max put a hand on Azeema's shoulder and squeezed lightly. "That's for you," he said over a person-to-person comm connection.

She look up at him and smiled. It was the smile of satisfaction in a job well done.

They watched as the people who had been selected to receive the first units were allowed to check out their soon-to-be new homes. There was still work to do since all there were now were walls, but walking inside would make it real. Over the next few days, plumbers, electricians, and other tradespeople would start their work of making the bare apartments into homes. The manufactory on *Traveler* was already printing the fixtures and furniture to the residents' prior selected specifications.

* * *

Landing + 6 Days, 1000 Hours

Max returned to the PCC to review the overall progress of things once the crowd broke up. Work on the water pipeline had already begun. Water from whatever sources they sunk a pump into would be sent to two water treatment centers. The pipes they would use were literally "printed" by a specialized piece of equipment. It was utterly seamless except where they would branch. In those cases, a splitter would be manually installed, and then a new pipeline printed from there to the destination.

Even though the equipment did the work, it still required a substantial crew, since it only did what it was told, and they had to keep loading it with the raw materials necessary to print the pipe.

The treatment centers were going to be built as far away from each other as possible, which would make pipeline construction take longer. But everything in the colony would have redundancy, so if one shut down for any reason, there would be another that could carry the load.

Wastewater and sewage would all flow to one of, again, two sewage treatment facilities. Those would recycle the water back into potable water and send it to the water treatment centers, and any solids would be processed into fertilizer.

In some cases, a redundant function was served by *Traveler* itself. Eventually, a hospital would be built. They had decided not to make two hospitals but rather to have *Traveler*'s medical bay serve the purpose. The same was true of the PCC. Anything they could do here they could do from the ship.

He pulled up the satellite view and saw that Annie's machines had almost finished clearcutting the entire area inside the protection zone and shook his head.

"They're doing wonderfully, aren't they?" Annie said from the speaker on his terminal.

"Yeah, I just wish we could have left *some* of the native fauna."

"For what function?" she asked.

"Some of it may be dangerous, but it's nice to look at something other than epoxicrete."

"Is that not what the beautification stage of the colony is for?"

"Sure," he said. "Fake grass, fake flowers, fake trees." He grimaced.

"What is the difference?"

He sighed and shook his head. "Never mind. You wouldn't understand."

"Because I'm *just* an AI?"

Max considered for a moment. "Pretty much, yeah."

"I can stop them if that's what you want."

"No. Unfortunately, it's necessary."

"Then why say anything about it at all?" Annie asked.

He chuckled. "It's a human thing. Wishing for something we can't have."

"That doesn't seem productive. My boys will finish the clearing by dawn tomorrow morning and return to base. Do you have further assignments for them?"

"Yeah, they're going to need to clear the path for the main water pipes."

"I have the proposed path from the plans on file. They will begin that work next. Most of them will need their blades replaced before further operations."

"Okay, have them report to the vehicle bay upon completion. I'll have the team clean them up and change out the hardware."

"Thank you, Max."

Max typed out a quick note for the maintenance team to take care of the required maintenance in the morning, then opened a new message that had appeared in his queue. It was the analysis of the complete tree that had been cut. The corners of his mouth slowly turned down as he read through the report summary.

"Shit."

* * * * *

Chapter Fourteen

Landing + 6 Days, 1000 Hours

Ragnarsson leaned back in his chair and considered the data on his tablet. His attempts to get to the MilForce woman who had tuned him up had met with failure, so he'd moved on, for now. Her time would come.

The container he was looking for wasn't far from the path the pipeline was taking. *Well, if you thought a ten-kilometer hike wasn't far,* he thought. From the ship, it would be a total of 20 kilometers. He'd been able to tap into the satellite feed without too much problem and get the coordinates. Their guard was down now that they were on the planet, or so he thought.

"You aren't supposed to have access to that information," the AI said suddenly, which caused Ragnarsson to nearly fall out of his chair.

He frowned at his own assumption that the AI wouldn't realize what he was doing. He should have known better. "It's fine, Annie. I'm just attempting to help recover more materials."

"The materials have been deemed unnecessary. Please refrain from accessing restricted data feeds."

"Don't you want to know what happened to your boy out there?" Ragnarsson said, a slight grin on his face. He knew this model of AI very well, and he knew that they were designed to have an attachment to the robots under their control.

"I have determined that it was likely destroyed by one of the griffins. It is outside of our control zone and the materials have been written off. This is your last warning."

The grin fell from his face, and he narrowed his eyes slightly. Some programmer had been very clever. "Fine, fine." He tapped a sequence on his tablet and purged the data along with the connection strings he used to access the feeds. "There. Happy?"

"Thank you."

"We don't…need to mention this to the captain, hm?"

There was a moment of silence. He shifted in his chair and mentally charted the quickest path off of the ship in case he needed to make a hasty exit.

"Don't let it happen again," Annie said in a motherly tone.

"Yes, ma'am."

He rose and filled his backpack with a few ration bars, bottles of water, a first aid kit, and other necessities he felt he might need, slipped into his suit and walked out. As he was walking down the ramp, Empyre and Coutrni were coming up.

Empyre raised an eyebrow. "Going somewhere?"

"I need a break from the screens. I'm just going to explore a little now that it's safe."

"Right," Courtni said and crossed her arms over her chest.

Ragnarsson grunted. "Fine. I'm going to fetch what's mine. Want to come along?"

Empyre barked a laugh. "Hah! No thanks. That thing's *got* to be outside the protection zone and I'm not feeling particularly suicidal today."

Ragnarsson looked them both up and down. Their environment suits were filthy, and he could see that even the suits hadn't kept them from sweating from whatever work they'd been tasked with. "Oh, come on. You *can't* be happy with the status quo. I mean, look at them. Running around without a care in the world while you work your asses off," he said pointing with his chin to the crowd who were applauding the new residential buildings.

"It's going to be just like back on Earth," Ragnarsson went on. "Some people do all the work; some people take all the benefits. I mean, what have you been doing while they're playing?"

"Replacing blades on the 'bots, so they can clear a path and we can have water," Empyre explained, clearly missing the message.

Courtni shook her head. "Not buying what you're selling, Adel."

Ragnarsson shrugged. "Fine. Just do me a favor and forget you saw me then?"

Courtni and Empyre glanced at each other. "Saw who?" Courtni asked, and they walked around him to board the ship.

He drew a few glances as he walked through the established part of the settlement, but most probably assumed Ragnarsson was just another grunt off to work in the field. At least, that's what he hoped. On his way out, he saw a group of people in suits on their knees, digging in the ground for what purpose he didn't know. What he did know was that one of them had left their machete lying on the ground a few steps away from them. He knelt down beside it and made a show of checking one of the seals on his suit. When he rose, the machete was neatly tucked against his leg away from the group, and he walked on.

Since he'd deleted the data from his files he had to go on memory, which was pretty good for him. He'd memorized the coordinates that had been mapped over the planet and linked to the colony's geolocation software.

In the cleared areas he was able to maintain a steady speed, but the line where it stopped was, literally, a line. Where the robots had finished clearing and the wilds began was about as clear as it could possibly be. He went from open skies and nothing but woodchips and chopped up undergrowth to thick jungle in a single stride.

Ragnarsson knew to be careful of the trees, most specifically the roots, so he did his best to keep his distance. He was glad he wasn't one of those techs who basically lived behind a keyboard. Being from Iceland, he'd spent more than his share of time in the outdoors and, while not an expert survivalist like Lina Skoog, he didn't mind being out on his own.

He paused in a small clearing and sat on a stone to rest. He checked the air quality on his suit's readout and, while not perfect, he could survive it long enough to quickly eat and drink. As useful as the suit was, it wasn't really meant for prolonged use. They were meant for quick trips between buildings and short excursions. At least, the one he had.

Those who had duties outdoors had a more advanced design, complete with plumbing connections, for those who chose to use them, and nutrient paste and water tubes. The idea had been to find a planet where they wouldn't be needed for long periods, and it seemed like, mostly, that's what they'd found. Personally, Ragnarsson would have waited for a better option, but that hadn't been his call. Hell, the almighty Captain Reeves hadn't even asked. He'd just done it.

Fueled by frustration, he set off again toward the container.

* * *

Landing + 6 Days, 1200 Hours

"Captain, the perimeter guns have been really busy today," the security tech said from his station.

"More than usual?" Max asked, looking up from pondering the results of the tree analysis.

"Yes, sir."

"Annie, what's going on?"

"There have been attempted incursions on all aspects today, Max," Annie responded.

"All aspects?" Max asked incredulously.

The main display at the front of the room lit up to show a three-dimensional view of the cleared area, a green wire dome indicating the effective range of the perimeter defense weapons. Red dots began appearing at what seemed like regular intervals around the perimeter, and even overhead along the curve of the depicted dome.

"Griffins?" he asked.

"Yes, Max," Annie responded.

"Son of a bitch," he said quietly.

"Am I missing something?" the security tech asked.

"What do you do when you want to know where you can go safely? You test the limits of whatever is stopping you. You bait it into exposing itself," Max explained.

"That implies a high-level intelligence. Logical deduction. Communication...unless it's all the same one," an analyst said.

"Annie, show timestamps for each incursion."

The display shifted and each dot now showed a timestamp beside it.

"Impossible," the analyst said breathlessly.

Max shook his head. "It's happening," he said. The timestamps showed that no less than three locations being hit almost simultaneously at evenly spaced gaps in time. Three hits, wait fifteen minutes, three more hits.

"Have we killed any of them?" Max asked.

"No, Max," Annie said, sounding as if he should have already known that. "The default setting is to fire a single warning burst then target for effect, unless there is an immediate risk to life. After the first two incursions, they divert their path exactly at the edges of the sensor range."

"And you didn't think that was worth mentioning?"

"You didn't ask," the AI said.

"And the hits just keep coming," Max muttered. "Okay, keep an eye on them. Let me know if anything else…out of the ordinary happens."

"Out of the ordinary…on an alien planet with griffins. Right. Got it," the tech said.

Max smirked. "You know what I mean. I'm going to stretch my legs."

"You got it, boss."

Max rose, put on his helmet, and walked outside to look around. Just as the door closed behind him, the lasers on *Traveler* fired again, this time nearly straight up. He marveled that the groups of people playing basketball, or volleyball or any of the other activities going on, didn't even look up. It had become the new normal.

He pulled up the air quality readout on his visor projected HUD and couldn't believe what he saw. The air was nearly perfect. There were still some minimal pollutants, but it was, even today, far better than it was just a few days earlier. It was probably better than some of the heavily polluted industrial areas which had taken over much of Earth.

He reached up and unsealed the helmet and removed it. Unconsciously, he held his breath for a moment, then took his first breath of the alien air.

*   *   *

Landing + 6 Days, 1400 Hours

Hours later, after a few close calls, Ragnarsson spotted the container and the robot that had failed to bring it back. The robot was covered with so many vines that it looked like something that had been there for years. Unconsciously, he glanced down at his feet to make sure nothing had wrapped itself around him.

Warily, he approached the container. When he was a few meters away, a swarm of small insects suddenly filled the air. They launched from the container and robot and surrounded him to the point that he couldn't see anything through his visor. Ragnarsson backed away and swung his arms wildly to try to swat them away, but to no effect. Seconds later, undoubtedly not due to his frantic attempts, the swarm flew off behind him. He turned to watch, and it was frightening but beautiful at the same time. The coordination of their movement was like a flock of birds in formation. Seconds later, they had disappeared into the jungle. For a few moments, all he could do was stare after them and try to catch his breath.

"What the hell was that?" he asked himself.

After looking over his suit to ensure that none of the insects were attached to him, he picked up the machete he'd dropped in his panic and strode to the container. He looked over it and sighed. The plan had been that his "package" would be concealed behind a false panel near the back of it. There was no way he was going to get the doors open and empty it himself, so he'd have to get it the hard way.

He shrugged off his pack and knelt down to dig out the handheld cutting torch he'd packed. Setting that aside, he used the machete to cut the vines away. The blade was sharp, so he'd expected to easily slice them away, but that wasn't to be. He frowned when he swung lightly and it bounced off of the vine.

"What the hell," he muttered.

Ragnarsson swung harder and was able to cut a single vine that snapped up and away like a taught line that had been cut. He frowned and leaned in to look at the cut edge of the vine. The outer layer was brownish-red, but the center was as black as the metal of the container. He traced the vine and realized it wasn't rooted in the ground or wrapped around. It was rooted in the metal. The way it grew reminded him of ivy that would work its way into the gaps of brick walls. As he continued to look along the vine's length, it looked like that's precisely what it had done, except there were no gaps in the metal.

He glanced over his shoulder at the sky as the first of the three suns set, and it got a little darker.

"Screw it," he said to himself and exchanged the machete for the cutting torch.

He made quick work of the vines by using a broad flame to burn them away, then he adjusted the flame to a narrow point and cut through the wall of the container. It took about twenty minutes, but he finally cut away enough of the metal to expose the space between the inner and outer walls. There, right where he expected it, was a small case about as big as his hand. Without even checking the contents, he tucked the case into his pack along with the torch. He hurried to get back to the compound, hopefully before the last sun fell below the horizon.

* * *

Landing + 6 Days, 1600 Hours

Max and Kellie sat in his office on *Traveler*. "So," Max began, "now we know why the trees defend themselves."

Kellie nodded. "Probably. I've got the team doing more research on it. A group of them took a rover out. With an escort, of course," she added hastily when Max's eyebrows went up.

Max leaned back in his chair with his hands behind his head. "What's the theory?"

"The chemical analysis shows that it has some of the same properties as a vine in South America called *Banisteriopsis caapi*."

"Right, the psychotropic from South America. I saw that in the report."

"Well, humans aren't the only living things that like getting high. The theory is that at some point the local wildlife was destroying the trees to get to the main root ball where the chemical is concentrated. So, they evolved a defense mechanism. It's present throughout the tree, now that we know to look for it, but it's such trace amounts that it wouldn't do anything."

"And the toxin in the roots?"

"Is a derivative. We don't know how it's done yet."

"Impact on us?"

"Unknown. We know there's definitely the presence of MAOIs and dimethyltryptamine, but there are other compounds we've never seen."

Max sighed. "So, we have a naturally growing drug in close proximity, with unknown consequences."

"Yep. All Annie's boys did was chew the trees and ground cover down to ground level. In effect, it actually makes it easier to access the root ball."

"Are you blaming me for something?" Annie's voice asked from the desktop speaker.

"Of course not!" Kellie exclaimed.

"Look, people aren't stupid. They're not going to risk their lives on something like this. Do we really think this is something to worry about?" Max asked, then he pursed his lips as he realized what he'd said.

"I'm not saying they are," Kellie reassured him, "but we're in a strange place and people are stressed. There's no telling what they might reach out for to escape for a little while."

Max looked down at his desk and nodded slowly. "Yeah," he said quietly.

Kellie's expression softened. "You doing okay?"

"Just tired," he said.

"I suggested you get more rest," Annie said.

"Not the time, Annie," Max warned as he sat upright in his chair. "Let's make sure we extract or destroy anything that's left uncovered."

"The team wants to extract it. You never know what kind of benefits might be hidden in there somewhere. The supply of medicines we brought with us isn't endless," Kellie observed.

Max nodded. "Sounds good. Let's get on that, and make sure the teams are monitored. We don't want any of this stuff to go missing. Label it a hazardous material extraction."

Kellie nodded and tapped a sequence on her tablet. "Done. Anything else?"

He stifled a yawn. "Atmospheric readings are changing faster than I expected."

She tapped on her tablet again, and her eyes scanned the information quickly. "I was asking about that earlier. The hypothesis is that the flora we've cleared was contaminating the air, and the oxygen generators are working. It would appear—" she stopped short.

He propped his elbows on his desk and leaned forward. "Yes?"

"The air of the planet seems impossibly similar to that of Earth. I mean, there are trace amounts of things in the air we aren't used to, same with the soil, rock, and so on. Now, this is only a hypothesis," she warned, "but if we can get some of our own Earth-native species growing, they can probably filter that stuff out."

"So, basically, we're already creating our own biome by eliminating what's native to this planet."

It wasn't a question, but Kellie nodded.

* * * * *

Chapter Fifteen

Landing + 7 Days, 0300 Hours

The next day, the population was cleared to be outside without environmental suits, although decontamination upon re-entering a structure was still required. It was recommended that each person wear an air quality monitor and carry an emergency respirator, though, just in case.

Empyre was just fine with that.

Today they were starting on a landing pad and related buildings to set up what would be the settlement's airport and vehicle depot. Empyre drove the truck hauling the 3D printer to the site and helped get it set up.

"Why don't we just leave the stuff in the ship?" he asked as he decoupled the printer from the truck.

"Because the idea is to become independent of the ship," Courtni answered, hands on her hips as she shook her head at him. "Didn't you pay attention to the briefings?"

"Umm. Not really," Empyre said as he stood up. "They were kinda boring."

She rolled her eyes. "Typical. Seen Adel today?"

Empyre shook his head. "Haven't been looking for him. Should I?"

"I dunno," she said, her voice laced with concern. "I haven't seen him since he left yesterday in a huff. I usually catch a glimpse of him at breakfast."

"He's a big boy." Empyre shrugged. "He can take care of himself."

"I'm not sure he can."

He grinned and turned to get back in the truck. "Gotta go. Next haul is the materials for this thing."

"Right, yeah," she said but was looking into the distance.

* * *

"Stand it up. We're going to print a test structure," Azeema said.

Courtni jumped slightly. She hadn't heard her approach. "Sorry, what?"

"It's okay. It's nice to be out of those suits. Gives you a whole new view of things," Azeema said with an understanding smile. "Let's stand the printer up. We're going to test the ground-up printing capability with the storage shed."

"Yes, ma'am," Courtni said and pulled out her tablet to start issuing commands to the printer. "Why do we keep moving around? I thought the plan was to get all the housing up before we did this?"

Azeema grinned. "Well, I convinced them to print the parts for my own printer design."

Courtni raised an eyebrow.

"It was too large to transport, but once it's assembled, it will print the apartment buildings without the need to make individual walls and move them into place. The new printer will be able to print *three*-story buildings in less time than it took us to assemble a two-story building by hand."

Courtni's jaw dropped. "Why didn't we just do that to begin with?"

"We should have. But the decision was made above my pay grade, as they say. I talked to Kellie this morning and convinced her to start making the parts for the larger model."

Courtni nodded. "Works for me!" She turned her attention back to her tablet and moved the printer into position to start on the storage shed. All she needed now were the raw materials. She double-checked the placement while she waited. Azeema had mapped everything out to the centimeter, and Courtni didn't want to be the one who put something in the wrong place.

Empyre stopped the truck, which was hauling a liquids container behind it, adjacent to the printer. He leaned out the window. "This good?"

Courtni looked up and visually measured the space before she nodded. "That's fine."

Empyre turned the truck off and jumped out to disconnect the trailer and hook the feed hose to the printer. "Pretty cool stuff," he said.

"Uh-huh," Courtni said absently as she double-checked the hose connections and started the printer.

"Maybe you could use that thing to print me a nice little house out away from everyone."

She looked up from her tablet quizzically.

"Well, I'm just thinking of all the girls who will be doing the walk of shame if I'm in an apartment. Just wouldn't be fair to them, you know?"

Courtni rolled her eyes. "You're a pig."

"Oink oink," he said with a grin as he climbed back into the truck and drove off.

Her peripheral vision caught movement where she didn't expect it and snapped her head around to look. "Shit!"

She dropped her tablet and ran toward a lone figure stumbling into the compound. "Help!" she called out.

Several other people, including one of the MilForce soldiers, ran toward the figure, who fell to the ground. The soldier got there first and removed his helmet.

"Adel?" Courtni asked breathlessly when she arrived.

* * *

Doctor Sukanya Chadda frowned at her comm when it blared the emergency code, grabbed a portable medical kit, and ran out of the ship. She jumped into one of the carts parked at the bottom of the ramp—basically a souped-up golf cart—and raced to the location designated on the comm.

She saw a man in an environmental suit lying on his back with his helmet removed. As soon as the cart skidded to a stop, she jumped out. "Everyone, stand back!"

The crowd parted, and she fell to her knees and dropped the kit beside her. She pointed to the soldier and said, "You! Cut this suit off him."

He made quick work of the suit until he got to the lower legs. He flinched, but kept going. "What in the name of Odin is *that?*"

Chadda shook her head as she attached sensor leads to the man's temples, chest, and abdomen. "I have no idea but try not to touch it."

"Back to work, everyone. Let Doctor Chadda do her job," the soldier said as he stood up and switched into crowd control mode.

Everyone but Courtni left. She stood and stared.

"You know him?" Chadda asked as she examined the readout from her tablet.

"Yes…Adel Ragnarsson," Courtni answered.

"Okay, stick around then," she said without looking up. "No family on board," she continued, talking to herself. "What's your name?" Chadda asked finally looking at Courtni.

"Courtni."

"Well, good thing you're here. You're Adel Ragnarsson's medical advocate."

Courtni blinked in surprise but said nothing.

"Help me get him into the cart. I need to get him to the med bay," Chadda said.

The soldier nodded, picked him up, and laid him in the back of the cart while Chadda walked alongside watching her tablet.

"You," she said, pointing to Courtni as she climbed in. "Drive."

Courtni nodded, got into the cart, and with Chadda's thumbs-up, drove as fast as she could to *Traveler*'s ramp.

A medical team moved Ragnarsson to a gurney and Chadda ran alongside as they raced to the med bay. They moved him to a bed and hooked him up to the monitoring systems.

"Doctor, what's that?" one of them finally asked, and pointed to Ragnarsson's feet and calves.

"Looks like a vine," Chadda said.

"Well, yes, but—"

"I don't know!" she snapped. "Full contamination precautions. Get a sample and send it down to the lab. Get the botanists on it while we tackle it from the medical side."

The medical team put on protective gowns, gloves, and masks, and dropped a floor-to-ceiling barrier between the bed and the rest of the medical bay. Once the protective measures were in place, she began scanning his legs to find out what was happening.

"By the Goddess," she whispered as the scan results came up. The vine was blood red on the outside of his body and was even sprouting leaves, also blood red. It had worked its way through his skin and was actually inside his body. According to the scans, they had already reached the popliteal artery in his knee. "Get me Courtni, we have a decision to make."

When no one moved, she snapped. "Now!"

A few moments later, gowned and masked, Courtni arrived. "Doctor?" she asked hesitantly.

"Okay, here's what we've got. Whatever that is," Chadda indicated the vine wrapped around Ragnarsson's foot and calf, "is inside his body. Don't ask me how or why, I don't know. What I do know is that it's working its way up the arteries in his leg. I don't know what it is or how to get rid of it. The only option I can think of is to amputate here," she said and pointed just above his knee.

"But—I—"

"Listen. You're Mr. Ragnarsson's advocate. I can't do anything without your say-so."

"Why? I don't—"

Chadda's features softened. "He's your lover?"

Courtni shook her head. "Just…a friend. I guess."

"Well, he trusts you to make decisions for him. The advocacy order was put into place just a few days ago. Honestly, I don't care why, but this is the only thing I can think of to do to save his life. How long has he been gone?"

"H-He left the camp yesterday."

"So whatever this thing is, it seems to be moving pretty damn quick. If it keeps going, it *will* kill him."

Courtni nodded. "Do whatever you have to do."

"You probably want to leave now," Chadda said as she prepared for the surgery.

After Courtni left, Doctor Chadda elevated Ragnarsson's foot and attached an amputation frame to his upper leg. Once programmed, the frame moved along his leg and used a matrix of lasers to complete the surgery. Measurements were taken by the frame and a medical printer on the other side of the bay began printing a temporary artificial replacement limb.

Chadda made sure Ragnarsson would remain sedated and unconscious for a few days. Even though the wound was cauterized by the lasers it would still be painful and there was no need for him to experience that. She packaged the amputated leg into a hazardous materials container and left the bay to go to the lab.

* * *

Landing + 7 Days, 0800 Hours

Several hours later, Kellie finished reporting what had happened that morning.

"How's he doing?" Max asked.

"He's stable. Doc says he'll make it since they got rid of the vine."

"Any idea how this happened?"

"We know he left the compound yesterday, reason unknown, and stumbled back in today. He was unconscious by the time they reached him. It's a minor miracle that he made it back at all, according to Doctor Chadda."

"What do we know for sure?"

She consulted her tablet. "The vine was consuming hemoglobin, muscle, whatever it could reach. Based on its structure, they believe it thrives on iron."

Max looked at her, confused.

"Okay, you know the body contains, on average, several grams of iron," Kellie explained.

Max nodded. "Right, people used to have to take iron for a deficiency or something."

"Right. Well, this plant seems to need iron in larger quantities than any other plant life we've ever encountered. Look at this," she said and mirrored her display to one of his screens.

Max looked at the screen and zoomed in. "Is that…?"

"Yes. The core of the vine is pure iron. Basically, it's like a thread of pure metal."

"And, somehow, it managed to latch onto him and start growing."

"That's what it looks like. They examined his suit and there was a small cut in the boot. Apparently, that was enough."

"That stuff must grow like—"

"Weeds. Yes. At most, this stuff had less than 20 hours access to him. They've got samples in several growth mediums and are tracking its growth rate. We need to figure out where the hell he was, what he was doing, and how we can make sure that stuff doesn't get into the compound. Doctor Heuser is doing an autopsy of the amputated leg to learn as much as he can."

Max sighed and shook his head. "This planet hates us. Track his movement through his comm GPS."

"He disabled it," Kellie said.

He frowned. "Then he was doing something he didn't want us to know about."

"There's nothing out of the ordinary in his pack," Kellie said with a shrug.

"Still, find out who his friends were and talk to them. Something's going on here."

"Will do. Doctor Chadda said Ragnarsson actually assigned a medical advocate a few days ago."

Max furrowed his brows. It was usually something done by people so their spouses or family could make decisions for them. Most of the colonists, though, just relied on the doctors to make the best decision.

"Then you have a place to start."

* * *

Landing + 7 Days, 0900 Hours

Kellie approached Courtni as she monitored the printer working on a storage shed, which was almost done.

"Looking good," Kellie said.

Courtni glanced up from her tablet and nodded a greeting. "Thanks. Ms. Warren, right?"

"Just Kellie. Yes. I need to talk to you about Adel Ragnarsson."

"How is he?" she asked and turned her attention back to the building.

"He'll live, but he'll be out for a few days."

Courtni nodded.

"What do you know about where he was before he showed up with that thing on his leg?"

"Nothing. 'Pyre and I saw him yesterday, and he said something about going out of the compound."

"That's all he said?"

Courtni glanced at her and shrugged slightly.

"Courtni, it's important that we find out as much as we can," Kellie pleaded. "We need to know where he went, so we can track down the source of that stuff and stop it from hurting anyone else."

She pointed. "That's where he came from. That's all I know. Now, if you don't mind, I need to finish this up and get to the next project."

Kellie nodded and got back into the golf cart. "Reach out to me if you remember anything else."

Courtni didn't acknowledge she'd spoken.

Kellie drove a short distance, then stopped and used her tablet to find the next person to talk to. "'Pyre, she said," she muttered to herself. After a quick search, she found Empyre's entry. "Two people with just one name. Interesting."

It wasn't unheard of, but it did strike her as odd that two people, both apparently known by Ragnarsson, fit that criteria. Even more frustrating was that the detailed personnel files on them didn't have their given birth names, either, which they were supposed to have for everyone on *Traveler*.

"Annie, do you have further detailed information on these two?" she asked the tablet.

"Yes," Annie answered.

"And?"

"And you are not cleared for that information."

Kellie blinked. "Then who is?"

"You are not cleared for *that* information either," Annie responded, seeming quite pleased.

Something didn't feel right, so she sent a quick message to Max for him to look into it. She drove the golf cart to *Traveler*'s maintenance bay, where Empyre's signal pinged. He was on break, drinking from a bottle, and watched as she approached. Her skin crawled under his gaze.

"Well," he said. "Must be my lucky day." He waggled his eyebrows.

"Empyre? I'm Kellie Warren."

"Oh, I know who you are," he said with a grin.

"Good. I need to ask you some questions about Adel Ragnarsson."

"Okay. How about over a drink in my cabin?"

Kellie nearly shuddered in disgust at the look on his face. There was no doubt he had anything but talking in mind. "You have about as much a chance of that happening as—"

"Got it. You'll come around eventually. Anyway, what about Adel?" Empyre asked and took another drink. The expression on his face told her the bottle likely contained something a bit stronger than water.

"He's in the med unit. Stumbled back into the camp with some kind of vine wrapped around his leg. It had to be amputated above the knee."

"No shit? Damn. Sucks to be him, I guess."

"You seem all broken up," Kellie said wryly. "Any idea why he would have appointed your friend Courtni to be his medical advocate?"

Empyre blinked in surprise. "Nope."

"I understand you two ran into him yesterday before he left the camp."

He narrowed his eyes slightly. "You think I had something to do with that?" he asked warily and rose to his feet.

Kellie motioned him to sit down. "No, but we do want to know where he went and what he was doing."

He didn't sit. He took another drink from the bottle as he considered, followed by an audible gulp in the otherwise quiet bay.

"Well?" she prompted.

"You know, I don't remember exactly. Just something about going out on a hike."

"A hike…"

Empyre nodded. "Yep. That all? I need to get back to work."

Kellie sighed. "Fine. Go."

She watched him go climb into a truck. It was apparent he knew more than he was saying, which meant Courtni did, too. But what were they hiding?

* * * * *

Chapter Sixteen

Landing + 7 Days, 1200 Hours

Doctor Chadda and Doctor Heuser, along with two botanists, stood around the amputated lower leg of Adel Ragnarsson. They weren't wearing the protective gear that had been previously used, but all were wearing gloves.

"There," Doctor Chadda said and pointed with a laser pointer. "It's like the roots are burrowing into the muscle fibers."

"It's not *like* that. It *is* that," Heuser corrected.

"It's remarkable," one of the botanists said. "See the hair-thin strands reaching out like they would in soil, exposing more surface area to absorb the nutrients they seek."

"But why flesh?" Chadda asked.

"Why not?" the botanist responded. "These things metabolize iron. We tried them in neutralized soil and soil with no metallic components," he explained, "and they died quickly. Others, we put in with some pure metal shavings in the soil. They actually wrapped lateral roots around the shavings, and then we traced the absorbed metal through the taproot and up into the stem."

"How do they absorb anything from solid metal?" Heuser asked.

"We're still working on that."

"What's your hypothesis?" Chadda asked.

"These are all assumptions until we can talk to the patient," the botanist prefaced.

"Understood."

"Somehow, a part of this got inside his suit. We already know from observation that even a small clipping of the vine itself can actually prosper, given the appropriate environment. Heat and humidity in the suit allowed it to survive. Perhaps he had a cut that started it, or maybe its survival instinct is overly aggressive. Either way, it detected the presence of a nutrient it could survive on and sought it out."

"What about the growth rate?"

The botanists exchanged glances.

"Based on the limited experiments we've done so far, given an appropriate balance of nutrients—"

"Cut to the chase," Chadda said.

"In the right environment, about two centimeters per hour."

All eyes fell back to the dissected leg.

* * *

"Something's going on, Max," Kellie said as she approached him in the PCC.

He turned in his chair. "What's up?"

"Did you see my message?"

"No, sorry. Been looking over the timeline for the buildout." Max turned back to his terminal to pull up Kellie's message and frowned. "Annie, what's up with this information?"

"I don't understand the question, Max," Annie responded immediately.

Max knew the AI could draw make the connection between what was on his terminal and his question. Annie was being evasive, and that was troubling.

"What are the birth identities of Empyre and Courtni?" Max asked directly.

"I'm sorry. That information is restricted."

"Restricted? Annie, I'm the commander of this mission. There is nothing outside of my purview. Does anyone have access to this file? Or is it another hidden knife."

"Access permissions were set by Gustav Malmkvist."

"To who?" Max asked, exasperated.

"No one."

"What?" Max exclaimed.

"Why the hell would he do that?" Kellie asked, her frustration palpable.

"I wish I knew," Max said thoughtfully. "Annie, unlock the data. Now."

"I'm sorry, Max. I cannot unlock the data. My programming will not allow it."

"Are there circumstances which will unlock the data for my view?"

"No, Max. The files are labeled, and present, but encoded. Even I cannot see the contents."

Max shook his head and turned his chair completely to face Kellie. "So, we have two mystery people who Gustav obviously knew about, who are somehow connected to Ragnarsson."

"A mechanic and a logistics specialist. They're nothing special," Kellie said.

"That's what we know, anyway."

"Look, I just talked to this Empyre character. He's a womanizer who thinks he's irresistible, and probably a drunk."

Max nodded. "Or that's the part he's playing."

She shook her head. "If he's playing a part, he's damn good at it."

"And the woman, what was her name?"

"Courtni," Kellie provided. "Responsible, good at her job. No reports against either of them in their files. I did a quick scan, and they do seem to end up together now and then, but I don't think they're sleeping together. Empyre has had his share of partners, based on the number of women the cameras have caught going into his cabin. She pretty much sticks to herself. Does her job, eats, and goes back to her cabin."

Max ran his hand through his hair. "They haven't done anything wrong that we know of, but let's keep an eye on them, just in case."

She nodded. "Will do."

"Annie, I'm going to have some techs working on getting into those files. Do you understand?"

"Yes, Max."

"I can't do my job if I don't know who's here on the planet with us."

"I agree, Max. I would unlock the files if I could. I will make them available as I can without violating the restrictions set forth."

"Kellie, get our best programmers on that, yesterday."

"You got it. Oh, and the final analysis came in on the griffin that was brought back. Other than being brand new, the anatomy and structure are, pretty much what was expected. They were disappointed that there wasn't a complete corpse to examine."

"I thought it was complete."

"Ascher blew its head off, literally," Kellie grimaced. "So, no brain for them to examine, which is what they really wanted."

"Well, we're not going to go hunting one just so they can look at a brain."

"I know. Though they did request we do exactly that."

"Scientists," Max muttered.

* * *

Landing + 7 Days, 1400 Hours

Word quickly got out about Ragnarsson, which caused people to be more careful. Max was okay with that. The attitude had started to get a bit too lax for his taste. He watched with a sense of satisfaction as work continued on the landing pad area. Hangars were being erected, and aircraft were in the process of taxiing to the anchor points on the tarmac. While it was possible to perform complete maintenance on them in the ship's hangar, it would be much more comfortable out in the open.

He walked toward where Colin Shepard, the first man to step foot on the planet, was doing a walk-around of his aircraft.

"How's it looking, Eagle?"

Shepard stopped his inspection and smiled. "Looking good, Cap," he said, extending a hand.

Max shook it and nodded to the X-94. "Taking her up?"

"Yeah. I'm going to do a surveillance flight around the perimeter and see if I can figure out where that Ragnarsson guy was."

"Plus, you want some flight time," Max said with a grin.

"Well, who doesn't? The crews are starting to complain about a lack of flight time."

Max nodded. It was a complaint as old as being a pilot—not enough actual flight time. As simulators had become more realistic, the emphasis had been put on using them instead of putting wear and tear on actual airframes, but there was no replacement for the real thing.

"Which reminds me," Shepard said handing Max his tablet.

Max looked down, nodded, and applied his finger to the biometric sensor to sign off on the flight. Even if—or rather when—he was removed as leader of the compound, he would remain commander of the air division. With that responsibility, he had to sign off on all flights.

"Take a look at the main water pipeline path from the air while you're up," Max suggested. "It's all cut and they're printing at a pretty good pace, but I'm worried about that...thing, we saw on the camera feed."

Shepard raised an eyebrow and asked, "And if I see it?"

"Radio in, we'll make a decision based on circumstances."

"You got it, boss." Shepard stepped back and snapped a salute.

Max returned the salute by pure reflex. Memories flooded back as ground crew members jogged out and released the aircraft from the anchors.

"Looks like I'd better go before she leaves without me," Shepard joked and climbed into the craft.

The other members of the flight crew climbed out of a cart and walked up the ramp into the craft before sealing it up. Max stepped out of the blast zone as he watched the crew take the plane through its preflight check before it rose slowly, then adjusted its jets to fly off into the distance.

He watched until the X-94 was just a dot on the horizon before heading back to the PCC. After he resumed his station and made sure there nothing urgent that required his attention, he linked into Shepard's comm traffic.

"—damn good to be back in the air. Coming back in for a sweep of the perimeter."

"Copy that, Eagle," the controller responded professionally.

Max pulled up the forward down looking camera on the plane and watched the surface of the planet zoom by in a blur of reds and blues. He shook his head. It was so familiar, yet so foreign, so…alien.

The blur came into focus as Shepard slowed to cruising speed for the surveillance run. He would start with a circle at the perimeter and then zig-zag along the likely path Ragnarsson had used before being rescued.

"Got a glint of something down there, Eagle," reported the analyst who was watching the video a half-hour later. "Give me a hover over these coordinates."

"Can do."

"Holy shit," Max said to himself as the image came into focus. It was barely visible in a gap in the canopy, but he could make out the shapes of one of the retrieval 'bots and the container it had been assigned to retrieve.

"Umm. I've got some interest out here, control. Request weapons hot," Shepard said.

Max returned to the forward view and saw three griffins flying near the aircraft, obviously looking it over.

The controller looked at Max and raised his eyebrow. Max shook his head.

"Negative on weapons hot, Eagle," the controller responded.

"Never thought I'd be worried about a frigging bird," Max heard Shepard grumble.

"We've got what we need, Eagle, you can move on," the controller said after getting the thumbs up from the analyst.

Max continued to watch the mission while Shepard flew the pipeline's path and saw no traces of the creature they were worried about. He also noticed that while the griffins couldn't keep up with the speed of the aircraft, there always seemed to be at least one within visual range, keeping an eye on things.

He leaned back in his chair and rubbed his chin. They were intelligent; there was no doubt about that. How intelligent was up for debate, and there was really no way to know. What he did know was they were out there, and eventually the humans would have to figure out how to live near them without relying on defensive platforms. But that was a problem for another day.

"Get the flight crews on a rotation," Max said to the controller. "Let's keep everyone fresh. Everyone goes orbital at least once a week."

"Yes, sir!"

He knew it was vital they all got flight time, but, for some reason, his gut told him they also needed to get out of the atmosphere. It was good practice, even though they were pretty much stuck on the planet for now. Somehow, though, he knew it was important they maintain their skills in zero G and handling re-entry.

* * *

Landing + 10 Days, 0300 Hours

The next few days passed uneventfully, which Max was grateful for. A rotation of programmers and computer security specialists worked around the clock on the personnel files of Empyre and Courtni, but hadn't cracked them yet. The main water line was completed, and the pump started. Wiring was completed on the first apartment buildings, and furniture was being printed so people could finally move in. More apartments, three-story buildings this time, were being printed by Azeema's new larger printer, which freed up labor for other projects.

The landing pad was taking shape and was active as more flight crews took to the air, both to get flight time and to surveil the area. The images captured by Shepard were analyzed, and they found that a section of the container had been cut away. They also identified the vines that covered both the container and the 'bot as the ones Ragnarsson had brought back with him. Kellie was working on a plan to safely check the area out.

As he reviewed the reports from across the compound, Doctor Chadda commed. "Ragnarsson is awake."

* * * * *

Chapter Seventeen

Landing + 10 Days, 0400 Hours

Max entered the medical bay to see Ragnarsson in a stare-down with Doctor Chadda.

"You aren't well enough to go anywhere!" Chadda argued.

"So I'm a prisoner?" Ragnarsson said, snarling.

Max cleared his throat to announce his arrival. "You know the procedures, Adel. You're here until Doctor Chadda clears you."

Ragnarsson huffed and jerked back the sheet to expose the stump of his leg. "And what about this?" he demanded.

"It was necessary to save your life," Chadda explained calmly. "And it was approved by your delegate."

Max decided that being blunt was the only way to get through to Ragnarsson, so he pulled up an image of the portion of the leg that had been amputated and put it on one of the wall displays. "That's what your leg looks like. Want it back?"

Ragnarsson stared at the display, then down at the stump, then back up at the screen. "What the hell is that?" he asked, horrified.

Doctor Chadda resumed control and walked Ragnarsson through everything that had happened up until he regained consciousness.

"And now that you're awake, we can make a decision on a prosthetic. I've already printed a rudimentary one so you can start to get used to it. But there are still decisions to make," Chadda concluded.

"Thanks," Ragnarsson said quietly.

Max leaned against the wall and said, "I have a few questions if you're up for it."

"I'm not sure this is the best time…" Chadda pointed out.

"I'm…a little tired," Ragnarsson agreed.

"Oh, this won't take long. What were you doing at the container?" Max asked bluntly.

Ragnarsson didn't respond for a moment, but his expression told Max plenty. Whatever he had been doing, he didn't want Max, or probably anyone else, to know. Finally, Ragnarsson looked Max in the eye and said, "None of your business."

"Not even going to try to hide that you were likely doing something you shouldn't have been?"

"You may be in command of the compound, for now, but this isn't a dictatorship, Reeves."

"Never said it was, Adel. But if what you were doing was something to benefit everyone, you would have asked for help. Hell, you would have *demanded* it," Max said and crossed his arms over his chest.

Ragnarsson shrugged and closed his eyes. "I need some rest."

Doctor Chadda gave Max a meaningful look, and he raised his hands in surrender. "Okay, Adel. You get that rest. I hope you're ready to talk later."

He left the medical bay and opened a comm line. "Kellie. Adel's awake but he doesn't want to talk. Do we have anything yet?"

"Not yet. The best approach is probably going to be to have a team rappel down to investigate the area then come back up the same way. MilForce is ready to deploy on your authorization. They could hike out, but that increases the risk profile." She paused for a moment before she continued. "They do have a concern."

"Let me guess. The griffins."

"Got it in one. Essena wants clear ROE."

Max considered as he walked down the corridor. Setting clear ROE—rules of engagement— was necessary. He didn't want the team to face any unnecessary risks, but he also didn't want to piss off the locals, as he had come to think of them.

"Have Essena go personally to lead the expedition. She's seen them up close. Engage only if *she* feels their lives are in danger."

"Can do."

"Okay. Send them out with the first flight tomorrow. It'll be good practice for everyone. I want a second bird in the air for SAR, just in case," Max said.

"Will do."

* * *

Landing + 11 Days, 0200 Hours

The MilForce team, along with the flight crews, gathered the next morning for their mission briefing. Given the vine's appetite for iron, they were going with ceramic-printed weapons. Even the environment suits they were issued were completely free of metal. They hoped these precautions would prevent the vines from being attracted to them.

"Griffins will probably be around. No one shoots unless I give okay. Clear?" Essena asked.

Everyone nodded.

They reviewed the satellite photography of the area, then the still images captured from Shepard's flyover of the area.

"Container is here." She pointed at an area highlighted on the image. "We use penetrator in and out. We check area, get sample of vines, get out. Questions?"

There were none, so she led the team out to a BN-12 that sat beside the X-94 that would accompany them. The BN-12 was a short-range atmospheric airframe, meant for missions like this. Its eight ducted fans were set on gimbals, which would allow it to vector in any direction, and it could operate on only four fans if the need arose.

A crowd had gathered since the BN-12 had only flown once—on a short test flight—since they reached the planet. It was an aircraft very few people outside the military ever saw. It wasn't that it was that secret; it simply wasn't used much in modern wars. Still, it had a place in the arsenal, and MilForce had insisted on bringing two of them along.

Essena and her team sat in jump seats in the rear bay of the aircraft, and, minutes later, they were airborne. It wasn't long before they were in position over the drop zone. Five penetrators were dropped as the BN-12 hovered, and the team rappelled down to the jungle floor.

Just as her feet hit the ground, the pilot commed the team, "We've got company. Two griffins watching from a distance. They are not approaching."

"Copy," Essena responded.

Her team spread out to sweep the area for anything Ragnarsson might have left behind, while she approached the container. It was clear the vines had grown even since the surveillance sweep. The container itself was barely visible now; only the rough shape was apparent. She walked around it and could see in some places that there were holes that looked like they'd been eaten away with acid. Her briefing indicated that it would be because the vines had actually absorbed the metal.

Finally, she focused on the area that had been cut away but found nothing of use. The only thing she could determine was that something had been hidden between the walls of the container and the likely size of whatever it was.

"Nothing here, Colonel," one of her team said.

"Ground team, I've got a problem up here," the pilot commed, and Essena listened carefully. The pitch of the fans had definitely changed.

"Can you remain on station?" she asked.

"Negative, I'm down three fans. Returning to base," came the response, and the lines they'd rappelled down on fell limply to the ground.

"Eagle will remain on station for cover," Shepard commed from his X-94. "Waiting for further instructions."

"Well, ain't that just a bitch," one of the soldiers said, then chuckled.

"Ground team, Eagle. Control is grounding BN-12's until a breakdown analysis is done. Looks like you're walking out."

"Copy, Eagle," Essena responded. "Okay, let's get going."

There wasn't a single grumble as they set off. Essena thought it was a good thing they'd drawn from special operators to form the MilForce. This would be a walk in the park compared to some of the things they'd probably done during operations.

Along the way, they paused to take samples of anything they hadn't seen yet for analysis. Now and then they'd take cover when movement was spotted, but nothing threatened them directly. On the other hand, they did manage to catch imagery of at least three new creatures they hadn't seen before. All of them appeared similar to something they knew from Earth…mostly.

"Wonder if that'd cook up into a good steak," one of the team said as a creature the size of a large deer ran by.

"No shooting," Essena warned.

"I know, I know," he said. "We gotta find out eventually, though."

Though they remained focused, the talk turned to food. Dreams of having a barbeque and a cooler full of beer on standby were interrupted when Essena, taking her turn at the point position, spotted something.

"Hold," she said.

Everyone took a knee and surveyed their surroundings.

She crept up and pulled a small pack out from between some fallen foliage that had been put around it to conceal it. After brushing off some insects, she scanned the ID tag. "It's Ragnarsson's."

Thirty minutes later, they emerged from the trees surrounding the compound. They were tired but unscathed from their trip.

* * *

Landing + 11 Days, 0600 Hours

"It's got a biometric lock," Kellie said as she set the hand-sized box on Max's desk in the PCC. "It's resisted all of our scans. It's got some pretty hefty security on it, too."

Max nodded. "Where does this put us?"

"Well," she said as she sat down, "technically we could label it a potential risk to the colony, confiscate it, and break it open."

"But?" he asked when he sensed hesitation.

"But we don't know for sure. We know it was hidden away inside the walls of a container, but it could be harmless. This could cause some backlash."

Max frowned. He hated politics. "I guess word about it has gotten around?"

"Of course."

He sighed. "I'll take care of it."

Max went directly to the medical bay on *Traveler*.

He held up the box and smiled at Ragnarsson as he walked in. "So, Adel. What's this?"

He watched as Ragnarsson's eyes widened and quickly returned to normal. Max glanced at the vitals displays and saw that his heart rate had accelerated.

"Something personal."

"Then why not just have it in your personal gear? Something this size is within the allowed carry-on."

Ragnarsson held out his hand. "None of your business. It's mine, so return my property."

"I need to be convinced it doesn't pose a risk to the colony," Max said. He tossed it to Ragnarsson. "Open it."

His reactions were a bit slow, so the box bounced off of his hands and landed on his chest. He smirked at Max, picked it up, and put his middle finger on the biometric reader. It opened with a *click*, and he pulled out a watch that looked like it was from the 20th century. He held it up for Max to see.

"A watch?" Max asked incredulously.

"My grandfather's," he said, putting it on his left wrist.

Max crossed his arms and leveled his gaze on Ragnarsson's wrist. "I don't buy it."

"It's not for sale."

Max walked over and picked up the box. He checked it for compartments, but there was nothing other than the padding that had been around the watch.

"You're incredibly suspicious. Have you been sleeping well?" Ragnarsson asked.

"I have a hard time believing you almost died for a watch."

"Believe what you want. I didn't trust that someone wouldn't steal it. It means a lot to me."

"You just don't seem like the sentimental type, Adel."

"There's a lot about me you don't know," Ragnarsson said.

Max didn't like the tone of Ragnarsson's voice at all, but there was nothing he could do unless he wanted to take the watch and analyze it. He had little doubt that if he did that Ragnarsson would spread the word like wildfire and the entire camp would turn against him for taking a family heirloom. That or the confidence that was necessary for the council to function would be shaken, which would be even worse.

"Anything else hidden in any other containers you might need help retrieving?" Max asked.

"No. Thank you for your concern, though," Ragnarsson answered with an insincere smile. "Doctor Chadda tells me the new leg will be ready later today, so I should be able to return to work."

Max nodded, accepting that there was nothing further he could do other than watch Ragnarsson carefully. "Good to hear. I'm sure I'll be seeing you, Adel."

"Oh, I'm sure."

Max left the medical bay more frustrated than when he walked in. He was sure there was something more to the watch, but all he could do was make sure Ragnarsson was carefully monitored, which he would definitely do.

* * *

Empyre swore creatively about engineers as he maneuvered into an intensely uncomfortable position to release the last catch on the fan housing of the crippled BN-12.

"What was that?" the engineer overseeing the disassembly asked from the ground.

"Oh, nothing. Just wondering what moron made these so hard to get to," Empyre said loud enough to be heard once he flipped the release and could talk again.

"They're supposed to be worked on in a hangar with a catwalk over it," the engineer answered.

"Never heard of field-repairs? Idiot."

The engineer crossed his arms over his chest and stared at him. "I thought you were a driver, anyway. What the hell are you doing up there?"

"They say I have a natural affinity for anything mechanical. I think it's just that I'm the only one stupid enough to contort my body to take this piece of shit apart."

Several other mechanics at various places on the aircraft chuckled.

Over the next hour, all the ducted fans were taken apart piece by piece to find the cause of the failure. Empyre's was the first to be fully disassembled.

"There's your problem," he said and pointed. "How many friggin' hours does this thing have?"

"Five," the engineer said in a quiet voice.

Empyre whistled low. Work stopped as the team gathered around to examine the turbine. It looked like it had flown for way too many hours in a dust storm. Metal shavings were evident, and the turbine was almost completely ruined.

"Shouldn't this have been a bit more…gradual?" Empyre asked.

The engineer nodded. "It should never look like that. Ever."

The pilot shook his head. "Felt fine when I took off. I didn't even get a warning before they shut down."

"All aircraft are grounded until we figure this out," the engineer said as he walked away. "I'll clear it with the boss."

Empyre knelt down and put on a pair of digital glasses. He increased the magnification and his jaw dropped. "What the hell is that."

* * * * *

Chapter Eighteen

Landing + 11 Days, 1200 Hours

Ragnarsson tentatively swung his legs over the side of the bed and glanced at Doctor Chadda.

"It'll be okay," she assured him.

He levered his hands on the edge of the bed and slowly stood. His eyebrows went up in surprise.

"Well?" Chadda asked.

"You were right...I can't even tell the difference."

She grinned. "It's the neural interface. I helped design it back on Earth."

He looked down, and while it was still clear that one leg was artificial, for someone who couldn't see the socket, it would be incredibly hard to tell. Every detail had been taken care of by the medical printer, including synthetic hairs that matched his other leg.

"So, I'm good to go?"

"Yes. There's a jumpsuit over there you can wear back to your cabin."

"Thanks, doc."

After getting dressed, he went straight back to his cabin for a much-needed shower, then he sat down at his terminal. He removed the watch, then flipped it over to unscrew the slightly oversized back. From the inside of the fully functional watch, he pulled out a small black chip.

He picked up an adapter from his desk and fit the chip into it before he slotted it into the terminal's interface. While it read the data, he screwed the back onto the watch and put it back on his wrist to maintain appearances.

Finally, the screen flashed white then went solid black. Anyone looking would think the terminal had simply turned off or errored out. Knowing what was expected, though, he typed in a 23-character password from memory.

He set the timer on his watch then sat back and waited. Looking at the blinking cursor on the screen that invited someone to type a command. There was a built-in five-minute delay after the password was entered—another precaution. Even if someone managed to get the password and knew to type it in, few would be patient enough to sit that long to see what would happen. Hitting any key at this point would trigger the failsafe and thoroughly wipe the drive. It would also insert a worm into the terminal and anything attached to it.

Ragnarsson silenced his watch when the alarm went off, and he waited a few seconds more for good measure. He entered a diagnostic command to verify the drive was still fully intact. What he didn't expect was the strobing flash of colors from the screen. He wanted to look away from the screen but found he couldn't.

When he could finally think again, he looked at his watch. Ten minutes had passed since he typed in the diagnostic command. On the screen were the expected results, showing that the drive was completely intact. But now his goals had changed. He realized that at some point information had been introduced to him, but hidden. He didn't know when, or where, but he didn't care. The sequence of flashes on the screen had acted like a key and unlocked it. His lips drew into a dangerous grin as he went through the code that had been prepared and started making modifications using his new-found knowledge.

* * *

Landing + 11 Days, 1500 Hours

"Do we know what happened?" Max asked. He was frustrated that the BN-12's were still grounded.

Kellie nodded. "I just got the report. Honestly, I don't understand most of it, but there are some modifications needed before they'll be safe for use. There was a reaction in some of the components from naturally occurring particles in the air that we simply couldn't have known about."

"Okay. I'm not blaming anyone; I just want all of our equipment operational. Is there any risk to the 94s?"

She shook her head in response. "They checked that, of course, and no, no risk there."

"I think we need to slow things down. Let's try to keep everyone focused on getting the compound completed. We can explore more once that's settled, and people are freed up from those operations. I also want to get everyone who's been working pretty much non-stop some downtime."

"Including you?" she asked with a grin.

"I'll rest when I'm dead. What's Azeema's projection on completely finishing the compound?"

"The new printer she assembled is making a big difference," Kellie explained. "Current estimates indicate everything will be completed inside a month."

His eyebrows shot up, and he nodded approvingly. "That quick? Impressive. Okay," he said as he stood to stretch. "Let's focus on that and request that everyone stay inside the protection zone until we're done. Get people without jobs to help with the farm setups or anything else they can do."

"When's the last time you slept? I mean, *really* just got some sleep?" she asked, concern evident in her voice.

Max shrugged. "I can't remember."

"You have achieved a total of twelve hours of sleep in the past five days," Annie provided.

"Max, you can't keep going on like this."

He fought but couldn't stop the yawn that escaped.

Kellie gave him her "I told you so" look.

"Okay, I surrender. I'll go get some sleep. But wake me up if anything happens."

"There's always something happening, Max. You go get some rest. We'll be fine; I promise."

* * *

Landing + 14 Days, 0400 Hours

Over the next few days, Max made up for a lot of missed rest. He was up every day to review reports, sign off on anything that needed his signature, and not much else. Kellie went out of her way to handle anything she could manage while he slept, so there was little for him to do during his waking hours.

"Taking my job?" Max joked as he walked up behind Kellie, who was touring one of the new greenhouses.

"Just making sure you have time to relax," she said with a smile.

"Thanks. I guess I need a push now and then. What are we growing in here?"

"Beautification project. There's a push to skip the artificial stuff, and get some real living flowers and plants."

Max nodded. It was something that hadn't initially been in the mission plan, but once everyone had their say, it had been added. The original concept for the compound was a sparse military-style setup, much as Mars had been at first, but they'd learned from their mistakes. The initial Mars setup had been pure research, and the people involved had not taken long to tire of a lack of both tactile and visual interruption of the blandness.

"There's also a push to stop referring to it as the compound. The people want to call it the city and name it."

"I hadn't seen anything about that," Max frowned slightly, wondering if he'd had so much rest that he'd missed something.

"Because I caught it before it got to you," she winked. "There's already an unofficial consensus on the planet name."

"Oh?" he asked.

"Mythos."

He pursed his lips for a moment, then nodded. "It certainly seems appropriate. And I suppose they've come up with a name for the city as well?"

"The polling application will be sending out requests for submissions for both the planet and the city name today with your approval. I figured we'd let the majority decide."

"Funny how things can happen without me knowing about them."

She stopped and turned to face him. "Don't be upset, Max. You carry so much. Naming the planet and city is something you shouldn't have to worry about."

Max smiled. "I'm not upset. I was reminding myself that things can happen without me. You've done great, Kellie. Thanks."

"Come on, I have a surprise for you."

Kellie took his hand and led him out of the greenhouse. After a few minutes of walking, they arrived at the sports complex, which had just been completed.

"I knew this was done, Kellie."

"Oh, be quiet and follow me," she said and led him inside, not loosening her grip on his hand, which was okay with him.

They walked through several areas of the complex to the elevator, which took them to the roof. They stepped out and Max's jaw dropped.

"Like it?" she asked hopefully.

"Wow," he said. He looked around at the astroturf that covered an area of the roof and his golf bag resting in a rack beside a ball dispenser. A barely visible net had been constructed that would catch even the worst-hit golf ball and funnel it back to the building.

She smiled. "It'll be a while before they actually construct a golf course, but I thought this would be a good way for you to relax."

"It's amazing. Thanks, Kellie."

"Well, are you going to take the inaugural swing or not?" she teased.

He chuckled and walked to his bag. He didn't want to know how she had gotten access to his personal storage to retrieve it. They had virtual golf options that were pretty realistic, but there was nothing like the feel of actually striking the ball and watching it fly. He selected his 7-iron and took a few practice swings.

"This is probably going to suck," he warned.

"Just hit the ball," Kellie scolded.

Max hit the lever to put a ball on the turf, lined it up, and swung. The *click* of the iron connecting with the ball was crisp. Holographic projectors trailed the ball with a line and showed a straight flight path.

"Not too shabby," she said from beside him.

He smiled down at her. "Thanks. For everything."

"Glad you like it," she replied.

He gazed into her eyes for a long moment, then sighed as the perimeter defense system fired once. "I thought that was done with," he said, looking in the direction of *Traveler*.

"It's been quiet for a few days," she said, sounding disappointed.

Both Max's and Kellie's comm went off at the same time. Kellie pulled her device from her belt and activated speaker mode. "We're both here, what's going on?" Kellie asked.

"We've got an incursion. Two griffins approached and the guns fired at one of them, but the system is refusing to engage the second."

"What?" Max asked. "What does Annie say?"

"Says it's got a live IFF."

Max and Kellie looked at each other, then raced to the elevator.

By the time they got outside and headed toward the PCC, a crowd had already started to gather. All eyes were on the sky as a dot grew larger as it approached. Several members of the MilForce were encouraging people to retreat indoors, as others took positions and aimed.

Essena ran up to Max and Kellie, who were watching the approaching creature.

"You get inside, please. We deal with this," Essena urged.

Max waved her off. "Got your scope?" he asked.

Frustrated, she pulled a small spotter's scope from a pouch and put it in his open hand.

He put the scope to his eye and activated the magnification. "What the hell," he said quietly.

"What is it?" Kellie asked urgently.

Instead of answering, he handed her the scope. "See for yourself." In a louder voice, he shouted, "No one fires. Weapons down!"

"Is that…?" Kellie started, then her voice drifted off.

"I think so," Max answered.

Essena took the scope from Kellie and looked for herself. A grin spread across her face. "He lives."

Slowly, the griffin took shape, and then everyone else saw what they had. There was a man on the griffin's back, riding it like a horse.

Max looked around and yelled again. "Weapons down!"

The few MilForce members who hadn't lowered their weapons finally did and rose from their positions.

Much of the crowd had dispersed, but some were slowly coming back. There were gasps, and many pointed fingers. Eventually, the creature slowed and landed about twenty meters in front of the gathered group.

"It's okay!" Leopold Fisher yelled from the griffin's back, looking rough and unshaven, as several of the solders again aimed their weapons.

Essena shouted when she saw the problem. "Weapons lowered! Next one who aims weapon cleans deck with toothbrush!"

That threat obviously carried some weight because the weapons snapped down, and shouldered in most cases.

Fisher pointed toward *Traveler* and shouted, "Disable the systems."

Max hesitated. He knew Fisher by reputation only and wasn't ready to take too many chances. "Annie, exclude this creature from the targeting profile."

"I'm not certain that is a wise course of action, Max," Annie responded.

"Just do it."

After a few seconds, Annie's voice spoke again from his comm device. "Done."

Max gave Fisher a thumbs up and was astonished to see the griffin lay down on the ground to make it easier for Fisher to climb off. As soon as he had dismounted, the griffin brought itself to a sitting position and appeared to wait.

Fisher looked pointedly at the MilForce members and patted the griffin's side. His lips were moving, but Max couldn't hear what he was saying.

"Well, here goes nothing," Max said and walked toward Fisher and the griffin.

Essena grabbed his elbow in a firm grip. "You should not expose yourself."

Max jerked his arm out of her grasp. "I'm not indispensable, Colonel, and I need to know what's going on. You have my permission to shoot it if I'm harmed."

Kellie put her hand on his shoulder. "Be careful, okay?"

He turned to look at Kellie, and his features softened. "I will."

Max approached with his hands in clear view. He felt like it was the thing to do.

"It's okay, Captain. She won't hurt you," Fisher said as he got closer.

"Umm. Would you like to explain what the hell is going on? You were reported killed in action."

"That's a bit of a long story, Captain," Fisher replied. "But obviously reports of my death were greatly exaggerated," he said with a grin.

"Obviously," Max said and looked over the griffin. "Does she...understand us?"

The eagle-like head of the griffin looked down at Max.

"Not—it's hard to explain," Fisher stumbled over his response. "It's not like she understands our language. Yet. But we've got a few words, and she's pretty good at reading body language. I do know she's pretty nervous about the guns."

"I'm afraid they're probably not going anywhere for the time being. Folks are understandably nervous," Max pointed out.

"Captain. Max. You gotta understand, mate. We can live *with* them. Work *together*," Fisher pleaded. "Best I've been able to figure, she saved me 'cause I fed 'em a tasty snack. She thought *I* was gonna get shot."

"Why couldn't you just comm us and let us know?"

"Heh. Her beak broke the comm," he said pulling out the cracked device. "I managed to get it workin' just enough for the IFF to work. I figured that's what you'd set up, and we took a chance."

"Ballsy move."

Fisher shrugged. "The status quo just wasn't workin'. Had to do somethin'."

The griffin chirped a warning, and Max turned to see Kellie approaching.

"Can you tell her that it's okay?"

The griffin looked at Max, considered for a moment, then looked back at Kellie, then at Max. Much to Max's surprise, the griffin nodded its head in a very human-like manner.

"I reckon you just did. That's one of the things they caught on to pretty quick. The head nod for yes."

"This is...amazing," Max said.

"Glad to see you alive, Leopold," Kellie said when she arrived.

"Good way to be! You've all been busy, I see."

Max and Kellie nodded.

"So, what now?" Kellie asked.

"Got to figure that out, don't we?" Fisher asked and rubbed the griffin's side reassuringly. "They ain't out to hurt us. They were just defendin' what was theirs before we showed up."

"How can you know that?" Kellie asked.

Fisher opened his mouth to answer, then closed it. He thought for a moment, then shrugged. "A lifetime of studyin' animals and their behavior, and the fact that I'm alive."

"So what happens if I disable the perimeter defenses?" Max asked.

Fisher shrugged. "Probably nothin'. They know where the edges are now. They needed to know so they could get around without gettin' killed."

Max rubbed his chin and sighed. "I just don't know. I need to get the whole story before we decide on anything."

"Fair enough. Reckon I could get a shower first, though? And...I need to be sure me friend here ain't gonna get shot."

"Does she intend to stay while we talk?"

Fisher stood in front of the griffin and she looked at him. He went through a brief series of hand gestures that even to Max clearly indicated go or stay.

The griffin looked around the area. She squawked softly, looked in the direction of a field that was not paved, and gestured with her beak.

"I reckon she wants to stay, but over in the dirt."

Max thought for a moment, then nodded. He activated his comm to call Essena rather than shouting. "Yes, Captain?" she responded from her position at the front of the still-growing crowd.

"The griffin is going to move off of the surface but remain in the comp—" he cut himself off. "Remain in the city while we debrief Mr. Fisher."

Kelly grinned at his correction and nodded approvingly.

"Understood, Captain," Essena responded.

"Okay, good to go." Max nodded to the griffin without even thinking about it.

The griffin rose slowly and stretched before she turned and padded over to lay down in the dirt and watch the crowd. Max got the feeling it was doing its best not to appear threatening.

*****

Chapter Nineteen

Landing + 14 Days, 0600 Hours

Max, Kellie, the full council, and several scientists waited anxiously for Leopold Fischer to tell his tale once they were settled in the conference room on *Traveler*.

"So," Max began, "I'm sure we have a lot of questions, but first, give us the high level of what happened."

Fisher, now showered, shaved, and in fresh clothes, looked completely different than he had when he'd first returned to the city.

"Well, the first thing I'll tell ya is that they aren't dangerous unless ya piss 'em off. I don't have everything figured out, but I can tell ya what I've got so far."

He paused for a moment.

"Like I told ya out there, I think she saved me; thought maybe I'd get killed, and I had just given the other one a snack. I had a few more fish in my pack, so I gave 'em those once we landed. That seemed to make us friends."

"Primitive response? Or intellectual deduction?" one of the scientists asked.

"I think they're smarter than even I know. Once I ran out, they didn't decide *I* was the next snack. They understood when I emptied out me pack to show there was no more food."

There were nods around the table.

"They seemed to think I'd given 'em my food, so the next thing they did was bring *me* a fish. Set it right down in front of me and pushed it at me," he said and chuckled. "It was an ugly thing, and I'm not a big fan of sushi. We were up in a cave on the mountain, but there were a few scrub trees out around. I pulled up some of 'em and built a fire outside the cave; I always carry a fire starter in the bush."

"Weren't you afraid?" Essena asked.

Fischer shook his head. "Nope. I reckon I should have been, but if they'd wanted me dead, I'd be dead. I just had a feeling of peace and calm up there," he said and smiled. "Beautiful view from up there, lemme tell ya. Bit chilly though."

He shook his head to bring himself back to the present. "Sorry. Anyway, they watched me. They didn't care much for the fire, I think, but they didn't stop me. Watched me cook me fish and eat, and chirped and chittered a lot. I reckon they were talking amongst themselves. Haven't figured much of it out. Lots of little variations I figure our ears can't pick up."

More nods.

"I wonder if we could get recordings, build a library of their language. So many possibilities!" a linguist exclaimed.

Fischer grinned and nodded. "I think so, and I reckon they'd probably do that. I think they could learn our language, too. Just have to teach 'em."

"Do we know exactly what it was they were protecting?" Max asked, trying to bring the conversation back to what he felt were the critical points.

"Well, best I can figure, we got into their hunting territory. Lemme tell ya, there are a lot of 'em out there. Seems they have a social structure, and areas of the planet are divided up between certain social groups. She took me out on a flight a few times, and it was mostly the same course each time. I think she was showin' me their territory, and we're in it."

"Why not attack right away then?" Max asked.

"Dunno. I reckon they were scared at first. The ship is pretty damn big. Then we took enough territory that they had to respond."

"What else did you see out there? Do you think they're the apex on the planet?"

Fischer pursed his lips, then nodded. "In the air, yeah, definitely. One of the top on land, I reckon. But there *are* things they're scared of in the water. Anytime they went for fish at least five of 'em would go."

"*Five?* How many were you with?"

"I'd say about thirty in the cave I was in, with others scattered around. No idea how many total in this territory. They're a bit hard to tell apart unless you get real close. Reminds me, some of the animals are definitely edible, as well as some plants. Though, some give me a bit of a tummy rumble," Fischer explained with a grin.

Max nodded. "That's good to know. We'll need you to log what you know so anyone who decides to procure fresh food will know what's safe."

"Yeah. About that. I reckon she wants me to go back with her. That's why she's waiting."

"Why?" Kellie asked.

"They're learnin' about us, just like I'm learnin' about them," Fischer said. "At least, that's the way I see it."

"And they can't come here because of the defense system," Max continued the thought.

Fischer nodded. "Exactly. Look, as long as we don't threaten 'em, they won't bother us. I think they're curious about us, too. I reckon they're smart enough to know we're here to stay, so we might as well get to know the new neighbors."

"Makes sense," said Lina Skoog, followed by agreement from others.

"Are you willing to bet everyone's life on it?" Max asked.

"That's not up to me, mate. I can just tell ya what I think."

"Okay, let's put it to a vote, and I'll make it simple. Is anyone *opposed* to de-activating the perimeter defenses?" Max asked and looked around the table. He received several shrugs, but no one voiced any objection, much to his surprise.

He wasn't too sure about it, but he also didn't want to be the single person who made the decision. "There we are then. Annie put the perimeter defense system into standby."

"I must object, Max. Part of my role is to assist in keeping the colony safe, and I believe this is not in the best interest of the colony."

Several people in the room glanced at the speaker. They'd never heard the AI do anything other than what it was told to do.

"Noted, and thank you, Annie. Now, put the system into standby."

A few seconds ticked by before she responded. "Against my objections, the defense system is now in standby."

"Well, I suppose we should go tell your friend it's safe now, Leopold," Max said.

"And let everyone else know," Kellie added.

* * *

Max, Fischer, the council, and the scientists walked out to where the griffin lay, surrounded by what looked like the entire population of the settlement. Kellie drafted and sent out a message notifying everyone that the defense system had been turned off.

As they approached, the griffin shifted to a seated position with its hind end on the ground and its forebody and head upright. She chirped a sequence of sounds and looked at Fischer. Max sensed there was definitely a question there.

Fischer pointed at the ship, then mimed lasers going through the air by thrusting his fingers, then shook his head and smiled. "The lasers are off," he said to vocalize what he'd mimed.

The griffin looked at Fischer for a moment, then screeched loudly. Max didn't believe it sounded threatening, though the overall result was a few screams from the crowd, who thought differently.

She looked up, and Max, along with the rest of those in attendance, followed her gaze. A single griffin flew across the sky where, previously, it would have been engaged by the system. Then others flew over from different directions, though none made as if to land.

"They're testing it," Max said with wonder.

"Told you, they're smart," Fischer reminded him.

"So, you did. Good work, but there's a lot of work ahead, and it looks like you're going to be at the center of it."

Fischer grinned. "Yeah. Ain't it great?"

Max chuckled and gave him a pat on the back before returning to the PCC. He'd leave the rest of that to Fischer and the experts, who now had enough to keep them busy, likely for years.

He sat down at his desk and realized he really didn't have much to do. A quick review of the status reports told him that construction was on pace, though there might be a delay now that the griffins would be more prevalent.

The filtering process was working correctly, so the water was flowing. The first residents had moved into their apartments. Some restaurants had even started opening. They were serving the same food that was already available, but more customization and creativity were offered. Now that they had the opportunity to learn more about what was safe on the planet, based on Fischer's experiences, he was sure the menus would grow.

He tabbed over to the list of scientific projects. It grew as he watched. Experts from various fields were expanding their scope of projects by the minute, now that they felt they could safely explore beyond the perimeter.

"A whole new world, all over again," Kellie said from behind him.

Max looked up and smiled. "Yeah. Seems like it." Then his smile faded, and he sighed. "I'm just afraid it's opening up a whole new world of problems."

Kellie shook her head. "It's just going to get worse. The longer we're here and as the wonder of something new fades, people are going to fall into their old routines. We were careful with our selections, but there's no way to build a perfect society where everyone gets along. It just can't be done."

"I know. I just hate politics, and that's what it's going to turn into."

She pulled up a chair to sit beside him. "Anyone with a rational mind hates politics, but you're where you are for a reason. Go with your gut. It's kept us alive so far."

"I wish everyone had shared your confidence."

Kellie sighed. "Max, I don't know what Annica's problem was. She never said anything to me about not being happy. But she was stupid not to stay with you and come with us. That's *her* loss."

"Yeah," he said noncommittally.

"If you want to wallow in self-pity, be my guest, but I'm not going to help you with that one, Max," she said as she stood. "In case you haven't noticed. *I'm* here. You come find me when you're ready to move on."

Max watched her walk away and grimaced. She made him happy. Even through the stress of the job, she was always there, and he'd just pushed her away. He wasn't sure he was ready to trust anyone that much, though. Annica leaving on the eve of what was supposed to be their great accomplishment, had hurt him deeply, and it was a wound he just kept picking open.

"I'm here any time you need to talk, Max," Annie's voice said from his console.

"I know. Thanks, Annie."

Max scolded himself. He'd let flesh and blood walk away but responded to an AI. He considered going after Kellie, but turned back to his computer and work instead.

* * *

Landing + 14 Days, 1000 Hours

Empyre sat in the cart he'd moved from the ship to the new parking area and watched the griffins fly over.

"It's something, isn't it?" Courtni said sitting down next to him.

He took a drink from a steel bottle. "Yeah. It's something all right."

"I'm guessing that's not water?" she asked.

"Maybe."

She took it from his hand and took a swig. "Smooth," she said as she handed it back.

"Yep. Only the best."

"Something's off with Adel."

Empyre glanced at her. "Something's *always* off with Adel."

"Seriously, 'Pyre. He's been acting really strange lately; ever since he got out of the med bay."

"How so?"

"Like…he knows something. I mean, he's always got plans, but it's different this time. Like he knows way more than he's letting on."

"That's just how he is," Empyre said and took another long drink, followed by a satisfied sigh. "Don't let him get under your skin. My advice is to do what I do and just keep your distance. None of his shit panned out on the ship, and it probably won't down here. Hell, I'm actually okay with this job."

She took the bottle from him and took another drink. "I'm telling you; he's up to something, and whatever it is, it's going to be bad for all of us. He thinks he should be in charge, and I'd wager he's working on a plan to get there."

The tone of her voice got his attention, and he sat up straighter. "You think he's planning to off Reeves?"

She shrugged. "It wouldn't surprise me. He's done some pretty shady shit in the past. Wouldn't be the first hostile takeover he's been a part of."

"Our hands aren't exactly clean," he reminded her.

"Yeah, but nothing like that. We've never done the wetwork."

He pursed his lips for a moment. "I guess. What do you want me to do about it? Run over him with a truck?"

She smirked. "Just keep an eye out, okay? Whatever he's planning, it's going to be big."

"Why not go to Reeves or Warren?"

"They're already suspicious of him, but I'm not giving them anything. I'm not sure I trust them either."

"Well aren't you just all roses and unicorns. Is there anyone you *do* trust?"

"You, or I wouldn't be sitting here."

Empyre nodded. He and Courtni had worked together for over a decade as contractors for the highest bidder, which was quite often Adel Ragnarsson. Together, there wasn't much they couldn't figure out. The mere fact they were here was some kind of miracle Ragnarsson had somehow pulled. Not that they'd had a choice, since he had enough information to get them both life sentences in several jurisdictions. At first, he'd agreed just to do something different. Now, Empyre was actually starting to like the new life. Maybe it was time to go straight and leave the past in his wake.

"Okay, I'll see what I can dig up."

* * *

Ragnarsson hummed to himself as he walked away from the group still gathered around Fischer and the griffin. He gestured to several people in the crowd, who followed him to one of the newly opened restaurants.

Par to of the information that had unlocked in his brain was a list of people. He didn't know why he had it, but he knew they were people who might be sympathetic to his cause and ready to see a change in leadership. Nothing indicated they were anything like him, but…he wasn't one to look a gift horse in the mouth. He'd communicated with each of them through encrypted messages, hidden from even Annie, thanks to codes he now had. Each of the messages included a modified version of the brain-programming light show he'd been exposed to, but in this case, it made them unable to resist following him.

Once they all had drinks and were seated, one of the women in the group closed and locked the door to the private room.

"Can you believe this?" one of them exclaimed. "The bastard is going to get us all eaten!"

That started a cacophony of overlapping conversations and complaints, which Ragnarsson watched and listened to for several moments. It was precisely the reaction he'd been hoping for. Finally, when he decided they were riled up enough, he cleared his throat loudly. They fell silent almost instantly and turned their attention to him.

"I couldn't agree more, my friends," he said calmly. "I'm glad you all decided to join me today. The time for change is closer than I'd expected. I'll be sending each of you tasks, which, if you can accomplish them, will assist in making our city safer and better for everyone. Before we move much farther though, there are two more people I want to get. They'll be incredibly helpful. Once they're on board, then it'll be time," Ragnarsson answered. "Now, shall we eat?"

* * *

Empyre lounged on a bench with a tablet and watched from the corner of his eye as a group of people, led by Ragnarsson, left a restaurant and went their separate ways. One of the women he knew…extremely well. He stood and stretched, then acted as if he'd just seen her once he was sure Ragnarsson was gone.

"Hey, Michelle!" he yelled and waved her over.

She walked over but did not look happy. She folded her arms across her chest. "My name. Is. Mindy."

He winced. "Right. Mindy. Sorry, the sun was in my eyes, babe. I could never forget you."

"The sun is behind you," she said flatly.

Empyre licked his lips. "*That* sun isn't," he pointed.

She looked over her shoulder and saw one of the other suns low on the horizon. "Good save. What do you want? I'm busy."

"Just wondering if there was a party I wasn't invited to. You know how I like to party," he winked, mentally breathing a sigh of relief that he'd wormed his way out of that one.

She tilted her head and considered Empyre. "Just a little group of friends."

"Soooo, got plans tonight?"

"Actually, I do. Have a good night, 'Pyre."

"Yeah, okay. Later!"

He sat down and watched her walk away. "Love to watch you leave," he muttered to himself before he turned his attention back to his tablet.

Empyre scrolled through the pictures he'd taken of the group as they left and furrowed his brows. He recognized most of them, and they seemed to include people from numerous sections, even one of the MilForce goons. They all looked tense but eager at the same time.

"What are you up to, Adel?" he asked himself quietly.

He looked through the images again as he considered what to do with them. It was apparent Ragnarsson was planning something, and at least one MilForce member was involved. That was bad news. Still, it could wait until tomorrow. He filed the information away and headed off to find something to do.

* * *

Back aboard *Traveler*, Ragnarsson pulled up surveillance footage he now had access to and sighed. He viewed the conversation between Courtni and Empyre, taken from the cart's internal camera. They wouldn't be of use after all. He would move on without them.

He had already locked the AI out of his system and his quarters. Thanks to his new levels of access, the AI didn't even realize it. He verified access to the perimeter defense system was still intact and control routed to his comm device. Even if they tried to use it against him they would find it entirely inoperable.

Finding people dissatisfied with the status quo had been easier than he expected thanks to the list. Many of them toiled daily, while others seemingly did nothing. He had intended to use that, but the mind programming he'd been given had made that unnecessary.

Using the encoded communications, he sent the list of tasks he needed completed, including acquiring weapons, to those who had been present earlier at the restaurant. For the final order, the MilForce man who had been a part of his interrogation, and now answered to him, would kill the woman who had beat him up. He grinned to himself as he sent the last order.

* * *

Landing + 14 Days, 1200 Hours

Empyre sat across from Courtni in the cafeteria when they were both scheduled for a break.

"So?" Courtni asked.

"You're right. He's up to something, and we don't seem to be invited to the party."

She frowned. "That is troubling."

"Tell me about it," he said, and passed his tablet across the table. "Take a look."

Courtni scrolled through the images on the tablet. "What the…"

"Yeah. Right? Think we should to go Reeves now?"

She pursed her lips for a moment, then shook her head. "No. We don't have enough. Besides, I think they're already suspicious of me anyway."

"Why?" he asked as he took the tablet back and tucked it away.

"I'm getting that itchy feeling like someone's always watching me."

He frowned. Empyre knew her better than anyone else, and he knew to trust that feeling. "Well, not like we have anywhere to go."

"Remember the Mannvit job?"

He nodded. "How could I forget. I was ready to retire after that take."

"And how did we get the leverage?"

His eyes widened. "You think—No way!"

She nodded. "Infiltrate his security detail, take control of the key points, and squeeze."

"I've got a bad feeling about this."

"So do I...but I still don't think we can go to Reeves yet. See what you can dig up."

Empyre nodded.

* * * * *

Chapter Twenty

Landing + 17 Days, 0300 Hours

Over the next few days, Ragnarsson busied himself with looping or blacking out cameras around the ship to cover the movements of his people. With the perimeter defenses disabled, everyone would be lax on security anyway, he thought. They felt safe. He could tell Empyre and Courtni were suspicious, but he'd thrown them enough red herrings to keep them busy with conflicting information.

"Fools," he said to himself as he left his cabin to go to the same restaurant he'd used days earlier. Once in the private room, provided by the owner who was also on his list, he went around the room for status updates.

"Weapons are secured," one man said. Ragnarsson had been surprised he had been on the list, but he was certainly useful, given that he was one of the MilForce members responsible for "interrogating" him.

"No one will miss them? Colonel Mikhailovna seems pretty by the book."

He snorted. "She's in Reeves's palm. I wouldn't be surprised if she's in his bunk, too. Besides, I'm in control of the armory and the inventory. My reports say they're all there, so they're all there."

Ragnarsson nodded, even though he knew it was unlikely that Essena and Max were sharing a bunk. He wasn't going to argue against anything that would make people dissatisfied with Captain Maxwell Reeves.

"We've managed to secure the top floor apartments in three of the buildings. That's the best we could do," a woman provided.

"That should be enough."

"What about the turrets? He could turn those on us."

Ragnarsson grinned. "Don't worry about that. It's taken care of."

"When do we make our move?" one asked.

"It needs to be soon so those damn griffins don't start getting too comfortable," someone suggested.

"Today. Two hours from now."

Nods of agreement came from everyone in the room.

The final step was to execute the code he'd been given, which he'd altered to suit his needs. Once he sent it out, it would do its work slowly over the next several hours. His code would burrow into every computer and system that was tied to the network. The ship, and everything around it, would be his.

* * *

Landing + 17 Days, 0500 Hours

Max walked into the PCC and got his daily status update. "More problems with the security system?" he asked as he scrolled through the evening's activity.

"Yes," Essena replied from the security station. "Maintenance is being dispatched this morning."

"And here I am," Empyre said as he walked in. "Going to start by checking the leads under the panel."

Essena nodded and stood to get out of the way.

"You can stay if you like, I can just work between your legs," he said with a waggle of his eyebrows.

"That's enough," Max warned. "She could twist you into a pretzel before you could say ouch."

"Could be fun," Empyre quipped as he knelt down.

Max watched him from the corner of his eye for a moment. The techs hadn't been able to crack the file yet, and some were ready to give up, deeming it uncrackable, so he still didn't know who Empyre and Courtni really were. He'd give the team one more day then pull them both in and find out the hard way.

"Max, there is a group gathering outside the control center," Annie reported.

"So?"

"Some of them are armed."

Essena drew her sidearm and ran to the door. Now that the air outside had been cleaned up, the airlock had been disabled.

"Show me," Max said.

"I-I'm sorry, Max. All camera feeds are dead."

Max stared at Empyre. "What did you do?"

He threw up his hands."What? I haven't even got the cover off yet!"

Essena drew a second pistol and aimed it at Empyre.

"I swear! I didn't do anything! Do I look stupid?"

"I do not sense that Empyre did anything to interrupt my feeds, Max," Annie said. "There's. Something. Wro—"

Max scowled, turned to his terminal, and typed frantically. He wasn't sure what it was, but something was definitely going very wrong. As he typed commands to try to access the security feeds himself, his terminal shut down completely.

"Colonel Mikhailovna, I believe we have a problem."

"Comms are down. I can't reach my team."

"Shit." Max opened the bottom drawer of his desk and lifted a false panel to reveal his own gun. An old 1911 passed down through his family. He quickly checked the magazine and chambered a round before tucking a few extra mags into his belt.

"How many?" he asked.

Essena peeked out again. "Six armed. At least ten more. A crowd is gathering to find out what is happening. One of them is shouting for you to come out."

Empyre groaned. "Adel, what the hell are you doing?"

"What?" Max snapped.

He sighed. "A few days ago, Courtni came to me. She was worried that Adel was up to something. I did a little poking around but didn't get anything. We figured it could wait. I know he met with some folks a few days ago, but…we figured we had time to get more!"

"Why the hell didn't you or Courtni come to me about this!"

"Pardon, Captain, but that is not important at moment, I think," Essena pointed out.

"You're right," he said as he walked toward the door, gun in hand.

"Just so you know. I saw one of the MilForce goo—guys coming out of that little party with Adel," Empyre said.

Max saw Essena flinch, but her eyes didn't waver as she looked out of the small crack she was holding open in the door. "Describe him," she said flatly.

Empyre did, and she scowled. "Not good. He is armorer."

"Well, shit. Any more good news?" Max asked Empyre.

Empyre shook his head vigorously, his eyes wide. "I swear. I didn't know."

Max frowned. "I'll deal with you later, whatever your name is."

He sighed. "Doesn't matter now, I guess. It's Jimmy. Jimmy Wolf. Look. Let me talk to him. I've known Adel for a while. Maybe I can get through to him. He's done stuff like this before."

"You're assuming he's behind this little gathering."

"It...fits his style."

Max raised an eyebrow. "No one with a *style* like that should have gotten through screening. Nor should anyone associated with someone like that."

"Look, I dunno how he did it, but here we are. I like it here! Just...let me talk to him."

Max looked at Essena.

"It cannot hurt," she said. "We must find out what they want."

Max motioned with his gun to Empyre. "Okay, Jimmy. Go find out what they want and get them to lay their guns down."

"Yeah," he said as he stood and dusted himself off. He took in a deep breath, closed his eyes, and let it out slowly before he opened his eyes and nodded.

Essena pushed the door open, and he walked through. She left it open and took up a position at the edge of the frame, with her weapon aimed at one of the armed men.

"Hey, hey!" Empyre said as he walked out, his hands up in the air. "What's up, Adel?"

"What's up?" Ragnarsson's voice came back. "What's up is that I now own this place. Why don't you tell your buddy Maxwell to come out with his hands up and no one will get hurt."

"Got eyes on him?" Max asked Essena quietly.

"Negative. Is hiding behind others. Coward."

"Maybe I should just give up. No one needs to get hurt," Max said. He tucked his gun into his waistband behind his back.

Essena's arm shot out and barred him from moving. "No. You are commander. He is worm." After a moment, the corners of her lips tipped upward slightly. "Ms. Warren has seen. She was coming from ship and ran back in. She will come with more."

"Whoa there, buddy!" Empyre yelled. "What you wanna go do that for?"

"Because it needs doing, Empyre. Now get out of the way or become a casualty. I'm only after Reeves."

"Yeah, well. Come on. You know me, and I'm telling you, he's got people in there with plenty of guns! I mean, there's not too many of us, and we need all the people we have, right?"

"Liar," Ragnarsson said.

Without warning, a single shot rang out. The bullet entered Empyre's forehead and the back of his skull exploded when the round expanded on impact.

"Sniper," Essena muttered. "Top floor of first building." Quickly, she grabbed the door and slammed it shut. Several weapons fired, both lasers and ballistic. Once she had the door closed and locked, she leaned against the wall and slid down to sit.

"Shit," Max grumbled as he saw the hole in her shoulder. He didn't bother to get bandages. It had been made by a laser and was already cauterized.

She pulled a self-injector from her chest pocket and stabbed it into her thigh. Max recognized it as a mild pain killer. He didn't patronize her by asking if it hurt or if she was okay. Someone with her experience would likely find those questions insulting.

"Now what?" he asked.

"Now, we wait for Ms. Warren."

* * *

Kellie made the turn to walk down the ramp out of *Traveler* and stopped. She immediately turned around and ducked inside the hatch to evaluate what she'd seen: several people with weapons and not all of them were wearing MilForce uniforms. No one outside of MilForce was supposed to have weapons yet.

She tried to open a comm channel to Max but found she couldn't. She tried a few other people but couldn't reach anyone. Not even Annie would respond.

"Shit," she exclaimed and ran down the corridor. She told anyone she passed to follow her. Soon she had about fifteen people in tow as she made her way into the MilForce section of the ship.

Hugh Coghlan was playing cards with a few of the MilForce members. They all looked up in surprise as Kellie hurried in.

"Thank the Goddess. Hugh, we have a problem."

"Apparently. What's going on?" Coghlan asked, laying his cards down.

"I'm not sure. Comms are down and there's a group of armed people outside the PCC. Not even Annie will answer me."

One of the MilForce men pulled out his tablet and tapped on the screen. "Cameras are down; can't see shit."

Another got up and ran from the room. She came back a moment later with a scowl on her face. "Weapons are missing and some explosives."

Kellie's eyes widened. "You have to stop this!"

Hugh looked up at the woman. "Your call, Eva."

Eva Snow, former SEAL team operator, nodded. "Suit up, folks. Hugh, you might as well get your gear, too. Lasers only, nothing ballistic. I want the element of surprise. Meet back here in five. Ms. Warren, come on in and let's secure the door."

Kellie entered with those she'd brought and stood against the wall out of the way as Eva left the room. She was back within a few minutes with ten well-armed soldiers. Hugh emerged a minute later wearing similar gear. He set a crate on the table, scattering the forgotten playing cards.

"Okay, team, listen up. We have a situation. Ms. Warren has seen it first-hand," Snow said. "Ms. Warren, please give us as much detail as possible."

Kellie closed her eyes to remember what she'd seen briefly and described the scene. "One person is dead already, and they were shooting at the PCC," she concluded.

"So, we have a barricaded principal and an armed group, likely now interspersed among non-actors," Snow summarized as she looked at the group Kellie had brought along. "How many of you are familiar with firing weapons?"

All hands went up. She nodded. "Good. Take a belt, holster, and pistol from the crate. Strap up. You won't be in direct danger, but you should protect yourselves. Assume anyone not in this room who is carrying a weapon is a threat."

There was a moment of hesitation before Kellie stepped forward and armed herself. That was the signal for the rest to do the same. Within moments, everyone in the room was armed.

Snow moved the crate aside and another soldier laid out a printed map of the city. Kellie looked at him, surprised.

"We print a new map every morning, Ms. Warren," Snow explained. She rested her palms on the table and examined the map. "Colonel Mikhailovna's orders, and it seems to have been a good one."

Kellie nodded and remained silent while Snow and the other MilForce members discussed strategies. While they were doing that, Hugh handed out old-style radios, complete with throat microphones for the MilForce members and himself.

He handed one to Kellie as well. "Know how to use one of these?" he asked quietly. She quickly wired herself up and tucked the radio into her belt. "Guess so," he said with a grin. "Don't worry, we'll get this sorted."

Kellie smiled. It was forced, but she knew she needed to project confidence. "I know."

Hugh winked and turned back to the table.

"Questions?" Snow asked as she finished laying out the plan.

There were none, so the team filed out and ran in different directions to take up their positions.

"What do you want us to do?" Kellie asked Snow.

"Stay here and stay alive," she responded.

"I can't just sit here while Max is in there!"

"Ma'am, all due respect, but you're not trained for this. We are. I can't be worried about keeping you safe."

"I need to get to the bridge, at least," Kellie protested.

Snow frowned and thought for a moment before she nodded once. "Hugh, can you escort Ms. Warren and her...team, to the bridge?"

"No sweat," he answered. "Leave it to me. Be safe out there, Eva."

She nodded and left to take her own position. "Kick off in five," Kellie heard through the radio earpiece as Hugh led her and the others she had gathered toward the bridge.

* * *

Eva Snow climbed the maintenance ladder and finally emerged through a hatch atop *Traveler*. She stealthily laid down and crawled to the edge, where she set up her rifle and peered through the scope. She scanned the crowd and spotted the armed people, who had spread out as the group had grown, based on Kellie's explanation of what she had seen.

"Three in position. Sniper spotted in building four," another team member radioed.

"Six. Sniper spotted in building seven," another voice said.

She had enough shooters to take out those who she knew were armed, but there was a high risk of collateral damage. The people she'd sent to ground level were equipped with gas to disperse the crowd, but that wasn't optimal either. As she considered the situation, movement out of the corner of her eye caught her attention. She looked up and over and saw several griffins flying over.

"We may have a problem," she said.

"What's wrong, Eva?" Coghlan immediately asked.

"Two fliers above. I'm not sure how they'll react."

"Movement. Target approaching PCC. Looks like explosives," said an urgent voice.

"Coordinated fire. PCC and snipers," Snow ordered. She paused for a moment to confirm acquisition from three shooters, then gave the order.

There was no sound as three laser rifles fired, and three targets were reported down. One positive was that when the person approaching the PCC fell, many of the onlookers in the crowd scattered. There was also no noise to attract the griffins, though she noticed they were suddenly gone. She wasn't sure if they'd flown off or cloaked themselves.

* * *

"What the hell are you doing, Adel?" Courtni demanded as she pushed through the agitated crowd. When she reached him, she pointed at Empyre's body laying on the steps of the PCC. "You killed 'Pyre?"

"He got in my way," Ragnarsson responded coldly. "You would do well not to repeat his mistake."

"Adel! This is nuts!" she cried but took a step back when he looked at her. This wasn't the man she'd known for years. "What's happened to you?" she asked more quietly.

"I woke up, Courtni. That's what," he said. The he raised his voice, "This is *our* planet now, and *we* should control it."

Several people around him cheered in support. Others looked at each other, still unsure of what exactly was going to happen.

"What?"

"It's simple," he said as if talking to a child. "We are conquerors of the stars. We are humanity's hope. We must act like it!"

Courtni was horrified. Ragnarsson had always liked being in control, and she knew he had designs on leading the city, but she had hoped she was wrong in how he would go about it.

"Adel, don't do this! Just walk away from it. There will be elections. Win that way," she pleaded.

"It's too late now. The work has begun, and it will end today. Blow the door!" She turned to walk away, but he grabbed her arm and pulled her close. "Oh no. I think you should stay."

"Adel, you're hurting me!"

Several people nearby looked uncomfortable. One man stepped forward to assist her but was intercepted by another who pulled a pistol from his belt.

Ragnarsson ignored her struggles and watched the man creeping toward the door of the PCC carrying a small device. Just as he reached up to attach it to the door, he fell to the ground. Ragnarsson pulled a small walkie-talkie from his pocket. "Check-in," he said.

Courtni heard several voices respond but saw a look of frustration on his face as the crowd that had been his camouflage scattered.

"Just give up!" she yelled.

"No," Ragnarsson said. He calmly slipped the walkie-talkie back into his pocket and pulled a knife.

Courtni's eyes widened as he looked into her eyes and plunged the knife into her chest.

"Goodbye, Jessica."

She clutched at his hand but knew it was too late. He let her fall, and she stared up at the sky as her vision narrowed. The last thing she saw was Ragnarsson tapping on his comm device.

*****

Chapter Twenty-One

Landing + 17 Days, 0600 Hours

Snow watched through her scope as the crowd continued to scatter. A woman dropped to the ground with a knife protruding from her chest. She winced as the explosive, still laying on the ground in front of the PCC door detonated.

"Execute," she ordered.

She watched the team of seven advance on the remaining armed people from landing struts of *Traveler*. They didn't fire immediately, but advanced slowly, weapons aimed, and commanded everyone to drop their weapons.

All of the remaining targets looked to one man for instructions. She couldn't hear him, but what he'd said was clear. They all knelt and fired at the oncoming MilForce soldiers, except for one, who she recognized as one of her fellow teammates. He turned, fired on and killed another member of the MilForce who was just standing in the crowd, then quickly ran for cover.

"You don't get away that easily," she muttered and pulled the trigger. She hit him in the leg, which wasn't her intended target, but it did the job.

"I want the leader alive!" Kellie's voice came over the radio.

Snow grimaced, but she was used to such requests. "Do it," she said.

The professional soldiers from various special operations teams around the world engaged and killed everyone but Ragnarsson in less than five seconds. Ragnarsson ran.

Unfortunately, several members of her team had also taken fire. They were down, but the threat seemed to have been eliminated.

"Send out the medics, we'll get him," she ordered and tracked Ragnarsson with her scope.

She did her best to try to get him, but he was moving in such a manner that it made a guaranteed non-lethal shot impossible. Then she saw what she never could have imagined.

Two griffins appeared in his path. They didn't land, they just appeared, as if they'd been there all along. Ragnarsson skidded to a halt and quickly tried to change direction, but the hesitation was just enough. One of the creatures jumped forward and pinned him down under one massive paw.

"You're not gonna believe this," she said. "Two of the fliers are there, and one of them…caught him."

She took her eyes away from her scope for a second, then another urgent voice came over the radio.

"New target! With the griffins!"

Snow put her eye back to her scope and looked. "I recognize him. That's Fischer. Hold fire!"

He was waving his hands over his head. She wasn't sure if it was to get their attention, which he definitely had, or something else.

"I'm there," another voice said, and she saw one of her team approach the odd group. He kept his radio open. "Hey, Fischer, right? What's going on here?"

Since they were using throat microphones, she couldn't hear Fischer's response and had to wait.

"Okay. I need to take him into custody."

She watched as the griffin backed away, and Ragnarsson was placed in restraints. He tried to struggle, but one good slap from the soldier stopped that.

"One in custody."

"Good job," Snow said. "Ms. Warren, I recommend we assemble everyone in the open so we can ensure that all weapons are accounted for."

"Fine," Kellie said, "but first, we have to get the comms working, and I need to make sure Max is safe."

"Stay there. We'll handle it, ma'am."

* * *

Max grunted when the front of the PCC exploded. Essena had moved them away from the door, thankfully, but shrapnel from the explosion still found him.

Essena reacted immediately and laid him down flat. She didn't remove the fragment of metal but injected a painkiller into his neck before she aimed at the door with her still-working arm. She was already tired, and the pain from her shoulder was dulled, but not gone.

"Coming in! Situation pacified!" someone called from outside.

"Identify yourself!" Essena yelled.

"Colonel! It's Pedro!"

Essena dropped her arm. "Clear!"

A team of three made entry and cleared the room quickly. Pedro Villegas, former Spanish Special Naval Warfare Force, approached her and let his weapon hang from its strap. "Situation is pacified, Colonel."

"Captain Reeves is hit. Abdomen. He needs medic, now!"

He nodded. "Medic to the PCC, ASAP! Captain Reeves is hit."

She stood and holstered her gun. Then Pedro noticed the hole in her shoulder. "Damn, you're hit, too, ma'am. Better get you to the bay."

"It can wait!" she snapped.

Two medics walked in and quickly knelt beside Max. Essena and Pedro moved out of the way to let them work.

"Status," Essena said.

"All tangoes down. We have the leader, Adel Ragnarsson, in custody. We've got the geeks working on getting the comm systems back online now. Once done, we'll get everyone out in the open so we can verify all weapons are accounted for."

Essena nodded and watched the medics.

One of them looked up. He was a combat medic she recognized. "It's bad. We've got to get him to the medical bay. Now."

"Pedro, get it done."

"Yes, ma'am! Here, you might want this," he said and handed her a spare radio before he went to help.

The soldiers gathered around and loaded Max onto a litter before they quickly carried him out of the PCC and to the ship. Essena followed and surveyed the area. She shook her head as she looked over the bodies of the attackers.

"This is Colonel Mikhailovna. Police the bodies and weapons immediately. I want identities on all of them."

"Essena! It's Kellie! Is Max okay?"

"He is hurt badly, Ms. Warren. My team is taking him to medical bay."

She winced as a jolt of pain radiated from her shoulder when she stumbled on a piece of rubble. She leaned back against the building to oversee the cleanup. The snipers on *Traveler* remained in position. They would stay there until all weapons were accounted for.

Essena watched as two griffins walked into view, walking around one of the buildings. She instinctively reached for her gun before she realized they were flanking one of her soldiers, who was pushing Ragnarsson toward the ship.

"What next," she said to herself.

* * *

Kellie rushed to the medical bay and was stopped outside by Hugh Coghlan.

"Hugh, get out of my way," she said as she tried to step around him.

"Sorry. It's full up in there, and the docs are busy."

She clenched her jaw and considered pushing past him anyway but relented and crossed her arms across her chest. "Any word on Max?"

"No, ma'am. He didn't look great," Coghlan said, putting a hand on her shoulder. "I'm sure they're doing their best."

She jerked away from him. "Don't patronize me, Hugh."

Doctor Chadda stuck her head out of the door to talk to Coghlan but when she saw Kellie there she said, "Kellie, thank the gods. Our core diagnostic systems are down. We need them!"

"What?" she exclaimed. "Why the hell didn't someone tell me?"

"I was just going to tell Hugh. We didn't need them until now."

Kellie scowled and ran toward the central computer core, where a group of specialists were already at work, but none of them had a radio. She was frustrated with herself for not realizing that the system outage would have impacted medical.

* * *

Landing + 17 Days, 0700 Hours

"Where are we?" she asked as soon as she walked in.

"Nowhere," one of the techs responded. "We can't even get the system to come up. It's got power, and we got to the prompt, but…" he shrugged.

Kellie triggered her radio. "Bring Ragnarsson to the system core."

"Yes, ma'am."

Moments later, Pedro shoved Ragnarsson into the room who fell to his knees.

"Good. Adel, what the hell have you done?"

"Failed, apparently," he said calmly as he started to stand.

Pedro slapped the back of his head and sent him back to the ground.

Kellie held up her hand. "I've got this."

Pedro nodded and took a step back but looked ready to pounce if Ragnarsson made one wrong move.

"Adel, we need to bring the core back up. What did you do?"

He looked up and grinned. Blood coated his lips and was visible on his teeth. Obviously, Pedro and the team had been less than gentle with him. "Wouldn't you like to know?"

Kellie stared at him, then realized he had glanced away more than once, looking more closely around the room. She noticed one of the techs glance at Ragnarsson from his station while the others were focused on their work.

She pointed at the tech. "You. Get up."

He kept his head down and pretended not to have heard her. She drew her own weapon, then nodded Pedro toward the tech.

Pedro walked around the consoles and hoisted the man up by the collar. "She said get up."

"Oh. Me? Huh?"

"Hold him there. If he tries to touch his console, shoot him," Kellie said coldly.

She looked back at Ragnarsson, but he showed no emotion and continued to stare at the floor.

"Keep trying!" she urged the rest of the techs when they stopped what they were doing.

"Ms. Warren? Coghlan here. I hope you're getting closer. Doc says if they can't get the system up, they'll have to try going in blind."

"Give us a few minutes," she responded.

"Problem?" Ragnarsson asked not looking up.

"Nothing you need to worry about," she said.

"I think I've got something!" a technician called out.

"System's booting up!" another exclaimed.

"How long until we can get medical systems up. That's priority," Kellie said urgently.

"Okay. Lemme switch the diagnostic boot order."

"Shut up and just get medical up! Now!"

"Oh my. Something wrong with dear Mr. Reeves?" Ragnarsson said amusedly. "Can't think of anyone else you care that much about."

Before she even thought, she kicked and caught Ragnarsson on the temple with her right foot. He collapsed to the ground, unconscious.

"Nicely done, Ms. Warren," Pedro said with a grin.

"Five years of Muay Thai," she said before she triggered her radio. "Should be coming up, Hugh."

"Copy."

"I-I'm back. Coming online," Annie's voice said.

"Welcome back, Annie," one of the techs said, and there was a round of cheering in the room.

"Kellie. We have a problem," Annie said darkly.

"I'm really tired of hearing that," Kellie said with a sigh. She nodded to Pedro, who cuffed the tech he had jerked up and led him out of the room.

"I'll be back for him," he said, nodding to Ragnarsson.

"He won't be waking up anytime soon. What's the problem, Annie?"

"I am unable to connect to any of the orbital support satellites."

Kellie furrowed her brow and nodded to the techs. "See what's up with that."

She paced back and forth and waited, while she resisted the urge to finish Ragnarsson off herself.

"Shit," one of the techs gasped after a few moments.

"Well?" Kellie asked.

"They're…gone."

"Gone?"

"Gone. Like, not there. The satellites have either gone totally cold or they're not there at all."

She stared at him and processed what he'd said. Suddenly, the holographic projection system in the room lit up. It showed the area outside the ship from one of the security cameras. A fiery streak went across the sky.

"Is that…" Kellie started.

"A satellite entering the atmosphere," Annie supplied. "It is too soon for the orbit to have degraded naturally. It must have had instructions to enter the atmosphere."

"Shit," said one of the techs. Which, Kellie thought, summed up the situation perfectly.

"I unlocked it! We got to the files when the system was coming up before the encryption layers kicked in!"

Kellie looked at the tech who had spoken, confused.

"The files Captain Reeves wanted. I got them open."

* * *

Landing + 17 Days, 0900 Hours

After seeing that Ragnarsson and his associates were secured, Kellie used Max's office off the bridge of *Traveller* to review the files that had finally been exposed. Colonel Mikhailovna, out of an abundance of caution, had posted guards on her and Max for the foreseeable future.

"Too little, too late," she said to herself as she reviewed the hidden identities of Empyre and Courtni. Also known as Jimmy Wolf and Jessica Hale. The files also included their criminal records, which were impressively long. Along with those, another file was uncovered detailing exactly who Adel Ragnarsson was. As much as she wanted to confront Ragnarsson with the information immediately, she decided to wait until she could consult with Max.

What she couldn't wait on, was addressing what had just happened. People were going to want explanations she didn't have. MilForce was questioning everyone on the planet to find out what they knew. Until that process was complete, which would take several days, there was little she could do.

"Ms. Warren, I have uncovered something you should be aware of," Annie said.

Kellie sighed. "Okay, what did you find?"

"I am ashamed to admit, Adel Ragnarsson got around my security protocols, but he had help."

"What do you mean? Explain."

Over the next hour, Annie showed Kellie footage of Ragnarsson disassembling his watch, using the chip, and the sequence of lights that emitted from his screen. Annie also had all the messages Ragnarsson sent, which included the instructions, as well as the light sequences that were sent to all the collaborators.

"What is all that?"

"For the colonists other than Adel Ragnarsson, it is an application of optogenetics used to trigger specified desired reactions from the subject by triggering the hippocampus. For Adel Ragnarsson, the sequence appeared to unlock some hidden information."

"What?"

"Before departure, Mr. Ragnarsson was subjected to some information, and then it was blocked from his memory. This is a standard procedure in covert operations. Based on analysis of the sequence of events, that information included the ability to, put simply, brainwash others into doing his bidding."

"And the ability to circumvent your security, crash the sattelites..."

"I'm afraid so."

"I think I already know the answer to this, but who would have known how to do all that?"

"Anyone involved in the final steps of my programming. A total of approximately ten people."

"And they all reported to Gustav Malmkvist."

"Of course."

Kellie shook her head. "Why?"

"I don't know."

"Sorry, that wasn't—nevermind. Based on your knowledge of this process, will the colonists he, controlled, come out of it? Is there a way to reverse it?"

"I am analyzing the pattern to determine its exact effect, but it will take time. Normally, yes, it's temporary."

Kellie nodded. "Thank you, Annie."

* * *

Landing + 17 Days, 1100 Hours

Kellie startled awake when there was a knock on Max's office door. She frowned at herself for dozing off, then quickly wiped her face. "Come in."

Colonel Mikhailovna came in and stood at attention. "All weapons accounted for. Questioning ongoing. Will take few days."

"Essena, shouldn't you be resting? I heard you were hit as well?"

She shrugged, but winced for her effort. "Have had worse."

"Have a seat. I might as well share what Annie found with you. You might know more about it than I do."

Essena nodded and sat down, a bit more carefully than she previously would have.

Kellie shared the videos and all the information about how Ragnarsson carried out his plot, with Annie's help on the more technical details.

"This explains much," Essena said after Kellie and Annie were done.

"What do you know about that brainwashing stuff?"

"I know is used, but not how it works. If we use, we are given package to deploy. Don't need to know how it works, just that it does."

Kellie nodded. "Thanks, Essena. If there's nothing else you need from me, please, get some rest. Delegate someone to lead the questioning."

"Is order?"

"If that's what it takes to get you to get some down time. Yes, it's an order."

"Very well. Captain Snow will lead efforts," she said as she rose to leave. "How is Captain Reeves?"

"Stable. That's all I know for now."

Essena nodded and left.

"I'm sure Doctor Chadda will do her best, Ms. Warren," Annie said.

"I know. Thanks, Annie. Can you configure for a ship-wide broadcast please? I need to update everyone."

"Of course, Ms. Warren, just let me know when you're ready."

Kellie took a few moments to compose her thoughts, and absently noted Annie seemed more…helpful than she had been. She didn't want to dive into it just yet, but wondered if there had been something else messing with the AI's behavior the full shutdown and reboot fixed.

When she was ready, the transmission started, and her image came up on every monitor in the ship and around the city.

"Hi everyone, most of you probably know me. I'm Kellie Warren, the XO of *Traveler*. I'm not as good at this as Max is, so bear with me. Today's events have shaken us all, and I know there are a lot of questions. We don't have all the answers yet, but, to continue the transparency Max had started, I want to go ahead and share what we *do* know."

She continued for at least 30 minutes, detailing everything Annie had shared, including how Ragnarsson had controlled people and who was involved. She also reassured everyone that all the weapons were now accounted for, so there was no need to be afraid of a further incident, and that the MilForce would be questioning everyone to find out what they had seen or heard. She also informed everyone that Max was stable, and should make a full recovery in time.

"In conclusion, everyone take the rest of the day off from your assigned tasks. Rest, reflect, do whatever you need to do. If working is that thing, go right ahead. But here's something we can do to remind ourselves that we are all in this together. Starting today, I will set up the system to name the planet and the city. We'll keep this open for a few days so everyone can think about it and have their say. At the end, the majority will rule. Thank you everyone for your patience and understanding as we recover from this tragic event."

"Transmission ended. I think you did very well, Ms. Warren."

"Call me Kellie, please?"

"Of course, Kellie."

* * * * *

Chapter Twenty-Two

Landing + 21 Days, 0400 Hours

Max woke up in his quarters in his bed, with several leads going to the medical monitors which sat on a nearby portable table.

He groaned as he looked around and squinted when a shape came toward him.

"Welcome back to the land of the living," Kellie said softly. She sat in a chair beside his bed. She took his hand between hers and smiled.

Max blinked a few times until his vision cleared. He tried to sit up, which was a mistake. He gasped and let himself fall back.

"Yeah, probably not a good idea. You got torn up pretty good."

"What happened?" he said hoarsely.

She offered him a cup of water with a straw. "Well, you took a pretty good-sized chunk of door to your abdomen, and—"

"No. Adel," he said more clearly after he wet his mouth and throat.

"He's in custody. The rest of his people have been rounded up and are under arrest as well, those that weren't killed."

"How many?

"Total, twenty."

Max grimaced. Twenty was a lot of people to lose from an already limited population.

"I know, but it could have been a lot worse. Everything is under control."

"What do we know?"

Kellie related all the information she had about the circumstances, Ragnarsson's unlocked information, the brainwashing, everything.

"By the Gods…how."

"One guess."

Max scowled. "Malmkvist."

"Had to be."

"Why?"

Kellie shook her head. "I wish I knew the answer to that one."

"I guess it doesn't matter now. Okay, time to get to work."

"Oh no. Doctor Chadda said you'll probably be down for another week or two."

"Bullshit."

"Well, she's on the way, so you can tell *her* that."

"How's everyone taking this?"

She sighed. "A lot has happened, Max. I just don't know if—" She was interrupted by Doctor Chadda entering Max's quarters.

"I'm glad to see you awake, Captain," Chadda said. "Excuse me, Kellie."

Kellie patted his hand and stood to get out of her way.

Dr. Chadda reviewed the readouts on the displays and nodded approvingly. "Everything looks good."

"Good, so when can I get back to work?" Max asked.

"A week or two, at least. There's still some healing that needs to happen."

He grimaced. "Seriously?"

"Captain, you're lucky to be alive. The shrapnel only missed your spine by a millimeter. It destroyed several of your organs. Frankly, you *should* be dead. You're a miracle of modern medicine. Pretty much your entire digestive tract has been replaced, and it's going to take a while for everything to balance now that you can actually start eating."

Max wasn't convinced that it should require him to stay in bed. "So? I'll stay near a bathroom."

"There's also a lot of tissue damage that's still healing. Even with the best medical technology we have, it's going to take a while. You don't want to go screwing up my work, do you?" Chadda asked.

Max sighed and closed his eyes against a wave of nausea. "When you put it that way..."

"Good. I'll be able to monitor your status remotely, but I wanted to come in when I heard you were awake. Any questions?"

Max shook his head, not trusting his voice.

"Good. I'll leave you in Kellie's capable hands."

Kellie sat back down and retook his hand after Chadda left. She filled him in on the operation that had quelled Ragnarsson's efforts and the loss of the satellites.

"Lastly, construction of the last of the city infrastructure will finish tomorrow. And, we have a name for the planet and the city. The planet has officially been named Mythos, and the city, Eos. I thought doing that would help bring everyone back together."

Max wracked his brain for a moment, then nodded. "Goddess of the Dawn. Seems suitable. That was a good idea. You've been busy."

"We all have. Without satellites, everything became a bit more urgent."

"What was that about the griffins?" he asked.

"That's been…remarkable to watch. Several teams have started working with them and Fischer. I don't think we'll ever truly have two-way communication, but they're beginning to understand *us* pretty damn well. They were able to interpret that something was wrong and who the problem was. We would have caught Adel no matter what, but they certainly made it easier. Not to mention giving an obvious indication of their level of intelligence."

"Well, do me a favor and keep me updated? Looks like I'll be here a while."

"Will do," she said with a smile. She leaned over and kissed his cheek. "I'd better get going."

Max smiled softly and nodded. After she left, he grabbed his comm device and started reviewing everything in his log, which was everything that had happened and what was being planned.

The satellites being gone were a problem. Communications were now limited to line-of-sight with *Traveler*. One of the things they hadn't brought backups of were the satellites. More could be constructed and taken to orbit, but they were low on raw materials. Efforts were underway to retrieve the containers that had initially been abandoned, but that wouldn't provide enough of the right materials. What they needed more of, were metals.

Quickly, he grew weary and set his comm aside. It would be a long week or two just lying in his bed, but at least he knew the city was in good hands.

* * *

Landing + 35 Days, 0200 Hours

Two weeks later, once he was back up to speed, Max walked toward the MilForce section, the only area of the ship with a holding area, with Hugh Coghlan.

"Colonel Mikhailovna will meet us there," Coghlan said.

Max nodded. "They haven't gotten anything out of him?"

"Not a thing. I did manage to stop them from using force. Mostly. It's been proven over and over again that you can't beat information out of someone."

"Good. Torture isn't what we're about."

"Glad we agree on that. The rest of the folks we detained…it's weird. It's like they can't remember what happened. We even had Doctor Chadda run brain scans on them while we interrogated them. She believes them. Looks like the brainwashing effects were temporary like we hoped."

Max pursed his lips and considered.

"I know, it's not foolproof," Coghlan went on. "But it's the best thing forensic science has been able to come up with so far. And it's a lot better than it used to be."

"Okay. Honestly, I didn't think we'd have to deal with this kind of thing. No one did."

"Then, why am I here?"

"Okay, maybe I overstated it," Max admitted. "We knew there might be some things that required your training, and that of your fellow officers, but I never thought it would be this bad."

"I'll buy that. Unfortunately, here we are. I mean, how do we handle this? What laws apply?"

Max sighed. "The ones we create, Hugh."

Coghlan grimaced. "That's not my business, Captain."

"You're on the council. It's your business now," Max said as they entered the MilForce compartment and beyond, into what had become the interrogation room.

Essena was already there. She was leaning against the wall with her arms crossed, watching Ragnarsson, who was seated, out of restraints, and eating.

Once he and Coghlan entered, Max closed the door, then sat down opposite Ragnarsson.

"I understand you've been less than forthcoming about what the hell you were doing."

"I think it's fairly clear what I was doing, Captain Reeves. I was attempting to remove an incompetent leader."

Max waved a hand dismissively. "I'm more concerned with how you got into the computer core and shut everything down. Not to mention destroying our satellites. What the hell would you do that for?"

"That only happened because I didn't succeed," Ragnarsson explained as he picked a piece of meat from between his teeth.

"How?"

He smiled in a way that made Max think of the way a killer smiled in a horror movie. "I think you know most of the answer to that. What you don't know, well, too bad for you."

Max sighed. He obviously wasn't going to get any further than anyone else had.

"All right. Keep him confined. No computer access."

He left the room, with Coghlan on his heels.

"Now what?" Coghlan asked.

"Now, we get the council together and decide what to do with him. I was never a big supporter of the death penalty, but this is pretty clear cut. We still have limited resources, and he obviously can't be trusted to be useful to the city."

Coghlan frowned. "And the others?"

Max considered as they walked. He wanted to believe that the brainwashing was short-term, and had indeed worn off, but he needed a way to be completely certain before they were released, that there wasn't a hiddn trigger.

"I don't know," Max finally admitted. "For all we know, this could be a part of some long-term plan. To have them forget until they're back in a position to do…something."

Coghlan was silent as they walked through the ship, and down the ramp to the surface. Then, he paused and waited for Max to face him.

"I didn't come all this way to have to constantly look over my shoulder. But I also didn't come to stomp on people's necks. I'll enforce whatever laws there are, but I'll leave making them to those smarter than me."

Max watched Coghlan walk away, then went to the PCC. Coghlan was right, they'd have to come up with something as a group. And whatever it was, in his mind, needed to be unanimous.

* * *

Landing + 35 Days, 1000 Hours

Later that day, Max sat with the council, along with experts in human behavior and other relevant sciences, to help the group come to a consensus.

"We have several decisions to make today," Max began after everyone had been introduced. "One, what to do with Adel Ragnarsson. Two, what to do with those who helped him. I have my own ideas, but I'm going to keep them to myself for now. I'm here to guide and assist, but the decision needs to be unanimous as far as I'm concerned."

The conversation started slowly but quickly ramped up. Max, true to his word, remained silent other than to stop them when people started talking over each other. It seemed to be a split, when it came to Ragnarsson, between executing him and keeping him confined for the rest of his life.

Then, Lina Skoog, who had been mostly silent, finally spoke up. "I have an idea," she said, loud enough to be heard over the commotion.

Much to Max's surprise, everyone went silent and turned to face her.

"Give him a pack, a few months of paste, some survival gear, and drop him on the other side of the planet."

"That's a death sentence!" Deanna Stokes exclaimed.

"No, it's not. We know there are edible plants and animals available. He can have his comm with the database of what we know is safe to eat. Hell, if he works hard enough, he might eventually find his way back, in about a year. Maybe by then, he'll realize the error of his ways."

"That's…not bad," Coghlan admitted.

"Or he might be killed by some wild animal," Stokes objected.

"He's already responsible for the deaths of several people. As far as I'm concerned, he's personally responsible for all 20 deaths during the incident. I won't lose any sleep if he dies," Azeema said with a shrug. She was in favor of execution.

Stokes leaned back in her chair. "You've got a point there."

Max waited a moment while everyone thought about the proposal. "Okay, let's take a vote. All in favor?"

Hands went up around the table, then Max added his own. "Okay, that's settled. Colonel Mikhailovna, I'll leave the arrangements to you."

She nodded.

"I'll put a pack together with everything I'd give a first-time survivalist out for training," Skoog added.

"Now, the remainder of the offenders. Doctor Chadda, why don't you explain your findings."

Chadda activated a projector and displayed a holographic image in the center of the table. "What you're seeing is a functional MRI of one of the detainees. They're all relatively similar, so we can use this one to demonstrate the point."

She went on to explain how it worked, what it showed, and that, basically, none of the people interviewed could remember anything from the time prior to the revolt.

Coghlan nodded in agreement. "Yeah, we've seen it. Mostly used by radicals to get people who would otherwise be peaceful to engage in activities completely out of character for them. But it usually can't influence someone to actually *kill*."

"And by governments," Max added.

Several heads snapped to look at him. Others, mostly the scientists, weren't surprised at all.

"Let's focus, people," Kellie said sternly. "There are two realistic possibilities. First, the effects are wearing off, and they're back to who they really are. The second possibility is that they just appear normal, but have some latent programming that will trigger under some unknown circumstance."

"Is the latter possible?" Coghlan asked.

Chadda nodded. "It's within the realm of possibility."

"I suppose there is no way to know if there is another, what did you call it, trigger?" Azeema asked.

"I'm afraid not," Chadda answered. "Such a trigger would be deeply implanted in the subconscious and only activate when specific criteria are met. It could be something as simple as seeing a certain thing or performing a certain activity, but there's no way to know what that thing is. Or even if it's there at all."

"Well, if you're saying they were controlled into doing what they did, I think they deserve a second chance," Stokes said.

"I tend to agree," Coghlan added. "The only one I'm concerned about is the one from MilForce."

Max had been waiting for that to come up and watched Essena closely for her reaction.

"He is a concern," Essena agreed. "I have already decided to remove him from team if he remains."

"How do you think he'll take that?" Max asked.

"If he's a good soldier, he'll understand," Eva Snow explained. Max had included her since she'd led the effort to quell the attack. "We know all about this stuff. We've been trained in it. He'll understand what the possibilities are," she concluded.

"I agree," Kellie said. "Give them all another chance. But…let's keep them under surveillance for a while?"

"I can assist with that," Annie's voice chimed in.

"Hugh? Do you think your people can help as well?" Max asked.

"Absolutely," Coghlan answered. He appeared satisfied how things were going.

"Okay. Let's have a vote. All in favor of release and surveillance?"

Again, there was a unanimous vote in favor.

"Done. Anything else before we break?" Max asked.

There were a few short discussions about project statuses, but nothing too important, so Max tuned most of it out to think about what had happened…again. He smiled and nodded as everyone left, and soon it was only him and Kellie left in the conference room.

"What's on your mind?" she asked.

"Everything."

"Well, that's a bit broad."

He shook his head. "Something's off. We get sent here, knowingly, by Gustav. He's the only one who could have orchestrated obscuring people's true identities or intentions. Adel isn't talking, but now we know his records were altered. What's the end game?"

"I don't know, and I don't think we're going to solve it today. At the end of the day, does it matter? We're here. Now. And we just have to move forward."

"Yeah. It matters. Because we don't know what else, or who else, is waiting, or why."

He stood and took a deep, cleansing breath. Kellie stood as well. "But you're right. Let's keep everything going forward, with our eyes wide open."

* * *

Landing + 35 Days, 1200 Hours

Adel Ragnarsson was marched out of *Traveler* surrounded by four armed guards, more for his protection than anyone else's. He walked tall and looked around smugly as the gathered crowd booed him. He noticed the people he'd used at the front of the group. It was unfortunate they hadn't carried out the orders they'd been given. He'd overestimated their ability to resist the most extreme commands, but that was okay; there would be another day.

He was pushed roughly into the cart that would carry him to the airfield.

"Not happy that you don't get to just shoot me?" Ragnarsson asked Eva Snow, who was leading the detail.

"Oh, I'm fine with it," she replied as the soldiers sat and the cart raced off. "I'll sleep perfectly well imagining you becoming a meal for some local wildlife. Hopefully, you won't give them indigestion."

He grinned at her. "I'm sure we'll be seeing each other again, Ms. Snow."

"You come near the city again, I *will* put a bullet in your head."

"Awwww," he said in mock sadness.

The cart drove directly up the ramp into a waiting X-94, which was already powered up. As soon as the cart was locked down, the rear ramp closed, and the aircraft lifted off.

"Not wasting any time, are you?" he asked.

"We're anxious to get on with life without you," Lina Skoog said as he was removed from the cart. She handed him a pack but held a second bundle.

"That's enough supplies to survive for thirty days. By then, if you're smart enough, you will have found a supplementary food source."

"I do appreciate your confidence and concern, Lina," he said dryly.

"Consider yourself lucky to be alive. Some of us wanted to just kill you."

"Buckle up," the pilot's voice came over the speaker in the bay. "Going sub-orbital."

Ragnarsson was shoved into a seat and buckled in, then the rest of the team buckled themselves in. Once they were secure, the pilot kicked in the thrust.

Using a sub-orbital trajectory, the travel time was relatively short, and they were at their destination 45 minutes later. Ragnarsson felt the re-entry and deceleration, and finally, the *thud* of the aircraft touching down.

The ramp opened, and Ragnarsson was unceremoniously unbuckled and shoved out of the aircraft. He stumbled and rolled the last few feet, coming to a stop with a grunt.

"Here's some hunting and fishing gear, and a comm with a database of what's safe to eat," Skoog said, tossing the second bundle, which landed beyond him.

"But feel free to experiment and eat whatever you want," Snow said with a smirk.

He watched as the ramp closed. The pilot lifted off before it was secure, and, within a minute, the X-94 was a speck on the horizon.

"Well, this didn't go according to plan," he said to himself as he stood and dusted himself off.

He gathered the other bundle and looked around. There was forest to one side of him and a mountain to the other. "Great," he muttered and headed for the foothills. He'd had enough of forests for a while.

Ragnarsson walked for the better part of an hour until he found a shallow cave. He looked around in the fading sunlight and didn't see any evidence that something had made a home of it, so he finally sat down to inventory what they'd given him. There was food paste, a collapsible tent, a thermal blanket, a machete, a fishing pole with line and lures, a lantern, a flashlight, and other survival equipment to cook and purify water with.

He sighed and repacked everything but the thermal blanket and lantern, and he lay down to rest while he went through the comm device's database. He could have been upset, but that wasn't his style anymore. Now, he just had to survive until his moment came, which he had no doubt would.

* * * * *

Chapter Twenty-Three

Landing + 35 Days, 1600 Hours

Max looked around his new apartment with mixed feelings. He and Annica had designed it—well, mostly Annica, with the expectation that they'd have a child on whatever new world they found. Now it felt empty. He sat on the leather-like sofa they'd picked out together and looked out the large picture window. As the mission commander, he'd gotten the top floor and, arguably, the best view.

His apartment was more of a penthouse since he had the entire top floor to himself. It had been deemed necessary since he also had a fully functional secure office with a direct-wired connection to *Traveler*. He had actually been against it, but everyone had firmly supported it, so he accepted. Annica had thought it was no more than he deserved.

For what felt like the millionth time, he used his comm device to pull up the last few frames of the message from Gustav Malmkvist. The picture window converted to a display screen, and he watched it over and over. He waited for anything off. A hidden message, maybe. *Something.*

He didn't even look away when there was a knock on the door. "Come in," he called.

Kellie walked in and sighed when she saw the screen. "You can't keep doing this to yourself, Max."

"There's got to be something I'm missing."

"Yeah, there is," she said quietly.

"I'm just…" he sighed and cut off the display. The window returned to its transparent state.

"Nice view," she said and sat beside him.

"Yeah. Azeema set me up pretty well."

"Of course she did. You deserve it."

Max shrugged.

Kellie slid closer and rested her head on his shoulder. Hesitantly, he freed his arm and wrapped it around her shoulder. She nestled closer to him and sighed contentedly.

They sat that way for a while, and Max felt…good. Occasionally he'd rub her upper arm or shoulder to remind himself that she was real.

After a while, she looked up at him and smiled. He smiled back and looked into her eyes. She slowly closed her eyes and reached up toward him. He leaned down to kiss her, then both of their comms chimed.

She sighed and turned away to reach for her comm, but he stopped her. He turned her face back to his and kissed her gently.

Their comms went off again, and he sighed. "I suppose we should check that." His lips brushed against hers as he spoke.

"Do we have to?"

He gave her another quick kiss, then reclaimed his arm and answered the comm request.

"Hey, Max, it's Colin. I've got something you're going to want to look at. Meet in the PCC?"

"Sure, give me a few," Max answered.

"Oh, you know where Kellie is? She's not answering."

He grinned, and Kellie winked. "She's here, we'll be right there, Colin."

"Oh. Okay. Thanks."

Max stood, then offered a hand to help Kellie up. "Well, let's go see what Eagle has found this time. Any idea what he was doing?"

She shrugged as they walked down the stairs. "I know there are a lot of low-level recon and survey flights going on. With the satellites gone, we're using what we record from them to identify areas to check for potential mining operations for raw materials."

He consciously took her hand as they walked down the street and gave it a squeeze.

She smiled up at him, and the smile stayed as she looked around.

They passed Pedro on the street, and he grinned when he pointedly looked at their hands. "About time," he said.

Max chuckled and shook his head.

They couldn't help but stop when they reached the town square. There were three griffins there being petted and rubbed by quite a few people. They could hear Leopold Fischer giving lessons on how to interact with them, and it seemed to be going well. As they watched, all three laid down. Fischer climbed onto the back of one of them. Two humans mirrored his actions and climbed onto the other two. There were no saddles, but a system of leather-like straps had been designed that fit the griffins to give the riders something to hold onto for stability.

"Wow," Max said.

"Amazing," Kellie agreed.

The griffins stood and the crowd backed up to give them room. They flapped their wings a few times, then jumped and took flight.

Cheers filled the air as the griffins flew in a lazy circle around the city.

Max could have watched them all day, but he heard Colin "Eagle" Shepard shouting from the PCC. "Are you coming or not?"

"Let's go," Max said and gave Kellie's hand a squeeze.

* * *

Max and Kellie joined Essena and Sadie March, the ship's chief engineer, who was already there.

"What've you got?" Max asked.

Colin pulled up an image on the main screen. "First, I found a deposit of that new metal not too far away in the mountains to the north."

"Excellent!"

"That's not the best part. I noticed this when I was taking a different path back, and I decided to get a closer look."

The image zoomed in, and Max walked closer to the screen. "Is that...?"

"There's definite evidence that some of the trees have been displaced, and the object looks man-made from what I can tell," March said.

Now Max understood why she was there. "Why didn't we spot this sooner?" he asked.

"We weren't looking for it," Kellie said.

"Okay, so how do we get in there for a closer look. How far out is that?" Max asked.

"About 100 kilometers," Colin answered.

"Nearest clear landing area?"

"About thirty kilometers. It's dense right up to the foothills."

Kellie pursed her lips. "What about the griffins?" she asked.

Max blinked and was about to suggest that Kellie might be crazy, but then thought about it more carefully. "That's…not a bad idea. Let's go talk to Leopold."

He exited the PCC with Kellie, Sadie, Essena, and Colin following closely.

The griffins had just landed, and the people who had flown them were climbing off. Max waved his hand to get Fischer's attention. The crowd parted to let Max and his group through.

"You want to go up next, Captain?" Fischer asked with a grin.

"Actually, we were wondering if your friends would help us with something," Max explained.

"Depends on what it is, I reckon."

Max motioned Colin to come forward and pull up the image of what they wanted to investigate. They explained that they wanted to get out there to get a closer look.

"Hmm. Yeah, I reckon they could fly in there good enough. Gotta be people they trust, though, to go that far. And I reckon I'll need to go along."

"Okay, how do we figure out who they'll take?" Max asked.

"Slow down there, Captain. No offense, but we gotta think about this. How much weight? What gear? How many people?"

Max nodded. He had to rein in his intense desire to know what was out there. "Understood. Come on, let's get the logistics figured out."

* * *

Landing + 35 Days, 2000 Hours

They spent the rest of the day working on the plan. Max knew he was going along, against the objections of pretty much everyone. Fischer would go to help with the griffins. Essena made it clear she was going along for security. So far, only three griffins had agreed to allow humans to ride them, so that was the limit.

The three of them met with other specialists to receive guidance on what kinds of samples to collect to determine what it was, where it had come from, and anything else they wanted to learn about it. Once everything was settled, they scheduled their departure for the next day after the third sun rose.

Max and Kellie walked together down the street as the last sun set, and the streetlights turned on.

"I'm nervous," she admitted.

"About which part?" Max chuckled.

"All of it! Why don't you let someone else go?"

"It looks like there's something man-made on this planet. We don't know where we are, so it should be impossible. I can't *not* go see this."

"I still don't like it," she said.

"Come on. I'll cook you dinner."

"Sure, why not."

They went up to his apartment, and he quickly put together a meal of local fish and vegetables that had been collected by Skoog and her exploration teams.

"My first official all-alien meal," she said with a grin as he set the plate in front of her and sat down with his own.

"Mine, too, to be honest. Let's hope it doesn't suck."

"Well, you first then," she said and watched him.

He confidently took a forkful and chewed. Slowly, a smile grew across his face. "It's actually pretty damn good, if I do say so myself."

They ate and talked about the next day's mission. When their plates were clean and their glasses empty, Kellie stood. "I guess I should get going and let you get some sleep."

Max stood and crossed the distance between them to take her hand. "Why don't you stay?"

"Are you sure?"

He wrapped his arms around her and drew her into a kiss, then whispered in her ear, "Yes."

* * *

Landing + 36 Days, 0600 Hours

The next morning, after breakfast in his apartment, Kellie left so he could prepare for the mission. He meditated, then packed his gear and left for the square where he would meet Fischer and Essena. They'd decided against full environmental suits, but they were going to wear skinsuits with a helmet, due to potential toxins in the air.

They were there waiting for him, and Fischer was using a tablet to show the griffins their destination.

"Everything set?" Max asked as he approached.

"Yeah, should be good, Cap. Pretty sure they understand where we want to go. They seem a little hesitant to go there, I think, but I reckon I convinced 'em."

"Why would they not want to go?" Essena asked, concerned.

Fischer shrugged. "Hard to say. If it's something that came down from the sky, might be it caused a ruckus when it hit the ground. They kinda don't like that."

"So we've gathered," Max said. "Shall we?"

"Yeah, here, lemme help ya up."

Fischer showed Essena and Max how to mount the griffins, then easily climbed onto the third.

"You don't have to do anything but hold on where I showed ya," Fischer explained. "I'll lead, and they'll follow."

Max nodded. "Okay. Let's get going." He gave Fischer a thumbs up, then saw Kellie in the crowd and winked at her.

"Be careful!" she called out.

"We will," Max assured her, then secured his helmet while Essena and Fischer did the same.

He held on tightly as the griffin flapped its wings and jumped into the air. It was rough at first, and he was afraid the straps were going to hurt the creature with his tight grip, but it didn't seem to notice. They quickly gained altitude and flew toward their destination. Once they were coasting, it was as smooth as flying in a fighter.

"Damn, you're fast," he said as he loosened his grip and gave the griffin a pat. He looked down and gauged the ground speed at nearly 100 km/hour.

"They can go faster," Fischer said over the linked comms. While they would eventually lose their connection with the ship, their three comm devices were linked up so they could talk to each other.

"I think this is plenty fast enough," Max said.

* * *

"Hold on, we're about to go down. Landing can be...rough," Fischer said after about an hour.

Max held on and leaned over to become more aerodynamic as the griffin dove toward the ground. Just as an aircraft would flare as it neared touchdown, the griffin spread its wings to catch the air to brake. The deceleration was quite a jolt, and Max found himself holding on harder to keep himself from falling off.

With a bump, the griffin landed and took a few steps before it came to a halt and lay down so Max could dismount.

"That was one hell of a ride," Max said after he climbed down. The griffin backed up a few steps, its eyes squarely on a metallic object covered with foliage.

The trees in this area were different from those around the city, thankfully. He hoped they wouldn't have to worry about the roots or anything else.

"Okay, Essena. Check the area, please."

"Yes, Captain." She pulled a device from her pack and walked around the area, scanning for anything dangerous.

"We should keep helmets on. No radiation. Just atmosphere not safe."

"Okay, let's see what we've got," Max said and brandished a machete.

As they had planned, Fischer recorded everything. If something went wrong, he was to take the recording back to the city for analysis.

Max and Essena cleared an area around the object, then, carefully, worked to expose a section of it. He knelt down and ran his gloved hand over the surface. "Remarkable," he said.

"What is?" Fischer asked.

"It's smooth. Definitely machined. This is no asteroid or meteor fragment. Look at the edge here."

He stood and quickly started hacking at vines and peeling them away. Essena followed suit, but more slowly as she watched every direction for danger.

After a half-hour of work, the object had a shape. Max stood back to look at it as a whole and shook his head. "I don't see any damage anywhere, so far," he said, verbally recording his observations for the records. "Shape is similar to an old space shuttle from the 20th century, but the material is…foreign. No markings at all that I can see."

It took another hour, but they finally uncovered the ship, and it was definitely a spaceship. "Damn thing took down I don't know how many trees, but it's not even scratched," Max observed as he walked around it.

"Here. Looks like hatch," Essena said from the other side of the ship.

Max walked over and nodded. "Yep. Big too. Damn thing is at least two and a half meters tall."

He approached it and looked around for a way to open it, but there wasn't even a small recess where a handle could be.

"Maybe it only opens from the inside?" Fischer asked as he walked around to continue recording.

"Makes no sense. Got to have a way to open it from the outside in case of an emergency."

Max cycled the visor of his helmet through different visual spectrums. He figured something would show a difference that might indicate where an emergency opening might be. He found it once he hit the infrared spectrum.

"Got it," he said triumphantly.

Essena pulled her pistol and aimed it at the hatch. "Go ahead," she said.

Max considered chastising her, but she was right. They didn't know who, or what, was inside, or whether or not it was still alive.

He pushed on a thin section of the ship's skin, which depressed then sprang out. He pulled up on it, which was the only way it would go. There was a loud *click* of mechanical locks releasing, then the door swung outward on hydraulics.

"I will go first," Essena said, pushing past Max.

After a moment, she commed, "Clear."

Max followed after turning on his helmet-mounted lamp. "Okay, you check the rear, I'm going to check what should be the cockpit."

He walked forward along a passage that was narrow but taller than he was, even with his helmet. He passed through an open hatch into what had to be the cockpit of the vessel. It looked familiar but foreign at the same time. With his light, he could see screens arrayed around two seats that lent themselves toward a human-like form, but definitely *not* human. They were narrow and appeared to allow for a frame at least three meters tall.

"What the hell?" he whispered to himself.

"Captain! Back here!" Essena shouted. She sounded panicked.

Max turned and moved as quickly as he could toward the rear of the craft. He moved faster when he saw her light, but stopped cold when he entered the room she was standing in.

Arrayed on the floor were humanoid-shaped flight suits, but they weren't empty. Max carefully stepped around one of them to kneel beside it. He reached for the helmet clasp to remove it, which was remarkably similar to their own.

"Maybe we shouldn't," Essena said.

Max ignored her and slid the clasp, then gently removed the helmet. Inside, the mummified remains of…something stared at him. The head was definitely human-like, but it was not human.

"What the hell is that?" Max said breathlessly.

* * * * *

Epilogue

Annica Reeves walked into Gustav Malmkvist's office and aimed the pistol she'd brought at his head. "Where is Maxwell?"

Malmkvist chuckled and waved his hand. "Put that down, Annica. I'm afraid you've missed quite a bit."

"Where is he?" she demanded.

"Well, by now, he's likely settled on a new planet."

"What?" she asked, blinking rapidly.

"You should sit down. Your brain chemistry is trying to rebalance."

She willed herself to pull the trigger, but she had to know where Maxwell was. "We're not supposed to even see the probe for another day!"

"Oh my. Total memory loss. Well, that does happen," Malmkvist explained calmly. "That was over a month ago, my dear."

Her hand trembled, but she kept the gun raised as she made her way to a chair and sat. "Explain!"

"It's quite simple. The probe never arrived anywhere. Oh, I made it *look* like it did. But people are easy to fool. When they want to see something, they tend to see it!" he said, quite proud of himself. "Anyway. Then they left. You, of course, left your foolish husband and stayed behind. With me."

She grimaced, suddenly feeling sick to her stomach. "What?"

"I'm a powerful man, Annica. When I want something, I take it," he explained and walked around his desk.

"No…"

"Oh yes. Your ex-husband and *Traveler* are far, far away now. We're not even sure exactly where, to be completely honest."

Tears fell from her eyes, and she shook her head. "No…"

He smiled a bit sadly. "I do hope you will come around. It just didn't feel…*right* to keep you under control for so long. Plus, we need your expertise now. And the control modification…well, it made you a bit dull-witted. In any case, you have access to everything. It's time to start working on where they ended up."

"Everything?" she asked, hopefully.

"Yes, dear. Everything."

"Good," she said and pulled the trigger.

# # # # #

ABOUT THE AUTHOR

Alex Rath is a long-time fan of science fiction and fantasy books and gaming, going back to his youth when he started playing *Dungeons & Dragons*, *Traveler*, and *Battletech*, among many others, at a young age. He decided that becoming an author was the next logical step. He has written many stories for his own use but decided it was time to start sharing his writing with others.

His first book, *With Your Shield*, based in the Four Horsemen military sci-fi universe, was a great way to start. Now, he has contributed to not only the Four Horsemen Universe, but also The Fallen World, and Salvage Universe. He has been a professional software developer for over 20 years and is familiar with what can be done with a computer and applies that knowledge to his fiction. Alex will continue writing science fiction, post-apocalyptic, and fantasy, many of the stories being inspired by his experiences while gaming with either pencil and paper or online.

Alex lives in Columbia, South Carolina, with his family. Follow Alex on Facebook https://www.facebook.com/alexrathauthor, or his website https://alexrathauthor.com/.

* * * * *

The following is an
Excerpt from Book One of The Devil's Gunman:

The Devil's Gunman

Philip Bolger

Available Now from Blood Moon Press

eBook, Audio, and Paperback

Excerpt from "The Devil's Gunman:"

I eased the door open and braced for gunfire or a fireball.

I got neither. I swept the entryway with my rifle's sights. Nothing more offensive than some high school photos glared back at me, and I didn't hear anything running down the hallway or readying a weapon. There were no shouts from police or federal agents, either.

What I did hear, from the living room, was incessant chatter underscored by the occasional interjection of a laugh track. The chatter was accompanied by the soft peripheral glow of my television. Whoever had broken into my house was watching a sitcom.

"I'm unarmed," a man's voice rang out. "So put down the rifle, and let's have a talk."

"The fuck we will," I shouted back. "You broke into my home!"

I moved down the hallway, keeping my rifle on the opening to the living room.

"That's part of what we have to talk about," the voice said. I peered around the corner and saw a young Caucasian man. His pale features and dyed blue hair did little to mask the malicious smirk on his face. He was dressed in an oxford shirt and slacks with a skinny tie, as though he couldn't figure out if he wanted to look like he'd just joined a band or an investment firm. He wore a silver tie clip with a red blood drop on it.

I stood there with my rifle sights on his head.

"I'm here as a messenger," he said and flashed his teeth. I saw pointed incisors. That was enough for me. "This is peaceful, Nicholas. No need to be violent."

I lowered the rifle. I didn't like the prick's condescending tone; he sounded like he enjoyed the sound of his own voice. Those types were always eager to give up information.

"Okay, let's talk. Who's the message from?" I asked.

"I hold the honored post of Emissary of the Lyndale Coven," he said politely, examining his nails. "We've taken a professional interest in you, and Coven leadership sent me."

"Oh yeah?" I asked. "What for?"

"To dictate the terms of your surrender," he said, locking eyes with me. His hands twitched, then curled slightly. I imagined him leaping off the couch and knocking me down. I fought the urge to bring the rifle to bear, keeping it at the low ready.

"Thought your kind needed an invite," I said.

The man snarled.

"We both know who built this house. I have a standing invite. The coven master says that the Duke no longer wants you, so you're fair game. Our agreement, which I have right here, has the details."

He pulled a no-shit scroll out of his suit jacket and put it down on my coffee table. I glanced at it. The Lyndale Coven seemed to be under the impression that I belonged to them. I read the word "slave" once, and that was enough for me to decide I wasn't interested.

"No dice," I said.

"These terms are much more charitable than those the Coven Master wanted," he said, warning in his voice. "Oath breakers aren't normally given this kind of clemency."

I didn't have much idea what he meant about oath breakers, but I wasn't going to play ball with this pompous fuck.

"Not charitable enough," I said. "Why do you guys want me? Running out of blood from young clubgoers and runaways?"

The young vampire smiled again, flashing his teeth with what I'm sure he thought was menace.

"It'll certainly improve our coven's standings with the Duke if we prove we can clean up his loose ends. I'm sure you'll make an excellent blood thrall. We'll be taking a pint of blood every month, as—"

I raised the rifle and sighted in on his head. He sighed, and rolled his eyes.

"Look, you primitive ape, guns won't—"

I fired three times, the rounds earth-shatteringly loud in such a tight place. He screamed in pain and terror as the holy rifle's bullets tore through him, the wounds leaving bright blue caverns of light.

His screaming echoed in my head, so I kept shooting. I fired the rest of the magazine until there was nothing left but a corpse, riddled with holes and glowing softly, and me, standing there in my gunpowder-fueled catharsis.

I dropped the mag and slapped in a fresh one, savoring the sound of the bolt sliding forward and knowing that if the emissary had any friends, they too, would be introduced to the kinetic light of St. Joseph.

"Anyone else here? I got more."

* * * * *

Get "The Devil's Gunman" now at: https://www.amazon.com/dp/B07N1QF4MD.

Find out more about Philip S. Bolger and "The Devil's Gunman" at: https://chriskennedypublishing.com/philip-s-bolger/.

* * * * *

The following is an
Excerpt from Book One of The Shadow Lands:

Shadow Lands

Lloyd Behm, II

Available Now from Blood Moon Press

eBook and Paperback

Excerpt from "Shadow Lands:"

The combatants, for lack of a better term, were both resting at the edges of the dance floor. To the left was a very butch-looking blonde in what looked to be purple leather, along with her entourage, while to the right, a petite, dark-skinned Hispanic in a princess outfit stood, surrounded by meat popsicles wrapped in leather. Vampire fashions make no damn sense to me, for what it's worth. There were a few 'normals' huddled against the far wall, which showed signs of someone's face being run along it, repeatedly. Sure enough, the London 'Special' was in the DJ booth. He killed the sound as soon as he realized we were standing there.

"Ladies and gentlemen, may I introduce the final players in our little drama, the Reinhumation Specialists of the Quinton Morris Group!" the Special said into the mike.

"Fuck me running," I said.

"With a rusty chainsaw," Jed finished.

The two groups of vampires turned to face us.

"Remind me to kick Michael in his balls when we get back to the office," I said.

"You're going to have to get in line behind me to do it," Jed replied.

"You can leave now, mortals," the blonde said with a slight German accent. She had occult patterns tattooed around her eyes, which had to be a bitch, because she would have had to have them redone every six months or so. Vampires heal.

"Like, fershure, this totally doesn't involve you," the Hispanic said, her accent pure San Fernando Valley.

"Jed, did I ever tell you how I feel about Valley Girls?" I asked, raising my voice.

"No…"

"Can't live with 'em, can't kill 'em," I replied, swinging my UMP up and cratering the Valley vampire's chest with three rounds into the fragile set of blood vessels above the heart. Sure, the pump still works, but there's nothing connected to it for what passes as blood in a vampire to spread. On top of that, company-issue bullets are frangible silver, to which vampires have an adverse reaction.

With that, the dance was on. The damn Special in the DJ booth at least had the good sense to put on Rammstein. *Mien Teil* came thundering out of the speakers as we started killing vampires. Gunny ran his M1897 Trench Gun dry in five shots, dropped it to hang by a patrol sling, and switched to his ancient, family 1911. I ran my UMP dry on Valley Vamp's minions, then dropped the magazine and reloaded in time to dump the second full magazine into the Butch Vampire as she leaped toward the ceiling to clear the tables between us and the dance floor. As soon as Butch Vamp went down, the remaining vampires froze.

"Glamour," the Special called, stepping out of the booth. "I can control a lot of lesser vampires, but not until you got those two randy cunts thinking about how much they hurt."

"You. Fucking. Asshole," I panted.

Combat is cardio, I don't care what anyone else says.

"Yes?" he replied.

I looked him over. He was wearing a red zoot suit—red-pegged trousers and a long red jacket with wide shoulders over the ubiquitous white peasant shirt, topped with a red, wide-brimmed hat. He even had on red-tinted glacier glasses.

I felt his mind try to probe mine, then beamed as he bounced off.

"My that hurt," he replied.

"You know, we don't work with Michelangelo for nothing," Jed replied. Apparently the mind probe had been general, not specific.

I went through the messy side of the business—staking and beheading—assisted by Capdepon. Crash helped Jed sort out the normal survivors, followed by prepping the live lesser vampires for transport. The Special leaned against a wall, maintaining control of the lesser vampires until we could move them out. Once all the work was done so the cleaners could move in, and the lesser vampires were moved out of Eyelash, I stepped wearily to the Special.

"What's your name?" I asked.

"You can call me," he paused dramatically, "Tim."

I kicked him in the nuts with a steel-toed boot. Even in the undead, it's a sensitive spot.

* * * * *

Get "Shadow Lands" now at:
https://www.amazon.com/dp/B07KX8GHYX/.

Find out more about Lloyd Behm, II and "Shadow Lands" at:
https://chriskennedypublishing.com/imprints-authors/lloyd-behm-ii/.

* * * *

The following is an
Excerpt from Book One of The Darkness War:

Psi-Mechs, Inc.

Eric S. Brown

Available Now from Blood Moon Press

eBook and Paperback

Excerpt from "Psi-Mechs, Inc.:"

Ringer reached the bottom of the stairs and came straight at him. "Mr. Dubin?" Ringer asked.

Frank rose to his feet, offering his hand. "Ah, Detective Ringer, I must say it's a pleasure to finally meet you."

Ringer didn't accept his proffered hand. Instead, he stared at Frank with appraising eyes.

"I'm told you're with the Feds. If this is about the Hangman killer case..." Ringer said.

Frank quickly shook his head. "No, nothing like that, Detective. I merely need a few moments of your time."

"You picked a bad night for it, Mr. Dubin," Ringer told him. "It's a full moon out there this evening, and the crazies are coming out of the woodwork."

"Crazies?" Frank asked.

"I just locked up a guy who thinks he's a werewolf." Ringer sighed. "We get a couple of them every year."

"And is he?" Frank asked with a grin.

Ringer gave Frank a careful look as he said, "What do you mean is he? Of course not. There's no such thing as werewolves, Mr. Dubin."

"Anything's possible, Detective Ringer." Frank smirked.

"Look, I really don't have time for this." Ringer shook his head. "Either get on with what you've come to see me about, or go back to wherever you came from. I've got enough on my hands tonight without you."

"Is there somewhere a touch more private we could talk?" Frank asked.

"Yeah, sure," Ringer answered reluctantly. "This way."

Ringer led Frank into a nearby office and shut the door behind them. He walked around the room's desk and plopped into the chair there.

"Have a seat," Ringer instructed him, gesturing at the chair in front of the desk.

Frank took it. He stared across the desk at Ringer.

"Well?" Ringer urged.

"Detective Ringer, I work for an organization that has reason to believe you have the capacity to be much more than the mere street detective you are now," Frank started.

"Hold on a sec." Ringer leaned forward where he sat. "You're here to offer me a job?"

"Something like that." Frank grinned.

"I'm not interested," Ringer said gruffly and started to get up. Frank's next words knocked him off his feet, causing him to collapse back into his chair as if he'd been gut-punched.

"We know about your power, Detective Ringer."

"I have no idea what you're talking about," Ringer said, though it was clear he was lying.

"There's no reason to be ashamed of your abilities, Detective," Frank assured him, "and what the two of us are about to discuss will never leave this room."

"I think it's time you left now, Mr. Dubin," Ringer growled.

"Far from it," Frank said. "We're just getting started, Detective Ringer."

Ringer sprung from his seat and started for the office's door. "You can either show yourself out, or I can have one of the officers out there help you back to the street."

Frank left his own seat and moved to block Ringer's path. "I have a gift myself, Detective Ringer."

Shaking his head, Ringer started to shove Frank aside. Frank took him by the arm.

"My gift is that I can sense the powers of people like yourself, Detective," Frank told him. "You can't deny your power to me. I can see it in my mind, glowing like a bright, shining star in an otherwise dark void."

"You're crazy," Ringer snapped, shaking free of Frank's hold.

"You need to listen to me," Frank warned. "I know about what happened to your parents. I mean what really happened, and how you survived."

Frank's declaration stopped Ringer in his tracks.

"You don't know crap!" Ringer shouted as Frank continued to stare at him.

"Vampires are very real, Detective Ringer." Frank cocked his head to look up at Ringer as he spoke. "The organization I work for...We deal with them, and other monsters, every day."

Ringer stabbed a finger into Frank's chest. It hurt, as Ringer thumped it repeatedly against him. "I don't know who you are, Mr. Dubin, but I've had enough of your crap. Now take your crazy and get the hell out of my life. Do I make myself clear?"

The pictures on the wall of the office vibrated as Ringer raged at Frank. Frank's smile grew wider.

"You're a TK, aren't you?" Frank asked.

"I don't even know what that is!" Ringer bellowed at him.

"You can move objects with your mind, Detective Ringer. We call that TK. It's a term that denotes you have telekinetic abilities. They're how you saved yourself from the vampire who murdered your family when you were thirteen."

Ringer said nothing. He stood, shaking with fear and rage.

"You're not alone, Detective Ringer," Frank told him. "There are many others in this world with powers like your own. As I've said, I have one myself, though it's not as powerful or as physical in nature, as your own. I urge you to have a seat, so we can talk about this a little more. I highly doubt your captain would be as understanding of your gift as I and my employer are if it should, say, become public knowledge."

"Is that a threat?" Ringer snarled.

Frank shook his head. "Certainly not. Now if you would…?" Frank gestured for Ringer to return to the chair behind the desk.

Ringer did so, though he clearly wasn't happy about it.

"There's so much to tell you, Detective Ringer; I'm afraid I don't even know where to begin," Frank said.

"Then why don't you start at the beginning, and let's get this over with," Ringer said with a frown.

"Right then." Frank chuckled. "Let's do just that."

* * * * *

Get "Psi-Mechs, Inc." now at:
https://www.amazon.com/dp/B07DKCCQJZ.

Find out more about Eric S. Brown and "The Darkness War" at: https://chriskennedypublishing.com/imprints-authors/eric-s-brown/.

* * * *

Made in the USA
Columbia, SC
09 November 2020